THE BROKEN COUCH

Paula Nicolson

The Fireside Press

Copyright © 2022 Paula Nicolson

All rights reserved

The main characters and events portrayed in this book are fictitious with the exception of those who took part in the trial. Any similarity to real persons, living or dead, is coincidental and not intended by the author.

No part of this book may be reproduced, or stored in a retrieval system, or transmitted in any form or by any means, electronic, mechanical, photocopying, recording, or otherwise, without express written permission of the publisher.

CONTENTS

Title Page
Copyright
PROLOGUE: Nuremberg, Germany, October 1946   1
PART 1 – THINKING ABOUT DREAMS   6
Chapter 1: Watching Television, South London, Present Day   7
Chapter 2: Dreaming about Death, Nuremberg, 1946   10
Chapter 3: The First Seminar, London. Present Day   19
Chapter 4: Unfinished Business?   24
PART 2: MAX   29
Chapter 5: Max's Story, Salzberg, 1939   30
Chapter 6: Travelling by Train   33
Chapter 7: The Man in the Car   37
Chapter 8: Work with Us   41
Chapter 9: Disclosures, London, Present Day   44
PART 3: ERIKA   53
Chapter 10: Erika's story – Vienna 1938   54
Chapter 11: Dream Sharing   59
Chapter 12: The London Clinic, March, 1945   60
Chapter 13: June 1945   64
Chapter 14: Pain and Death   69

Chapter 15: Talking to Erika	72
Chapter 16: Storytelling	75
Chapter 17: Max in London, 1945	78
Chapter 18: Psychoanalysis and Confession	83
Chapter 19: Hidden in the File, London Present Day	86
Part 4: THE DANGERS	89
Chapter 20: A Brush with Brutality, Berlin 1941	90
Chapter 21: Dachau 1942	98
Chapter 22: The Man with the Scarred Face, Berlin, January 1943.	104
Chapter 23: Thinking about the Past, London 1945	108
Chapter 24: Double Lives - London, Present Day	112
Chapter 25: Lunch with Marion, Present Day	115
PART 5: BEFORE THE TRIAL	120
Chapter 26: Erika and the Journey to Hell (August, 1945)	121
Chapter 27: The Prisoners Arrive, Nuremberg, August, 1945.	134
Chapter 28: October - The Palace of Justice	142
Chapter 29: Near Gartenstrasse	147
Chapter 30: The English Women	151
Chapter 31: Night	157
Chapter 32: Mary	164
Chapter 33: Helga	169
PART 6: CONNECTIONS TO THE FUTURE'S PAST	173
Chapter 34: A Diary, London Present Day	174
Chapter 35: 'Contacting J', London Present Day.	178
Chapter 36: Taken	183
Chapter 37: Lunch	191
PART 7: TRIAL, JUDGEMENT AND JUSTICE	202

Chapter 38: The indictments	203
Chapter 39: The American Psychologist	213
Chapter 40: One More Death, Nuremberg, 1945	220
Chapter 41: The Lawyer from Linz	224
Chapter 42: Another lunch with Marion, Present Day	236
Chapter 43 : The package	240
Chapter 44: Sharing Dreams of Salvation and Exclusion, Early in 1946	249
Chapter 45: Endings	256
EPILOGUE	258
About The Author	263

PROLOGUE: NUREMBERG, GERMANY, OCTOBER 1946

There was a strange feeling that night. A silence. A *loud* silence if you will. You could feel it. Hear it. Smell it. Palpable. The echoes of breath. For once his own breathing was coming easily and his heart was not fluttering as violently as it sometimes did. The shuffling outside got louder. Then the sharp clang as the guards peered into each of the cells. What was different? The routine hadn't changed but that feeling of peril stayed. That silence wouldn't be quiet.

He had felt irritated but now he had had enough. Talking, talking. All that talking. In the Courtroom. To those soldiers. To that doctor – the Jew. The woman – she was a Jew. Plagued by Jews. The only people who came to see him were Jews. And all they wanted was to hear him talk. And to watch him. Why? It was over. The Jews looked as if they had won this one. But was it true what those lawyers kept saying? So many dead? That was no victory then. But then that is probably a lie. Jew lies – he could tell. They always exaggerated. They couldn't consider anything in a calm and rational way like a true Aryan. They were a strange race. But he knew more about Jews than many. More than almost anyone. Surely there hadn't been so many deaths? That thought troubled him. A little. But he dismissed it successfully again. It was not possible. They always managed to get the most out of any situation. Ergo – they didn't die in those numbers or in those ways.

He was becoming very tired now and sat down heavily on the iron bed. It was late. He lay back with his head on the thin pillow, raised his legs onto the bed and took a deep breath. More like a sigh. Then the observation window crashed open, shrilly intensifying the sounds of the corridor. Its grinding metal screech was then outflanked by the noise of the door opening as two guards pushed their way into his cell. They materialized simultaneously. The lights were up now blinding him for a while but then he could see that another guard stood behind them blocking the door.

Was any of this necessary?

He wasn't going anywhere. He felt no desire to get up and had no intention of leaving the cell. He had just been getting comfortable. The noise grew louder coming now from beyond where the guards stood. It was pressing in from the corridor. Something had happened. It was all going wrong tonight.

'What's happening? What do you want?'

'Please stand Mr. Streicher.' They were military police – MPs - not guards. Americans. He registered that much. But everything outside himself was moving too fast, while his mind slowed down. This was an absurd consequence of this unwarranted disturbance. It took some while before he understood. Now he did. It had come. He felt nothing.

Streicher was wearing his only remaining suit, the one he had worn for the trial. He had always tried to remain as well dressed as he had done during the height of the Leader's power. It had been difficult, but he had looked after his suit and his favourite blue shirt. He did up the top shirt button. He had no tie. They had taken away all his ties and belts when they had brought him here to his cell.

What did they think I was going to do?

It was precisely ten minutes past two in the morning when the MPs entered his room. They gently, firmly, lifted him onto his feet. They manacled his hands.

What? Am I going to run away?

He was led down the corridor. He noticed that that still, heavy silence had returned. The cells were now like graves. It all seemed so easy. He was guided on towards the bright lights of the gymnasium ahead down the long corridor. This was where the guards took exercise.

I am tired I don't want to take exercise. Why here? Why now?

He was feeling confused. Two minutes later the manacles were removed and replaced by a leather strap. In front of him thirteen steps appeared. He didn't need to count them. Now he knew. He looked up noting that the steps lead up to a platform upon which three black-painted gallows came into view. Underneath the platform with the gallows was a black curtain. He was mildly curious, but a weariness overtook him. He had a sense that he had been here before.

He felt calm. He had no trouble with his breathing. It appeared to Streicher that he was looking at a stage with curtains in the wrong place. This was puzzling – you couldn't hide the drama if curtains failed to obscure the stage. He could not grasp the meaning. It was night. What did they want? What were they showing him? He then formed a thought.

It can't be right. Is this what happens? Is this what final moments are like?

But he didn't need to think or ask questions. He was well looked after. The MPs guiding him made him feel strangely safe. No more decisions. No choices. He was helped to the bottom of the steps and held tight. Still no need to do anything. He looked around. There was a small group of men and a woman holding notebooks.

That woman – the doctor. Jew. She was the one that had

come to see me. To talk to me about my life. The war. The Jews. Do they want me to give a speech about it all now? But the trial is over. What else to say?

Time came to a halt. He had been abandoned by those MPs now. At least he could not feel them there. He suddenly felt alone. It appeared that he now had choices. He looked up. There were people there. But it was strange. Suddenly different.

Where are the MPs?

These people staring down towards the floor were no doubt all Jews. Some stared at him. Others stole crafty glances. He knew all about Jews. He wrote about them. How amazing that they had come to dominate the world as they had done. Admirable. His efforts had been for justice, for a fairer world where the ordinary German could live free from Jewish and Bolshevik control. When he was thinking, deeply as he did now, he habitually looked at his hands. It helped concentrate the mind. But this was impossible now. His hands were behind his back.

What cruelty.

All he had wanted was for Jews to live in their own land. I made it very clear. In every issue. *'Der Stürmer'* was respected by Hitler and by the Party. Over one and a half million Germans, ordinary Germans, chose to buy it. Doubtless many more read it.

How could I be guilty of anything? Germans needed to be awakened to the attack on their noble culture.

His musings then came to an abrupt end.

'Heil Hitler!' he screamed it out. It was a comfort. Something familiar and something expected. The people with the notebooks wrote it down. Then an American army officer appeared at the bottom of the steps.

'What is your name?'

'You know my name! Julius Streicher'. Again. A yell. He had no idea where that voice was coming from. He began to ascend the thirteen steps. He halted near the 11th step up to the gallows. He could see the rope. A man holding back the rope – a heavy twisted rope strong enough to carry the weight of a man. To carry *his* weight?

Straight away he was grasped from behind by controlling, comforting hands again taking away responsibility. He was facing those Jews with the notebooks.

'Purim Fest 1946!' Another scream. He felt smug.

They can celebrate but they cannot stop the truth. These people don't even speak German.

'Ask the man if he has any last words' an American officer at the scaffold ordered from the translator.

'The Bolsheviks will hang you one day' Streicher replied.

The hood. Over *his* head now. A quick breath. Still calm. Near the last. 'I am with God'. The hood was adjusted.

'Adele, my dear wife'.

Quieter now. He paused longing to see her once more.

A loud bang as the trap door opened below him. A snap of the rope as it descended suddenly with the body. A groan. Another groan. The rope was moving but not for long. The hangman descended the gallows platform entering the curtained area and put an end to that piteous groaning and the movement from the rope.

PART 1 – THINKING ABOUT DREAMS

CHAPTER 1: WATCHING TELEVISION, SOUTH LONDON, PRESENT DAY

Wilson Coffey had an important decision to make. Should he have a beer and delay dinner, or should he put the ready meal into the microwave and start drinking the wine that had been sitting, breathing and eagerly waiting for him, on the kitchen worktop? Uncharacteristically he decided on the beer after pausing the television repeat of a compelling dramatized documentary on the Nuremberg Trials. He froze the program at one of the many points at which the actor playing Hermann **Goering** sprawled in his chair as he grinned at the judges, while occasionally turning to consider his fellow accused. **Goering clearly found them wanting.**

'For Heaven's sake, do you think I would ever have supported it if I had had the slightest idea it would lead to mass murder?'

Wilson snorted as he reminded himself of Goering's words in his own defence. He felt a deep disgust even now listening to evil. He rose slowly and painfully to his feet heading for the fridge returning, with a slight grimace, to his chair nursing the open bottle of beer. He resumed the broadcast with a flick of the remote and lowered himself carefully back on to his favourite armchair. It was always more difficult to release himself from the thirty-year old pain in his back than resuming his viewing.

His multiple agonies remained with him always, but they were more of a backdrop to his life now. He had to admit that and often felt ashamed by that acceptance. The pain had started when he had been shot in Berlin alongside his wife, Hanna the murderers' real target. It took many years before he could walk again but even now, several years since he had cast aside his crutches, there was pain to bring it all back into consciousness.

His decision to watch the drama about the famous trial, that dedicated an episode to each of the key defendants, was partly idle curiosity, but it also brought back memories of the time he had spent in Nuremberg when Germany was divided. It was there, as a part-time spy, in the American zone that Wilson had had contact with agents of the East and the West. It was part of the search for members of the neo-Nazi group calling itself 'Werwolf' the brainchild of Heinrich Himmler, that he and Hanna, a dedicated Communist, had chased and exposed the network hiding in the West. History now. In so many ways water under the bridge.

But Wilson was far more of a psychiatrist and psychoanalyst than he ever was a spy. He was old now, or so the calendar would have him believe. Born in 1942. Not long before he was to become 80 but like many, apart from the physical aching, his mind and aspirations were those of a far younger person. Hence, he had accepted the part time post at the Tavistock Clinic, the "Tavi", in north London. There, he worked with newly qualified psychotherapists particularly interested in linking the unconscious to the interpretation of dreams. Next week he was to run a session for around fifteen new graduates about social dreaming and their influence on social relations. It was seen to be particularly interesting now following a pandemic whose effect proved both divisive and unifying.

Very strange times!

But he was used to paradoxical events. And particularly now towards the end of his life. He turned off the television. He would catch up with Albert Speer and Rudolf Hess later – tomorrow probably. He had to eat now.

He dropped the empty beer bottle into the recycling bin, perforated the cover of his Tesco Finest lasagna, organized the microwave and poured a large glass from the awaiting bottle of Merlot.

Beer before wine …

As he anticipated the eventual ping of the microwave he wandered, wine in hand, towards the large picture window of his apartment smiling at the sight of the dark brown Thames as it moved quickly towards the estuary and the English Channel. There was slightly less to smile about in his reflected image. He stared at the "beer belly" that his younger self would never have accepted or predicted. More proudly he observed his shoulder length curly hair, totally intact, although only if you failed to notice the patch of skin gleaming from the back of his head. He sighed and for a brief, vain moment he felt pleased that Hanna had never seen him looking like this.

The apartment, with its view over the river towards Chelsea, the bridge and the northern embankment, had been his reward for spying activities and compensation for his life-changing injuries. Now, and for many years, it was home. He was happy and able to live with his heartaches.

But for much longer now? They will pass.

CHAPTER 2: DREAMING ABOUT DEATH, NUREMBERG, 1946

There it was again. I had that dream. Her dream – it belonged to Erika Adler. I know it wasn't mine. I wasn't born then so it couldn't be mine. So vivid. I woke yet again drenched in sweat. Fearful. It was horrible to see all of that, but I don't know whether <u>she</u> was fearful. And yet the dream signaled the end of that type of fear the fear and the fate that so many had endured. But what happened next? To her – the dreamer? I know what happened to all of them at least what happened in 1946. But is that what really counted? Perhaps a view of how they got there is more important. I found it easy to obsess about the trial and the sentences and along with her – or while I am in her dreams at least – I eventually breathed a sigh of relief. Now I am not sure I was wise to do so. But we shall know eventually - perhaps.

Dr. Erika Adler, psychiatrist and psychoanalyst, raised her eyes once again towards the gallows. This wasn't as easy as she had imagined. After Streicher came Saukel, the man who had been in charge of war-time labour camps. The man that Airey Neave thought had been at least partly conned by Hitler and Albert Speer. Saukel's slaves had made armaments for the Nazi regime. Saukel had been working for Albert Speer, Hitler's one-time favourite and the architect of the monuments to glorify Hitler and the, almost, Thousand Year Reich. But Albert Speer wasn't going to die on this occasion.

Speer was to face prison and die of ill health and old age. But that comes later than this story. And to my mind demonstrated justice as aberration.

And as she looked up again it was Jodl – Hitler's army General. Both Saukel and Jodl had tracked Streicher's footsteps up those thirteen steps followed by that strange deathly dance behind the curtains. But these deaths seemed mundane to Erika right now. An anticlimax. Almost pointless. She recalled talking to Streicher a few times over the past few months. Her colleagues had thought him vulgar and none too bright. She could understand exactly why they had thought that. In many ways so did she.

'But he was also pathetic. Sad. And he had loved his wife. Why do I think that matters? Something to be envied.' Erika thought about this a great deal.

How did I know so much about these people – who died before I had even lived? I dream about them. All the time. When I was very young, they chased me, and I had to hide. I was scared. More recently I have come face to face and challenged them. Seen them for what they are – or were - and they don't welcome that. I have always known about them but have no memory of who told me or what they told me about them. It was not a topic that entered my school History lessons. It was not something that anyone wanted to talk to me about when I was young – but I knew. The details of much of it I discovered over the years, but I was not surprised because I always knew.

Was I shocked when I first discovered what had happened? I can't recall. What I do know is that I wasn't born. Extended members of my family, who neither my parents nor I had known or would ever know, died. Murdered. They were the ones who had remained in eastern Europe and were brutally murdered because Stalin forgot to do anything to stop the German advance into Soviet territory. 'Forgot?' They are now buried in pits of death with all those others – children, babies with their brains dashed out, mothers, grandmothers, fathers and grandfathers.

As years went by interest in what we call the Holocaust increased. Scholarship, novels, films. Most recently – denial that it happened – or that it wasn't so bad – exaggerated fuss typical of those people. The suggestion that 'history is open to interpretation' from people who call themselves scholars! How could anyone think that?

But not everyone I have always known about was evil. Sigmund Freud – I've always had a sense of him. He died before most of those men's names – the ones who were brought to trial - were well known. Many of them killed

themselves towards the end of their reign. Most tried to escape. A number were captured, examined and sentenced. And it's only because they were brought here together that we can compare them and their crimes. A hierarchy of evil seems to be playing out here as the outcome from the trial will show us.
A lot of that evil was eventually pulled together in one place – at least it was a beginning – to find out – discover who else did things. Evil that had been scattered through Europe was put centre stage for a while at one of the places it had started and now it has been scotched forever. Never again. Do you really believe that? I no longer think I do.

Erika shook her head wondering whether this human feeling in Streicher for his wife made his rabid hatred of Jews even more despicable than if he had been a total, unloving psychopath. She thought about this. She wanted to understand – an intellectual project. But more so, she needed to understand for her own sake. How could they have done what they did?

They all had feelings. They all had lives. But their lives were so small, so twisted, compared to the lives they stole. So many stolen lives. And Streicher was also a pornographer. Streicher could not give up his sneering hatred even at the end.

It hardly matters now what she thinks or even what I think. At least not to him. But perhaps to Erika? It's her dream. I really don't want to have it again, but I expect I shall.

For Erika, practicing doctor and psychoanalyst, it was hard to move away from that conundrum. And it was not only her thoughts about Streicher that disturbed her. She had been sharing responsibility for the mental wellbeing of all these men during their imprisonment, trial and after sentencing. They were condemned. Either to death or most of their future lives were to be under lock and key.

'But' she wondered 'does that atone? What about the German people? The Austrian people?'

And then her mind jerked her back to her patients in London. Now temporarily abandoned. 'Could the death of these evil ones repair *their* lives?'

THE BROKEN COUCH

She brought herself back to the present. Sitting. Watching. It was hard for her to be there. But she had to know that these vile, venomous creatures had been scotched from the earth.

'This had to be seen. This had to be recorded.' But still she felt nothing. No pity. No fear. No revulsion. At least not for the events she was witnessing. It was surreal watching the guilty walk up to the gallows and hang. Die. In front of her. They dropped. One by one. Quickly, like a factory. The sound of the trap door, the rope, the grunts – each one different from the ones before. And she had got to know them well. She knew who liked whom and vice versa. The food they liked. Their health status. But still she felt nothing as she continued to stare at the gallows and their passing trade.

But this is not a death-factory. Not like Sobibor, Belsen or Auschwitz. But how much did she or any of them know about those places? Even then at the trial – I can't believe the full truth was known. And the men on trial could and would not believe what had happened – at least that is what they said. If they could believe it ... had known? What kind of evil?

Something snapped in her consciousness. Erika jammed her eyes shut, unsure how much more she could take. She heard another groan. She looked. She wanted to spit. At Streicher, Hans Frank, the man who had tyrannized Poland only to become a devout Catholic after his capture. The man who wasn't there but should have been. That man. The fat one. Piggy blue eyes. He had escaped justice. That was what they did – not here in this death chamber so much, but before here – another bunker. She shivered when she remembered the first time she had entered Goering's cell – but it was empty now except for his body, lying there so the world could see.

Then came Ernst Kaltenbrunner head of Reich Security – the SS. The Gestapo. The Criminal Police. A psychopath. A drunk. The man she had once known better than she knew any of the others. Max's boss – the one she investigated. Kaltenbrunner, the childhood friend of Adolf Eichmann – another coward who escaped justice.

He didn't in the end – and she, Erika, lived long enough to find that out.

She wanted to spit at all of them. Spit! But Kaltenbrunner. He had been important. To her. Only a few months ago. She knew him really well. Without him it would not have happened. He tried to appear so detached and even now, not everyone knows his name. He isn't one of the famous ones. But he was far worse than perhaps his reputation – or lack of reputation – his anonymity to the outside world suggested.

She didn't want to think about this anymore. Not now and not here.

Later. When I am more at peace. How pathetic to see them die so quickly. Easily. After what those monsters did. Is that all anyone can think to do to them?

But justice was worth more than her bitterness and she reminded herself that she had the privilege of seeing it done. But was that enough? So many died without knowing whether they would ever be remembered. Whether their bodies would be found. Whether the world would ever know or even care what had happened to them. Erika focused yet again upon the man who wasn't there. Hermann Goering. Ever the malevolent coward. But she had spoken to him. Listened. Often. To him. She remembered it all so clearly.

He had thought he had charmed her. To a degree, he had done. He had told her, and all the others who frequently visited his cell, that he had remained loyal to Hitler because he, Goering, was not a traitor to Hitler or more important – not a traitor to the German people.

How could he believe that? Did he expect his jailors to believe that? Did he expect what was left of the German people to believe that?

But as Erika reflected on that idea, the more concerned she became.

What did it mean to be a traitor? If you joined a group - if you were a Christian. A Communist. A Jew even. What would you do if the group violated your principles? If your leader breached your trust?

Erika had wondered about herself. About her mentor Sigmund Freud.

What would it mean to take on patients you knew you couldn't help? What if you preyed on their vulnerabilities? Not that Freud did anything like that. But that Swiss man? He seduced and cheated one of his protégées. Sabina Spielrein. He stole some of her ideas passing them off as his own to great acclaim. And then the Nazis murdered her. Not him. Not the Christian. Only Spielrein. For being a Jew.

Not many of us thought much about that even as the century wore on and people became increasingly interested in psychoanalysis. But later – as the years moved past the millennium - we heard much more about their relationship and Jung's diminished morality. But the photos of the kindly, elderly, white-haired man – that is who we remember. Not the anti-Semitic seducer. And he was. Both of those things.

Erika had to stop thinking. But it was impossible. She had wanted to see Goering again and again. To watch. To listen. She missed him. She felt a rage. Self-hate to a point. But hate for him and everything he was always keen to tell her – or she suspected – anyone who would take him seriously. The hangman – justice – had missed Goering too. He had thought until the last minute that he might get away with it. That the Court would accept his version of who he was and what he had done. Like Speer. Goering despised Speer. He had tried to persuade all of them – the military, the lawyers and the mental health staff, that he, Goering, was no common murderer. He had merely been chief of the armed forces – the Wehrmacht. He kept repeating to all who entered his cell before and after the trial and verdicts that this trial was about the "victors' justice". Not *pure* justice. Not the truth. Not *real* justice. His culpability, even in its very entanglement, was blatant.

Erika felt another surge of self-hatred. As if she were a traitor taking up the role she had done. Looking after these men. Caring. Inquiring into their souls. Their unconscious. She was planning to write a book on the death instinct and evil, based on some of these men. She had been singled out to carry out this work. It must have been because of her relationship with Freud she believed.

How could I do such a thing? Here? Profit from meeting them? Be interested in them? Care for them. But there was another reason. Something I had to find out. To know for sure.

And that was a private matter for her.

Erika had never been to Nuremberg before these trials. She was Austrian, born and raised in Salzburg who had later moved to Vienna to study. She had been one of the very first Jewish women to read medicine at the university of Vienna. It surprised her then to think her religion had ever been an issue. She knew different now. She didn't attend synagogue services other than on very special days, and then only to please her parents and catch up with friends. She didn't look especially Jewish – whatever that means. Her hair was dark, straight and shoulder length. Her eyes green, her skin pale and freckled and she was tall and thin. She rarely gave any thought to which of her friends and colleagues were Jewish. Nor did they. At least not until now. She was an Austrian and one among many others sharing her background. Nothing to think about then. But now she was ashamed.

She had loved medicine. Her teachers had told her that very few girls were good at science. Erika had been. Her parents were doubly proud of her accomplishments.

'You are to be special Erika' her father had told her. 'A Jewish girl at that great university'. He had been referring to the antisemitic laws that had prevented Jews from training in medicine up until over twenty years before. Recent in her father's memory. But his pride in her was tempered.

'But why do you want to do *this*? Looking after the insane. This witchery? This ....'

And here he would always look away in disgust muttering 'psychiatry'. It was, she knew, a controversial area that many argued was unscientific and a waste of medical talent. However, she had been determined.

'And now I am here in this place. Witnessing this. Thinking about this. For that reason.'

Her life had been something of a fairy tale at university and after, when she had met and impressed Dr. Sigmund Freud. But neither of them knew what was to come, there in their homeland. No-one human could ever have guessed. Not then. Not while she was studying a subject she loved. Some of her friends and colleagues may have peeked across the border in horror at the "new" Germany but then closed their eyes and let the evil sweep in.

'How could Vienna, this most beautiful and sophisticated city, in this wonderful and kind country, fall on its knees and let that poison in? But it had happened.'

How it happened is a question we are still asking today and asking with more urgency now. The first world war had devastated the Austrian empire – there was poverty to be seen and it didn't take much effort to notice it. Ripe pickings for those who wanted power and those who lusted to destroy. Now we understand and have witnessed what human beings are capable of doing to others. The evil has been allowed in. Will the human race be able to free itself? The people had listened to evil. They had watched. They did things that were far worse than listen. Such hatred. Why hadn't she seen immediately what was to happen? But even her mentor, Sigmund Freud hadn't fully grasped everything until it was almost too late. Until it had become personal. Shouldn't he have realized? It was Freud who drew our attention to the 'id' – the death instinct. Innate evil in humanity that both causes and desires death.

But now Erika had met these very men. These evil people who were driven to destroy. She had talked to them. Even felt for them - sometimes. Got used to seeing them every day over months. It is difficult not to feel something when people are telling you how they feel, what is upsetting them, why they are who they are. But they were monsters. And still she did not understand. Since her new life had begun in London, she managed to grasp the reality that she had survived and even flourished. She was a psychoanalyst. Everything she had always wanted to be before it had all started. Before these men. And here, in Germany, she had been caring for and analyzing the mental health of the defendants.

Has it been worth it though? Attempting to understand? We all need to think more carefully about this. Nothing is as simple as I had once thought it was. I think she must have felt the same. She was face to face with them. With evil.

Erika thought about the people she was treating in London. Refugees. Victims of these men. Survivors of such senseless and merciless evil it was impossible to imagine.

But one man in particular had intrigued her. He had turned up - *the only way to describe it* - in London at the end of February the previous year, as the war was drawing to its close. Before the liberation of Belsen. The total shock and disbelief that even the refugees from Nazi occupied Europe couldn't grasp the full extent of what had happened. It was unthinkable. Unbelievable. Even now it is hard to imagine but at least she now knew that it had all been true.

He had been held there he said. Because the Austrian people had fallen under the spell of the Germany? Because they had swallowed the lies of vermin like Streicher? Because Jews had never been truly accepted there? And he, Max wasn't even Jewish. It was just his grandfather.

'But no-one knew that did they?' Erika often thought about it.

Her life in Vienna and in London had all been part of the driving force that brought Erika to Nuremberg. Nothing could make up for her own losses. Her role here in Nuremberg, a sabbatical, almost a blessed relief from her everyday work, was based upon the promise to write a book about evil. It was integral to her own attempt to heal.

And to discover who Max really was.

CHAPTER 3: THE FIRST SEMINAR, LONDON. PRESENT DAY

He heard the noise – a shrill screech and a painful crashing sound. His eardrums ached and he couldn't hear anything else. But he felt the bullet that pierced his spine. Followed by nothing. Nothing but emptiness. So many years of absence. Pain in his mind. Pain in his back. His wife was dead. He had survived. That is what had hurt him the most.

Wilson's work at the Tavi offered opportunities that he relished. He was supervising trainee psychoanalytic therapists, running extra seminars for its sister rival, the Tavistock Institute of Human Relations, whose patrons shared a taste for examining the unconscious at work. His life as a reluctant spy was behind him allowing him to think about Hanna with warmth and love. Only when he was asleep did the figures in his dream world, who had brought about her death and his wounds, disturb him. Mental and physical. Nazis. *Werwolf.* The remnants of Himmler's plan to restore the Third Reich. It was hard to recall why he had become mixed up with any of it. He was a psychiatrist. He was now a qualified psychoanalyst as well. Politics generally were not his concern.

The seminars that had in part restored his 21st Century life, took place in offices shared with another psychological organization. The journey from his Battersea home demanded plotting an acceptable course to Old Street, an area adjacent to the City of London. The lack of any direct transit connections meant a train overground plus two underground changes. But at least Wilson didn't need to travel during rush hour where he would be pushed and stifled by the crowds.

Despite anticipating an irritating excursion, he managed characteristic good humour on the day of the first seminar. It was October, near the start of the academic year. It was a crisp, sunny, day so he didn't need to take heavy outdoor clothing that might prove burdensome. His back was having a good day. Pain only came during sudden movement. It was only the sickly type of ache that reduced his sense of wellbeing and energy level. Today he even thought he might leave his walking cane at home, although at the last-minute he thought better of it.

He checked that he had the necessary notes and memory stick for his presentation which was also on "the Cloud" if the system was incompatible with his iMac. The seminar was to explore social dreaming – the experience of sharing unconscious understanding, fears and desires with others during sleep. Wilson had surprised himself several years ago now, long after Hanna had died, with the realization that his dreams were highly connected with others'. While every dream has a meaning to its own dreamer, context brings about a strange kind of linkage.

'We are far from unique in struggling to understand where our unconscious mind leads us. We can share fears, expectations and beliefs particularly about the socio-political environment without realizing. In other words, dreams confuse us while enlightening us.'

'What exactly is meant by *sharing* dreams?' was one of the first questions his students usually put to him.

He usually suggested that they explore the content, style and colours of their own dreams. Whether making sense of the shared content of dreams could move people into emotional and social growth is what really interested him. His mind drifted further into anticipating the seminar.

Old Street, above ground from the Northern Line, always confused him, even when he was awake and alert.

I need to get an entrance to the south. Damn it I forgot to check the details.

Victorian buildings and concrete office blocks stood side-by-side but always one underground walkway or major road separated the unprepared traveler from the opportunity to take their bearings. The overall experience was complete disorientation. Old Street itself was a dual carriageway, anonymous highway and Tabernacle Street, his destination, was at the other side – but which other side? The station was in the middle of a roundabout, where four highways lead to all the directions of the compass.

On this occasion Wilson was saved by a familiar sight. Three women and a man all in their mid-thirties were moving purposefully, each carrying bags with a Tavistock Institute logo. He followed them with a feeling of gratitude and relief across pedestrian lights, over one part of the highway, and then zig-zagging through narrow streets. Most of the buildings were old and low rise, although some more modern blocks had been fitted into gaps caused by bombing during World War II.

The group ahead turned the corner into Tabernacle Street, negotiated the reinforced door, the intercom, the porter, the desk where names were taken, temporary passes given out along with instructions to reach the seminar room on the second floor via an elevator. There was also a promise that coffee and biscuits would be waiting.

The lift looked rather small so Wilson signaled to his unwitting guides that he would take the stairs. He didn't really like to meet students unofficially before his class – a strange inclination he knew as he would be happy to chat to them afterwards. *Provided it had gone to plan.*

He also needed to do a little bit of gentle climbing as often as he could as it kept his back mobile. So far, he hadn't felt the need of his walking stick. That felt good. The signs were positive as he reached the second floor and moved eagerly towards the trays of biscuits and cake, jugs of milk and flasks of coffee set out on a desk in a modern anteroom. From there he could peer through a glass partition towards an airy space with twenty desks in a U formation facing a computer, projector, whiteboard and in addition, he was pleased to note, a comfortable looking chair.

He began in his clear, albeit faded, Glaswegian accent telling them who he was and encouraging them to say as much as they wished about themselves. He told them he would provide a little bit of theory. They were a mixed bunch in terms of experience and age. One or two veteran psychotherapists in their late thirties and forties, several more, mostly at the lower end of the age range who were collecting credits for a postgraduate programme. The remainder comprised young, enthusiasts, eager to learn but initially with less to contribute.

Shy perhaps.

He noted that this seminar had attracted more women than the more traditional ones he ran at the clinic. In fact, out of the eighteen there were only six men.

'Ok guys. Let's begin. I shall be doing less talking than you, I hope. But, of course, I shall manage the boundaries - as we say!'

The therapists and a few of the others laughed politely.

'As you will know it was Gordon Lawrence, who is not only a former member of this exclusive establishment – the Tavi Institute - but perhaps more than that he has worked around the world. He's not like me or most of you – not at all like me - he's a man who has survived and thrived outside academia and psychoanalysis.' Wilson smiled to himself.

'Despite this he knew and thought more about psychoanalysis and dreaming than most of my colleagues or anyone else you might meet.'

Wilson looked around. They were engrossed and eager.

Well, everyone dreams. Everyone wants to make sense of their dreams.

'Today we are going to look at what happens when people meet to share their dreams. We're also going to sketch out the background to Lawrence's ideas. But the most important part is that we are going to be *a social dreaming matrix.* That means you share your overnight dreams, being open about what you dreamed to find links, make connections for understanding of the current socio-political environment. This is particularly interesting and a brilliant learning tool in times of crisis. Say for instance – during a war. London during the Blitz. Don't forget it's not too long since we all came out of months of social restrictions, fear and loss – a wee global pandemic. How that has influenced our collective unconscious we shall discover together.'

CHAPTER 4: UNFINISHED BUSINESS?

The seminar over, Wilson clambered onto a bus heading for Waterloo Station just south of the River Thames. It was a pleasanter way of getting home by far, than his earlier journey but not one to be relied upon if you had to be punctual. He loved buses but could only relax if he were going homewards. He reluctantly resisted the urge to climb to the top deck even though he had his walking stick. There were too many embarrassing memories from past years. Losing the power of his muscles half-way up the stairs. Worse – falling down from a few steps up and making a total idiot of himself.

No! I can only do the climb when the bus is stationery at the terminus and likewise at the end of the trip.

He acknowledged that looking a fool was not the worst thing that could happen to someone. He recalled travelling on the top deck into central Glasgow as a child. The smokers. The coughing. The other kids. And when he was alone – the views. Looking out over the tenements and beyond to the distant hills. He still missed being able to ride on the top deck.

He took his place quietly in one of the priority seats and turned the seminar over in his mind. It had been intended as a one-off for that group – giving them a sense of the power of the unconscious where dreams were a means of *concealing* desire as Freud proposed. Or, he asked them, was Wilfred Bion's view better - that dreams were about *thinking* about the unknown and drawing links with reality. But of course then came Gordon Lawrence arguing for dreaming as a means of understanding the social context.

'Think about what you have dreamed. Write them down. Most importantly note your *feelings*. Then the details – who was in them? Who did they represent for you? Scenery, activities, colours – or lack of and how you felt when you woke from the dream.'

He had been uncertain of his own thoughts as he ended the two-hour seminar.

Everyone had appeared to contribute and learn with enthusiasm and that was so rewarding.

He was tired by the end. He had listened intently to all the discussions and descriptions and held the boundaries as he had told them he would.

To ensure they feel safe sharing what represents a gateway to their inner beings.

He wasn't going to allow a free for all session about 'what *I* have been dreaming' without any further analysis or link to the others. This was a serious learning event. He knew what the participants needed to understand and think about. It was always hard work. It was nearly always satisfying. But he had wanted to leave when it was over. Something had been making him feel uneasy. As if there was a hidden detail lodged in his mind. A hint that he had forgotten or not spotted. Something either unfinished or not yet started.

What?

Tavistock rules demand that everything begins and ends on time. To ensure that people use the time to work. Don't hang back. Experience the benefit of boundaries. But as a visiting lecturer it was more difficult to sustain that rule – *or am I getting soft?* - and on this particular occasion the participants had had so many additional questions it was almost impossible to leave the room without appearing rude.

One of the psychoanalysts taking part, Dr Morgan – Marion – gripped his arm just as he had taken what he thought was to be his last farewell.

Now I think about it, she if anyone should have known better. Maybe that was why I still feel slightly uncomfortable. Why I am still going over this in my mind.

He had met Dr. Morgan a few weeks previously at the clinic. Since then, he had seen her walking around the long corridors and in the canteen. But their paths had not crossed in any more formal way until today.

'Dr Coffey. Please do you have a moment?'

Wilson looked at his watch.

That's unnecessary. I know the time.

'Okay. Let's sit down for a wee bit – just a short while out here.'

There were seats in the anteroom next to the tables where the cakes had been set out earlier and he pointed to them. He looked over at the remaining flasks hoping for a dreg of coffee. Marion spotted this and leapt up grabbing a plastic cup pouring him a still warm coffee.

'Milk?' he shook his head as he gratefully grasped the offering and sipped. Marion poured some for herself from another flask. Between them they had managed to mop up all the residual caffeine.

Wilson looked at Marion expectantly taking more sips. He was grateful he had stopped for a while now as he realized he was tired and certainly a little dehydrated.

'Forgive me – for breaching … I'm sorry.' Marion looked down into her coffee cup.

He felt perplexed, conscious of staring at her quizzically.

'That's okay.' He was met by her pale, thin face with a permanent tense, anxious frown above deep set blue eyes. Her thick dark auburn hair was caught up behind her head by a firm, ornate plastic clip. He guessed she was probably around forty years old. He had been told she was a talented analyst and teacher.

I doubt she would want to waste my time. I should be

attentive.

He manifested more enthusiasm than he felt though only because he was so tired.

'But what might I do for you Marion?'

'You mentioned in the introduction – do you remember – the work of Charlotte Beradt?'

'I do. Indeed. Her work on the dreams of the people of Berlin in the 1930s. Freud knew of her too. As I said. But …?'

'Well – this is difficult. Please don't judge what I'm going to tell you until I've finished. Explaining. But I need to show you something. Some papers. They are in my office. At the clinic. Someone my mother knew – or knew of – a Dr. Erika Adler a psychoanalyst who trained with Freud …'

'Really?' he felt a slight surge of energy as his interest grew.

Marion's face softened briefly for the first time during their conversation making him think that perhaps he had given something away.

She really ought to leave me alone. Let me go. What a strange set of words I've chosen.

'Yes. Not such a nice story though. But – well there's no reason for you to know about it - but my grandmother was murdered. In 1946. In Nuremberg.'

'What? Your grandmother?' Wilson recognized that this was a gauche intervention and tried to get around it.

'Er what was she doing there? Then?'

'Look. I'm sorry I troubled you – now I mean. I do need to see you. I think it was silly of me to try to tell you now.'

Wilson felt a mixture of relief and disappointment.

'I'm at the Tavi next Monday and Tuesday. First or last thing – any good?'

They agreed to meet. Wilson pushed himself out of his chair.

It's so strange. When I sit down for a while – resting – my legs are always more reluctant to move than when I am walking, standing or wearing them out.

Marion looked at him and smiled.

'I shall see you Monday evening then Dr Coffey I'll come to your office – I know where it is - but I do have to tell you now …. I don't want to deceive you …'

He stared at her sharply.

'I know who you are.' She moved away and into the corridor faster than he could follow.

Although to follow her would be rather a daft thing to do.

When he eventually did reach the corridor all he saw were the lift lights indicating that it had reached the ground floor.

What did she mean though? Grandmother. Nuremberg? Dreams? Hell, I hope this is not going back to somewhere I need to forget. But what the devil could it be?

His musings were interrupted by the electronic voice of the bus navigator letting the passengers know they were soon to reach Waterloo Station. Judging by the pushing crowd at the bus exit door, the automated route information was correct. He pulled himself to his feet, ensuring he had his bag and walking cane, before launching himself into the crowd of passengers leaving the bus, then carefully crossing the busy street. He headed towards the back entrance to Waterloo via the escalator seeking the first train to Queenstown Road, Battersea.

PART 2: MAX

CHAPTER 5: MAX'S STORY, SALZBERG, 1939

Everyone at that time had a story – they had to have a story. Max moved very near to evil. He acted as if he too were complicit. I peered into his dreamworld and am still unsure what he knew and what he did. I shall never know for certain what his motives were, even though I have shared so many of his dreams. His story is revealing and awkward whatever the truth about him. His dreams open a door to the minds that fed on death and evil but also the minds of those who struggled to resist. Men – not perfect men but decent enough under the circumstances perhaps - who were tortured and murdered by those who were so much worse. He had to watch and wait while this happened. He wanted Erika to understand. His absolution? Ask Canaris. Ask Kaltenbrunner. But more of them later.

Max Mayer had believed that there would be hope and excitement in Berlin. There was nothing in Austria for him right now. The German peoples had united and after so long in the shadows of defeat there were signs of regeneration and life. A future.

'Herr Hitler will accomplish great things Max' Helmut Mayer told his son. 'He has united our countries and our race. We shall rise again and do great things. The Aryan nations.'

'I don't want to hear this again. I shall have to leave!'

He had attended university in Vienna to study law but had not wanted to take a doctorate to qualify for practice. So, he joined the police in Salzburg. Where Ernst Kaltenbrunner, anti-Semite and lawyer, was a local Nazi leader.

'Just until I know what I really want.'

Max believed that his family had, for some time, secretly wanted to separate him from his friends including

Erika Adler, whose background was Jewish. Max couldn't understand the significance of this because all his friends were loyal Austrians with historical bonds to their country. The country they all shared. But he knew some of what was going on. He listened to speeches. Read the newspapers. He wanted to make things right.

'I would miss you all if I went to Berlin. You, my friends, Austria. Salzburg ....'

'And no doubt some of those particularly disagreeable people you spent your time with when you were in Vienna'.

Max sighed.

'Who do you mean? I like my friends. They are all good people'.

Helmut looked away.

'You need to spread your wings. You have talent. You could go far. Just listen to me!' The last few words were delivered with a passion Max had rarely seen in his father who was usually a kind, happy, family man lacking outward emotion.

'Is this what the new world is to be about? Hate?' His father sighed.

'I understand. And I shall try. Later, maybe, I might be a lawyer – or perhaps politics ...?' Max started thinking of the opportunities that might come his way if he should go to Germany. His father knew people – Austrians, mostly from the local Nazi party who had welcomed the Anschluss. Some had moved to Berlin and taken up important positions - several in the police force. That was the Mayer family's destination of choice for Max.

Not long after this conversation, arrangements were made for Max's move. The family had spent the Christmas of 1938 - together – not only his parents and sisters, but several aunts and cousins had joined them at their Salzburg home. To say good-bye. The warmth of the family was now replaced by an especially cold January. The only way to keep out the cold was to continue celebrations. That was the secret motto of the

Mayer clan.

'Eat. Drink. Stay merry - whatever the morality of it.'

In spite of his fleeting misgivings about the suffering of others, Max was the same as the rest of the Mayer family. He loved parties. He relished good food and good company.

Consequently, when the time was right, he embarked on the journey. First to Vienna, accompanied by both his parents and his two younger sisters, where they spent a celebratory, but sad, weekend in a famous luxurious hotel on the Ringstrasse. There they were treated to warmth, opulence, indulgent dining rooms that were shared with certain dignitaries - notably some prominent German politicians, actors, musicians and artists.

'I am saying goodbye to Austria forever – I feel it.'

On the Monday morning, very early, Max and his parents joined the crowd heading for the main railway station. Max had all his papers and first-class travel documents along with his two small cases.

'You must buy what you need once you reach your apartment. There are many wonderful places in Berlin' his mother emphasized. This was followed by tears, hugs slightly quelling sense of adventure along with pangs of anxiety. Also, there was something Max sensed but could not quite understand.

The twelve-hour journey across Czechoslovakia to Berlin promised to be comfortable and interesting giving him the chance to read newspapers, see the remarkable countryside and think about the new life that awaited. 'No doubt there would be interesting travelling companions as well.'

CHAPTER 6: TRAVELLING BY TRAIN

The first-class sleeping compartment his parents had booked for him was empty. The porter had led him away from his parents and the Viennese crowd, into the compartment with its gleaming walnut walls, putting the luggage into the built-in closet while indicating that Max should look around the impressive, comfortable-looking compartment. Two bunks were set in the wall above well-padded, facing bench seats. The carriage smelled of cleaning fluid and polish and the sheets and blankets of lavender. Max felt content. He handed the porter a generous gratuity, anticipating potential benefits from his gesture during the journey.

As Max leaned from the window to wave to the crowds, somewhere among which were his family, the train slowly chugged its way out of the station. He was expecting a travelling companion because he saw the small case of soft brown leather lying on one of the bunks. It was large enough to hold everything a man would need for a weekend away from home, and as Max couldn't see any other form of luggage, he concluded that his companion was probably on his way back to Berlin after a brief visit to Vienna. It was a Monday morning, so he guessed that Berlin was this man's home.

I'm going to have to wait and see. I hope he isn't going to regale me with Nazi propaganda. I would find that hard. It is all so confusing now.

He prepared to relax, maybe even catch up on some sleep. But before he felt comfortable enough to do that, he checked that both of his cases were safely stowed in the luggage locker. He noted to himself, again that his was the only substantially sized luggage in the carriage. All seemed well as he placed his small hand grip on the seat next to him, digging in to find the daily newspaper. As ever the content was depressing, lauding the Nazis and Hitler in particular. Max knew that it was not a good idea to express his personal views out loud.

He sighed as he came to the end of everything that he had wanted to read before ringing the service bell to order some coffee and cake. As the porter he had summoned left the compartment with detailed instructions, another man entered. He nodded to Max, taking his place on the bench seat opposite. Max returned the greeting lifting up his newspaper once again to see whether anything else might be of interest. It wasn't but Max took the chance to look at his companion in more detail.

The man's high forehead and spectacles made him resemble a university professor, although he looked more vibrant than many of those that Max had encountered. His companion here had full lips and a surprisingly ready smile. Max guessed he was in his thirties. He wore a well-cut suit of dark blue, a white shirt fully buttoned but without a tie. Neither was there any insignia to suggest his political leanings or nationality. Max's father often wore similar clothes which meant nothing other than he had a professional occupation.

This man doesn't look like someone who spends his time in an office though. The clue is in the absence of a tie. But neither does he look like someone who is afraid every day. Doubtless he's a member of the Party and I am guessing a German. He knows he's on the winning side. I need to be careful.

Something that Max had noticed in several of his

friends and some of his parents' friends was how they often hesitated before expressing an opinion. Their eyes would seek out the expressions and demeanor of those who were listening to them, while they mentally personalized what they were about to say.

The man in the carriage held out his hand to Max rising slightly from his seat as he leaned forward: 'My name is Gisevius – Hans'.

Max stood up and reciprocated noting the strong grip and the penetrating eye contact. He immediately felt a mixture of fear and excitement.

This is not a coincidence. No random assigning of this travelling companion.

Hans then lifted his case down from the bunk, took out a book to read along with what looked like a notebook. He then slowly placed the case in the luggage locker alongside Max's. The newcomer proceeded to flick through the pages of the notebook changing his expression according to what must have been on the page, eventually making a few notes at key points. Max was amused by what he identified as this show of what? Importance? Indifference to him? He wasn't sure.

Hans didn't speak until the waiter arrived with Max's refreshments. Hans then ordered coffee, brandy and some pastries for himself. When his drinks and cake arrived, Hans set his reading materials aside to focus his lively face on Max and his food.

'There are a few things we need to discuss.'

Max had no idea what this man, he had only just met, was talking about unless he was wanting to talk about sleeping or washing arrangements. But Max was wrong about that.

By night-time they had talked, eaten and even managed to laugh together. Max felt as if his brain had been through a sieve. But he didn't feel bad about it. Life was confusing right now. Hans, it seemed, was a friend of Helmut, Max's father

– more so they were working together on some "particular" projects. Max was astounded as he thought back over recent conversations with his father particularly since the Germans annexed his homeland. He had been convinced his father was a Nazi sympathizer but this man, Hans, made him doubt his former conviction. Hans was ambivalent about the Third Reich and its leadership, if not an active enemy of the Nazis.

Nothing appeared to be clear cut any more. Max's companion had revealed himself as a former member of the Gestapo, then he chose to leave it to work for the police service in the interior ministry. Then he was sacked by Heinrich Himmler after the latter had taken over the police service. Then Hans joined the German intelligence service – the Abwehr.

What does this make Hans? Not a fully committed Nazi – that's certain. But can I trust him with my views? Is he setting a trap?

Max was impressed, confused and amazed and no more so when he was asked to consider a similar type of career. As they continued to eat and drink Max was aware that Hans Gisevius was looking closely at him.

Trying to work me out? Check my response? I could have him arrested for what he has told me.

He then thought about his father thinking that he might have much preferred Hans' version of his father's politics than the one he had believed to be the case.

CHAPTER 7: THE MAN IN THE CAR

They arrived at the main station, the Anhalter Bahnhof, in Berlin soon after enjoying the appetizing supper served in the restaurant car. Max's head was reeling as his mind went over the conversations he had had with his travelling companion. The problem now though was that Hans had disappeared from the carriage about half an hour before the train arrived in Berlin. He was becoming increasingly concerned he had been led into a trap – revealing himself as a police recruit who was a potential security risk. He sighed and smiled to himself.

This is exciting! I feel things are so much better than I anticipated – regardless.

He peered out the window and looked around him. The lights were on across the station, illuminating the enormous vaulted glass ceiling and the high curved windows that cast dark shadows on the walls marking the end of the parallel tracks. The long-distance arrivals from the south all ended their journeys here. He picked up his cases just before he stepped out from his comfortable, warm, carriage onto the platform waiting for his chance to summon a porter.

Max was greeted instead by a biting wind, that had entered the station. He immediately retreated. Back inside the carriage his chest still hurt from that first bitter intake of breath. He waited before venturing out again. Other passengers streamed from their carriages, several of whom were met by friends and porters. Max was hesitant. He stood on the platform and looked around.

I'm not sure what to do now. Everyone else seems to know where they are and where they're going. But there are no porters! At least none available.

Then a young man in porter's livery appeared from the dimly lit platform end moving to lift Max's cases.

That is odd.

But there was no time to waste. Not much time to think either.

'Where to sir?'

Max indicated that he wanted a taxi. But now forewarned about the cold, he first lifted the collar of his coat, wrapping his headscarf, previously buried in his luggage, around his face. He felt better prepared for the short journey to the apartment he was to share with the son of one of his father's friends.

He followed the porter away from the trains across the wide, cathedral-like station concourse. The lighting surprised him a little as there continued to be much talk about war and Max had expected Berlin to be more subdued, at least at night. But there had also been talk of how Hitler and the Nazi Party had improved the lives of ordinary Germans. That was one of the reasons he was here of course. He was now feeling uncertain.

Did I make this decision? Was I pushed?

He dismissed these thoughts. Pushing them out of his mind as he could think of no reason that anyone he knew, especially his parents, would want him away from Salzburg.

'And they would want me nearby if there is to be a war.'

Max spotted a line of Mercedes cars in the street beyond the archways at the station entrance. He headed in that direction only to become disorientated by the porter who was heading further along the concourse where there were fewer lights.

'Sir, I know of a taxi that is quicker for you'.

He nodded and continued to follow the young man

whose pace had increased. He could see a smaller archway ahead of them. Max, stiff after his long journey, struggled to keep pace. Then he saw the car. A Mercedes, black as far as he could tell in the available light, with an enormous bonnet housing the engine, a high front windscreen, dark back windows, large running board with a man in uniform, smoking a cigarette and leaning against the driver's door.

He does not look like a taxi driver. But who knows? Germans are not like us.

Max headed towards the Mercedes. The smoking, uniformed man did not appear to notice his arrival. The porter put down the two cases while Max reached into his pocket to tip his porter guide. He counted some coins held them out towards where he had been. But the man had disappeared. Into the dark end of the concourse. The only person there was this strangely attired taxi driver.

'Friedrichstrasse please'.

The man looked at him. Dropped the cigarette on the ground. Stamped on it and opened the car door and got in. Max was left looking at the car with his mouth open.

At least that is what it feels like. What is going on?

He rapidly came to the conclusion that if he didn't put his own bags into the car and get into the passenger seat unaided that the man and car would drive away. He lifted the first of his suitcases into the back seat pushing it across the leather surface.

Then: 'Tch, Tch. Stop this.' There was a man there on the far side of the bench seat. He was horrified. Then, slowly, Max recognized the voice.

Could that be Hans the man from the train? But he left the carriage. Why didn't he come back? He could have helped me.

He then felt a little stupid. The man Max still believed to be the driver appeared at his side, gestured for him to retreat from his failing attempt to get into the car. He then slowly collected Max's two cases placing them in the trunk. Max suspected that the driver was sneering at him. The man in the car gestured to him to get in.

'Mr. Mayer? Please forgive me for deserting your railway carriage'. Max nodded, increasingly curious. Although his former travelling companion's face was in the shadows Max well recalled his features.

'My name you will remember is Hans' he sounded as if he smiled then and Max nodded slightly 'and you are well known to me, as since our time together, I am to you'.

Max was stunned. They had had a fascinating, although risky, conversation about Anschluss, Hitler, Europe. And his father. He now felt a chill creep from his stomach to his neck.

Has he trapped me? Is he Gestapo?

Max knew his father had friends and contacts in Berlin, but could they help him now? He was convinced he was to be taken for questioning. And what then?

Max's body felt as heavy as lead. Total exhaustion. As if his physical being had become welded to the seat of the car. And at that moment they drove off. He stared at his companion. Gradually, as they motored on he caught glimpses of Hans's face, completing the jigsaw from his memory. The thick brown hair that was receding over his bespectacled, square, pale, face made him look bookish. This contrasted sharply with the cleft chin and full lips. He also had incredibly long legs.

He looks like a civil servant. He probably is. High up in the Nazi party.

He had no idea how to behave or what to say. He simply gave in to the ordeal he was heading for. His knowledge of Berlin's topography was limited but he was convinced that they had crossed and left Friedrichstrasse behind and were heading south and east of the city. He tried to stop himself shaking with fear.

CHAPTER 8: WORK WITH US

The car drove onwards. They had left the civic buildings and the city lights behind them and were driving through a darker suburban landscape. Affluent houses with large strips of land surrounding them. Hans had been watching Max for some time. But Max stared ahead of him attempting to make sense of where they had been and were heading now.

This is not what I expected. I'm not sure it is what I want. Did my father arrange this? Have I been kidnapped?

After about an hour, with neither Hans nor Max saying a great deal to each other, the driver stopped outside what appeared to be a large detached house. As far as Max could tell there was one light on behind a blind in an upstairs room. That was all. Other houses shone brightly in their living areas, outside driveways and terraces. The driver switched off the engine, opened the door for Hans and then for Max before lifting his luggage from the trunk.

'Is this where I end my journey?'

Max felt afraid. Hans who may or may not have sensed this slapped him on the shoulder.

'Come on man – pick up your bags.' He then nodded to the driver who returned to the car as Hans marched towards the front door of the house rattling some keys as Max watched the car drive away. He noted Hans' self-confidence as he opened the front door beckoning to him impatiently, although still with humour. Max was holding his cases and staring up at the lighted window.

'This is where you will be staying for a few days, so come on in. Make yourself comfortable.'

Hans pointed out the bathroom and living room suggesting they might both benefit from a night-cap. When Max materialized from the bathroom, he found his former travelling companion in a large living room that stretched the length of the house. Hans was sprawling on a long russet coloured sofa facing an identical one. A coffee table was placed between them. He directed Max towards the sofa indicating a broad crystal tumbler containing clear yellow liquid – Max guessed it was whisky. It was. Max nodded before downing at least half of it gratefully and quickly. He leaned back on the sofa, mirroring Hans' stance, feeling the warm rush of the drink in his throat and stomach. He stared at Hans. He could think of nothing to say but was convinced he was due a detailed explanation.

Max realized that neither of them had ever exchanged the customary 'Heil Hitler' greeting which made him slightly wary.

Has he marked me down as disloyal? A traitor? Was he seeking me out on the train? But then he hasn't said that either. Neither did the driver. Christ. I am done for whatever, so I have to face up to what comes next.

'We want you to work with us.'

Max sat forward. His head was swimming slightly both from the long journey and his unexpected destination. And now this statement. It wasn't a request.

'What work? And who is us?' Max felt proud of his articulate and direct response to the question.

'Well the "us" is me. I have been in the Gestapo as you know. I told you. Now I work for the German intelligence service. We are loyal Germans and Austrians who desire to save our countries. I think I know your answer.'

Max also knew what his answer had to be. What he wanted it to be. He knew too much now so there was no choice anyway.

'From tomorrow you will have visitors. One at a time. This neighbourhood is safe. Mostly. If you are sensible. It will be about two weeks. Then an excellent position is ready for you in the offices of Prinz-Albrecht Strasse. You will be expected.'

'The Gestapo headquarters?'

'That's right.'

'But the secret police? I only wanted to be an ordinary – a straightforward policeman. Criminals – murder. Robbery. Hell - you know. You understand what I expected.'

'For sure. But we have far more important things. We have to save our nation. From war. From corruption. From hate. Very soon you will learn about the Gestapo. What you are to do. And how you are to help us.'

Max picked up his whisky glass and sipped its contents slowly. Hans stood up, moving towards a sideboard behind his sofa and lifting the decanter proceeded to top up the tumblers for both of them.

'Oh' Hans spoke as if in afterthought 'there is someone I need to introduce you to very soon. Her name is Mary.'

'That's an English name – at least the way you say it makes it sound like that.'

Hans smiled. 'It probably is. At least that is how you and I will address her.'

CHAPTER 9: DISCLOSURES, LONDON, PRESENT DAY

It was raining again.
So much for global warming.
The autumn term was gathering momentum meaning that it was about this time that everyone on the staff of the Tavi considered they needed to offer the students a "reading week". Everyone was tired. Wilson had just completed a run of five personal tutorials with some doctoral candidates which was interesting, encouraging but exhausting. Something he typically never realized until after he had stopped. After the adrenaline had dripped away and his back began to ache.

He decided to catch the lift to the top floor canteen to buy a coffee to keep him going because his meeting with Marion Morgan was almost due. Just time to catch up with the endless paperwork. *Maybe.*

The canteen was full of animated relatively young women and men, so he had a ten-minute wait in the queue.

> *Our dream flashed into his consciousness as he waited. A feeling of disdain. Well, in fact much stronger. There was good looking, dignified man standing before him smiling. Meeting his eyes. But I could sense Wilson felt disgust deep in his stomach. 'I was simply a good organizer – I made sure that my country produced the armaments we needed. We were at war.'*

And then fireworks, flags – red, black – and joyous shouts rang out. It was a work of art – only it was also a vision of the living Hell. I actually believe he knew I was there with him in the dream and in his contemplations. Then, as he began to puzzle out what this was all about, the queue moved forward.

A class of trainee psychotherapists were taking their mid-session break. Most nights students were in the building until seven p.m. After that the majority of lights were turned out, offices vacated while only the occasional door remained open to attend to the few trainees in the final leg of their qualifications.

Wilson would have loved to return home and watch more of the Nuremberg trial television programme that had become increasingly germane to his thoughts since his encounter with Marion Morgan. But that would have to wait. He had to find out what she wanted from him first.

What was she going to tell me? Or what does she want me to do more likely. I just want to go home! Am I wanting to flee? too scared to find out?

Wilson, coffee in hand, headed back to his small office on the 2nd floor that he shared with James Cook, another semi-retired psychoanalyst and lecturer. If you pressed your face against their office window, you could see that it overlooked the back of Freud's statue while also taking in a view towards the trees around Belsize Lane and Fitzjohn's Avenue. There were two full-sized desks either side of the room, each with an office chair behind it. In the small path between the door and the window was a comfortable green armchair. The intention being that either James or Wilson would most probably be there alone so were only expected one visitor at a time. It was more than satisfactory.

Unlike Wilson, James had worked at the clinic for around 30 years. As well as in his private practice on nearby Finchley Road ('not far from Freud's consulting room'), as he told everyone.

Well you have to go past Maresfield Gardens to get to Finchley Road I think James! But he's a good bloke for all the pretentions.

James, divorced several years ago and apparently happily single, spent the remainder of his time involved with a dog and cat rescue facility. Wilson admired him for this, often being tempted to adopt a dog himself but he resisted - aware that he could not provide the care and attention the animal deserved.

Wearing his Burberry raincoat with a man-bag over his shoulder, James was leaving the office as Wilson arrived after his longer than intended wait in the canteen.

'Excellent I don't have to lock up. But don't hang around too long old man. I hear the weather is getting worse. Go home and have some good Scotch whisky'.

Wilson saw the logic of that and wished he could. As he nudged James on the shoulder with a grin, risking potential spillage of his coffee, Marion came down the corridor carrying a box folder. James looked at her. Then at Wilson.

'Well!' and he smiled as he went away nodding to Marion as she stood aside for him to pass. Wilson felt he should protest to James about his assumptions but saw there was little point. He then felt embarrassed as he was holding only one coffee cup. Marion entered the office not waiting for an invitation.

'Don't worry – I'm all coffeed out.'

Is that a play on my name?

She took the armchair and waited for Wilson to get seated and as comfortable as he could be. He smiled and took a sip from the plastic cup. Marion looked at him and placed the box file on his desk, opening it as she did so but without letting go. It was full of ageing paper. The top sheet was in type face but there were several words scratched out and replaced and notes in the margins. He reached to pull it nearer to his side of the desk, but Marion pounced on it holding it even more tightly.

'Oh I am sorry. I didn't mean to snatch – er I thought it was for me to read.'

'Look Wilson you must please forgive me for the .... Well this cloak and dagger stuff. I feel possessive of this. Let me tell you what this is – then what it might mean.'

He looked at her and nodded noticing that the long-established anxious lines above her eyes had been replaced by a flushed eagerness.

She looks in charge.

'So, well, my mother died about nine months ago.'

He frowned but she held up her hand, palm towards him signaling that he should stop if he was about to offer condolences.

'It's Okay. You know she was a strange one. Kind. Well intentioned and all that but I hardly knew her. She was in her mid 80s when she died – heart problems. She, Susan Hart – that's my mother's name, was brought up from quite a young age by her grandparents – my great-grandparents – I hope you're following ....' Marion smiled at him gently.

'Her mother, Mary Hart my great grandparents' daughter, my grandmother, you see, had died. She was murdered in fact.'

At this point Wilson did intervene.

'Marion, what you are telling me is a tragic story. Please don't pretend it all washes off you.'

'Okay Wilson. Apologies – I didn't want all my losses and family history to get in the way here.'

She smiled and looked at the box file gently brushing her hand across it.

'Why do you think I am in this business? It takes a damaged soul to help find the flaws in others!'

They both grinned at each other. Rather too politely perhaps.

'Let me get it straight then. Before you reach the core of what you want to tell me, including what's in that file. You, Marion, are a psychoanalyst of note and a more than worthy colleague of mine.'

She began to relax.

He continued: 'You liked your late mother - Susan, she was a good person although, or in spite of the fact that she had had a difficult emotional life. Perhaps or likely because her mother Mary, your grandmother, died – unpleasantly – you're going to tell me the story – when your mother was a girl. I'm assuming her grandparents – your great grandparents were also reasonable human beings.

'As far as I know Wilson, I think so. But they would have been devastated too. A murdered daughter.'

'And I also note that your grandmother Mary and your mother Susan had the same surnames. Too early to be that kind of feminist so I'm guessing your mother didn't get married?'

'Nor did Mary my grandmother.'

Wilson smiled.

'And you are Morgan?' He hesitated. 'I don't mean to pry – and certainly I'm not judging – just wanting to get my head around the characters before you tell me the plot. And before you say anything – I'm not being flippant.'

She nodded giving him a faint smile of acknowledgement.

'My ex-husband. But I thought we Hart women needed a change of name!' She provided him with an uncomfortable grin.

He looked at her, nodding imperceptibly to encourage her to go on now they had established some rules.

'Well Mary, my grandmother worked for the British Government – Intelligence actually - during the war. My mother, Susan, was a young child and in most respects in the way of Mary's career.'

'Where was your grandfather? Who was he?'

'Not sure – I don't know much about him and my mother never talked much about him. But he may be an important part of this story. I think he was an Austrian.'

'Really?'

'This is why I want your help. He disappeared – and I

knew nothing about him other than he was called Max. And then I found these'. Marion gestured towards the box file.

Wilson reached for his reading glasses, perched them on his nose and watched her over the frame.

'I am guessing he – my grandfather - must have been – well some kind of spy. Don't you think?'

Wilson was trying to keep his mouth firmly closed but couldn't 'Well …. Errr …' He took a steadying breath 'what makes you think that?'

Marion let go of the box file for the first time and gently pushed it across the desk towards him. The papers here. I found them recently soon after my mother died. She was really untidy – and more than that – never threw anything away so I have been going through the papers for months. Whenever I had the time …'

Marion looked at her empty hands 'and whenever I could bear it. I am thinking that maybe he was – like – well what you might call a "double agent"?' The last few words were left as a question.

Wilson felt tired.

'Shall I get us some coffee? I could do with it.'

He stood up, grabbing his stick from the back of his chair. He felt a bit shaky, dismissing it as physical exhaustion after the long day. He was, as always, grateful for James' coffee machine and the pods. Wilson normally bought his coffee from the canteen as he didn't want to take advantage, particularly as James' need was greater and more frequent than his. But this was a slightly unusual event. And now the idea of a spy, double agent, betrayal and murder were making his mind spin. And he dreaded losing control of his thinking. As the steam died down he carried both cups and placed them on his desk.

'It is a bit of a fairy story – and in some ways I want to keep hold of it – let it stay like that because it is so much more – well glamorous – exciting – I guess than being the daughter of unmarried mother whose own mother never married either!'

Marion laughed but Wilson could tell it was somewhat hollow. It sounded like a strangled cry for help. He was leaning on his desk looking intently at Marion, while aware that she had let go of the box file that rested between them.

'This file. It's all about this man Max. I do believe he was my grandfather. But it seems very complicated.' Marion looked down and there was a pause. Wilson tried to work out whether she was lost in thought or had decided not to continue.

'But I know you will remember something I said to you last week. That I know more about you than you thought.'

Wilson straightened his back and stared at her.

'You look angry. I apologize. But I know Gabriel.'

Wilson frowned. He couldn't work out who that was or what this person might have said about him.

'British Intelligence – the priest from East Germany? Gabriel was there – when you came to identify the body. It's no longer classified.'

Wilson did a quick addition.

'I don't know what you are talking about Marion.' He wished he could get up and leave but he was in his office not hers.

Seven years is definitely not enough for information to be released.

'Okay. I understand. But please forgive me. Please. I know.' She stressed the *"know"*.

Clearly, she knows more than she should.

He wasn't certain how to proceed. If he read the contents of the box file on the basis of her understanding of his intelligence work, then he would be liable himself for breaching the Official Secrets Act. But he was curious now – although he remained uncertain still of what she wanted.

'Look I know, because you mentioned in passing to me – that you were fascinated by the first effort at post war justice – the famous first Nuremberg trials. I know you have spent time in Nuremberg. I know your late wife was actually from East Germany. You yourself have mentioned this in lectures and occasionally in the coffee bar. True?'

Wilson felt rather like a suspect.

Suspected of what for God's sake?

'Yes. Hanna was from East Germany. And like your grandmother Mary, she too was murdered.'

So, I've let her in.

Marion's appearance of being shocked seemed to be slightly over the top and Wilson recognized he had been led somewhere he had attempted to resist.

I give in.

'Look Marion – please get to the point. I am a bit confused – what do you want me to do?'

'Please don't look so cross. I am so very sorry that I have upset you – it's obvious that I have but ….'

She stared at the file before gently pushing it further towards his side of the desk.

'Thinking psychoanalytically, I would very much value your opinion on Max's story. This folder shows how he talked about his work when he was with the Nazi police – Gestapo. He might – he definitely was – a contact of Hans Gisevius – do you know about him?'

Wilson nodded. He had become aware of Gisevius through the drama documentary on the Nuremberg trial. He had been a witness, although he had had a background in the police and as a contact of the Americans in Switzerland. The box file, now so near to his elbows as they rested on his desk, felt as if it were burning a hole in the polished wood. He was very keen to examine the contents but also unsure how wise it would be to touch it let alone read it.

'But I wonder – I would please like your – advice or verdict I suppose I mean on who he really was. Was he on Gisevius side – against Hitler? Was he using his relationship with Gisevius to escape justice – or much worse? Did he betray Hitler's enemies – the people who tried to resist?'

Who would I be betraying if I took this? I am now a captive of my curiosity!

'And, well one more thing ...' Marion hesitated 'There are some documents in the archives at MI6.'

Wilson felt very tired and very irritable.

'I think they might help me in my search for my grandfather. And also my grandmother's murderer.'

'Ok Marion – you need to know that I have no access to any files – secret, open, archived or current. I can't help – I'm sorry but you've come to the wrong person.'

She looked as if she were about to cry which made Wilson feel even more irritable.

'But please then – let me have your opinion – please read these papers. They are just a background story. They are interesting – and just tell me your opinion of Max – was he a serious Nazi?'

Wilson nodded and agreed and began to feel guilty for being ill-tempered.

I know this is a bad idea. Something is very odd about this request – but what? It sounds so innocent.

PART 3: ERIKA

CHAPTER 10: ERIKA'S STORY – VIENNA 1938

I have frequently attempted to get myself into her waking, conscious mind. If I am to continue to have her dreams, even if they are now such old dreams, it seems sensible and even polite to think about the woman's rational world. Living in central Europe. A woman of certain privilege over and above the devastation. After the fall of Empire and universal economic wreckage. Health. Happiness and success. Part of me still envies her. But perhaps I should be a lot more grateful that I only have to share her dreams than I have so far given the impression of being. I do value them. How else might someone not born when evil entered our world, grasp what it felt like? I shall return to think about her life before it became important to me. Perhaps some answers lie there. Let me try anyway.

Erika made her way through the familiar streets of Vienna lined by their tall, majestic blocks of apartments. This city had always made her feel safe. Until now. The pavements were still sound. The buildings still solid, predictable and dependable, particularly here in old Vienna. But nothing was safe now. Not since the murder of Dollfuss, the Chancellor of Austria, four years ago. And then the constant threat of a German invasion. And now it has happened. It was hardly an invasion though. More like the acceptance of an invitation to Hitler from Schuschnigg.

'Please come and take us over! We have lost our empire and now want to be in yours.'

Erika was sickened. Schuschnigg - the man who had declared Austria a Christian country where everyone was equal.

Was he so stupid that he hadn't worked out what Hitler was all about? Come on – you can hardly believe that can you? And surely the Austrians who wanted to remain decent human beings – those who had been part of the Empire – surely they understood what might happen if they gave way to Hitler? And Kaltenbrunner – he was not exactly an also ran. Both came from

Austrian villages. But who knew that then? They all did of course but the rest of us – those of us not yet born, the Austrians who were Jewish the Austrians who were against the Nazis – maybe they didn't see them coming. I can't work that out. But it happened.

Nazi emblems decorated most houses. Small red and black flags hung from windows. Children waved them innocently as they walked to school. Large sheets adorned with swastikas dressed the outside of all public buildings. That day, the day they had marched across the borders, was etched in Erika's memory. Her homeland was no longer hers. She had tried to ignore antisemitism all through her life. But it seemed that there was little chance to do that any longer. Her parents had expected to go to New York at an uncle's invitation and their plans were now being accelerated. Erika had told them that she would choose England if she ever needed to escape and her parents seemed to accept the idea even though they were worried.

Erika was not so sure about the future though. Dr. Freud was planning to remain in Vienna, the home of his life and work. She wished to be as near as she was able to be to her friend and mentor.

He wasn't stupid but he was old, tired and ill. The cancer was virulent. And as you all know now, he didn't last too much longer even after he escaped the Nazis. But at least he died in freedom.

Erika felt that she too wanted to remain in her own country. That was where she belonged. Freud had disbanded the Vienna Psychoanalytic Society despite his own intentions to remain, thinking that some people might have to leave, although he had no specific plans for himself or even his family at that stage. Everyone from the Society had understood the need to move on and most of Erika's former colleagues were making their own arrangements to find more compatible places to live and work.

Freud was displaying his ambivalence to the developing situation you might think. Or maybe he really was just tired of it all by then. Maybe if it had not been for what happened to

Anna he would have succumbed to his own death drive.

Erika turned to walk along Berggasse to Dr. Freud's house. It was here, at number 19 that he had his home that he shared with Martha, his wife, Minna her sister and his six children - Anna, Mathilde, Sophie, Martin, Oliver and Ernst. More important for Erika though, it was here that he practiced his clinical work and wrote his papers.

And it is here that I meet him. Where he makes my brain hurt with the effort of thinking about my patients. I am so lucky. I don't want to lose this.

Despite being more than eighty years old Freud remained mentally alert and a deep, clear thinker as Erika knew so well. Despite this she sometimes thought that he protected himself from his unconscious anxieties about his cancer by his obsession with his work, defending himself from fear of his imminent death.

And protected himself from any thoughts of Nazi ideology while holding a further ambivalence about his Jewishness. Fortunately, fate was soon to intervene and spur him into his final life affirming actions.

Freud continued to treat patients, whom he saw in the consulting room at Berggasse 19, actively disregarding the Nazi insignia draped throughout Vienna. He also ran supervision meetings with students and favourite colleagues, including Erika, alongside clinical seminars in the small, cozy, but crowded office adjoining his clinical space. Furthermore, he continued with his writing despite the trauma from a few years ago when piles of his books were burned publicly by the Nazis and their sympathizers. Psychoanalysis – the hated *Jewish* science.

Erika's intention that day was to discuss two particular patients. One, a young woman who appeared to have fantasies about being dead. The other a man who was suffering from paranoid thoughts and related anxiety that had become so intense he was unable to continue work as a teacher. Both were Jewish and Erika considered that their symptoms had some basis in reality. Their anxieties and fantasies providing a warning of what seemed likely to come in this new Austrian state. They also had dreams that emphasized the central significance of their anxieties and fears for their futures. It was Erika's job to work with these patients to explore how their previous experiences and unconscious drives were manifesting themselves in these specific forms.

Erika arrived outside the tall, grey building, stood by the double doors and rang the bell that denoted the professor's apartment. One of the maids opened the door for her.

'Good morning Hilde' Erika smiled.

Hilde, recognizing who she was, directed her upstairs although she looked strained.

'He is not so well today, Dr. Adler. I hope you might be able to help him. He is in pain and ...'.

Hilde blushed slightly looking embarrassed that she had gone too far imparting such personal information.

'It's OK Hilde. I understand and will be careful. Thank you for the warning.'

Erika, familiar now with the grand, high ceilings of the wide hallway veered off towards the staircase a short way along the hall. Reaching the second floor she turned right into the waiting room and took a seat on one of the formal dark red chairs. She was always content to wait, enjoying the atmosphere of the room particularly the paintings and other artifacts that Freud had collected over his long career.

Across the corridor was the family apartment, although no sounds emerged from there. It was likely that Freud had a patient in the room adjoining the waiting room and had been working for several hours.

Shortly the door opened, and the professor came out walking towards her.

There wasn't anyone with him today. What has happened?

Each time Erika set eyes upon Dr. Freud his appearance

startled her. In his absence she envisioned him as well built, with white hair and beard, round spectacles and the ubiquitous cigar. Although not tall, he was sturdy with a commanding presence. At least in her ongoing thoughts of him.

But each time they met, just for the first few minutes, Erika was shocked. He was old. Sick. White faced and frail. His jaw looked strange and his speech forced and slightly slurred.

That prosthetic jaw. It must be so awful for him.

But once she was settled in her chair, telling him of her patients or herself, she saw him as he used to be – the man she recalled every time she was apart from him.

The cigar was no longer omnipresent, although he did defy doctor's orders on occasion, so that it was not unusual for him to be holding a cigar moving it round in his hand and staring at it. Erika knew he was sorely tempted to smoke but if he did, that might be the last thing he ever did. But today was different.

'Anna has been arrested. She's been questioned briefly by the Gestapo. They have let her go for now. I have to take her from this city. We are going to London.'

Erika, whose parents had chosen to leave Vienna for New York, was stunned. She felt the terror of her potential isolation. So many of her friends and colleagues had already gone. She felt his eyes on her. They were posing a vital question. She nodded.

'Yes. I shall come.'

CHAPTER 11: DREAM SHARING

There are other dreams too. Not just Erika's. Or maybe they are all hers. I can't always tell but I suspect they may be another's. There is a man – German speaking – Austrian accent I think. He dreams about her – Erika. And it is so strange. I see him and through him I can see her. He is tall – actually he is what I imagine to be a giant – not an attractive appearance. Far from it in fact. He is a lumbering ox-like man. He looks strong. His face is distorted by deep scars – alongside his nose and up through the left side of his face. His hair is thinning. His face might have been handsome. But it is too cruel and there are those deep scars. Already I don't like him. He sneers at me. He seems to like her for some reason. I would have expected Erika to be interested in similar people to the ones I like. Not this one. But that is the benefit of insight like mine - if you could call enforced dream sharing that. It is no longer my choice. I was curious at first – of course. I admit it. Wouldn't you be? But now I feel shame, unclean. But more than that – I am afraid. What is happening to me?

Erika herself is almost exactly like she is in her own dreams but when seen through <u>his</u> eyes there are things that are less clear. Less obvious. More questionable even. He appears to be uncertain about whether he can trust her. He is certain she doesn't trust him.

When I have <u>his</u> dreams, I know she should be more uncertain about him. But I become just as confused as each of those two when I think about it. I don't always have the time to give in to such contemplations but as they have forced themselves into my head it is important not to ignore what is going on. If I should do that, I am likely to be the loser.

I don't want to live in the past, particularly when it's not my past. Nor is it a past that occurred in my lifetime, but it is one that so many have told me about. There are so many stories – real and exaggerated. Misremembered although even when that is the case the memories that are retained shape the awareness of the thinker.

What I recollect from history, stories, films and books is that identities and loyalties shift when everyday realities are overturned. One day you are living in your own home, you are a success or a failure or simply ordinary. The next day you are an outsider, the enemy within, the enemy from afar who was never part of 'us', vermin, expendable, hunted, murdered. The lucky ones are exiles and consequently outsiders somewhere else. This is the case for both him and for her.

Power shifts. A failed artist, and a briefly imprisoned army veteran becomes an all-powerful dictator who changes history and raises questions for all of us about the nature of evil demonstrating the impossibility of human goodness.

You are the winner or the loser. Who is on the side of right? Are any of us?

CHAPTER 12: THE LONDON CLINIC, MARCH, 1945

Living in London's Camden Town meant that a brisk walk to Hampstead, for a young fit person was possible and even enjoyable when the rain and wind held off. Erika was forty now but energetically in denial about being *nearly* middle aged. She remained determined to get to work on foot. She had bad memories of the London underground and avoided using it as far as she could.

Gloria Mars, Erika's landlady, had been an air-raid warden during the Blitz. On many occasions, throughout the worst of the bombing, she had directed Erika and their neighbours to the safety of those underground platforms deep under London. Even while they were there, they could feel the thud as every explosion occurred. When each raid was over, they reemerged into the morning, where the smell of smoke and the silence ate into Erika's consciousness.

At least there were few bombing raids now. I think they know the game is up. They are trying to retreat and deny their actions.

Gloria declared: 'We've seen the last of them now. The Russians will see to that. The German military is destroyed.'

Visions of her homeland haunted Erika's almost unbearable dreams. She knew that the news was good, but she was terrified to learn the full details of the cost.

> *I too began to see fragments of her terror when I slept but it was too soon for me to recognize what was happening then. At that point I had not been to Vienna or Salzburg although I had done a little skiing near the Austro-Italian border. But that was not where or what Erika was dreaming about so there was little that I could recognize immediately. It was interesting though even then. It made me curious to discover everything about what had happened during those years.*

Erika couldn't imagine Vienna now at the end of the war. She felt grateful to the Red Army – it was Stalin who had frightened the British, not the Germans, at first. Now she couldn't imagine how anyone could have chosen Hitler over Stalin as a potential ally. And Stalin was hardly a political fool.

> *I expect everyone loved the Red Army then. I certainly still do. It helps me to overlook other aspects of Stalin's behaviour that were reprehensible. I often wish that Stalin had not murdered Lev Davidovich when he did. Or maybe at all! Then that man could have lived to witness what had happened to us – people with shared origins. People whom both he and Freud, shared an ambivalence. But I think Lev Davidovitch was even more conflicted about his identity than Freud had been. (Ambivalence or Oedipal tensions?) Trotsky, the name he stole and favoured over Bronstein, dabbled with psychoanalysis as did some of his children – well actually he forced it on them. He was a dreadful father – demanding, negligent and until he was forced to pay attention - he was too absorbed in his sex life and pursuit of power to care. I expect he might have denied it though. What is this conflicted pain with certain types of Jewish men - especially those who failed to live to witness the Holocaust? But Freud wasn't like that – not in the same way. But they were both dead before they were able to see what was to come.*

'I know Gloria,' Erika replied. 'Stalin and the Red Army are on the eastern edge of Germany now. The Russians have seen the hell of Auschwitz – what the Nazis had done. The Germans must surrender now. We can feel safe again very soon.'

She squeezed Gloria's hand. Gloria was hoping for her husband's safe return from active service.

'But how can those Germans live with themselves after what the Russians found?'

Could it be that bad? Could it all be true? It was in Stalin's interest to lie – or exaggerate. What was the truth?

It was early March and the weather in London had been described as "unsettled" which was no surprise. Erika had come to love her new home city despite the vagaries of the sun and rain. Today was warm, with weak sunshine pushing aside the early morning wet mists. In the distance she caught glimpses of broken, ravaged buildings that had survived the blitz and other later bombings. Far more of the city had been completely destroyed in the east of London. So many houses had been wrecked. So many lives turned upside down. So much ruined. A weak smell of burnt wood still lingered everywhere. Inescapable.

Erika recognized that these morning walks to work were probably the most peaceful moments of her day, an interval of tranquility before entering the hubbub that was the Tavi. Today, typically, she arrived shortly after 7.40 am. She opened the gate and walked up the short path to the open door. Her straight dark hair felt slightly wet. She knew the offices would be cold and damp and it was unlikely that she would feel completely dry at any point during the morning ahead. As she entered the main house, she heard women's voices, running water along with the smell of burnt toast. It made her slightly hungry and slightly nauseous.

The Westfield Women's College buildings in Maresfield Gardens provided a home for the beleaguered Tavistock clinic. The Bloomsbury department had been bombed out earlier in the war. Everyone was hoping to return to their base as soon as possible, mostly to avoid the frustrations of sharing these two Victorian houses with those noisy young women from the YMCA and the navy. There was also a financial shortage, so clinicians were unpaid. Such were the problems of war time. But despite these difficult working conditions there was a poignancy to working so near to Freud's former home and consulting room. Freud's presence was never too far from her consciousness. The new psychoanalysis was exciting.

Since arriving in pre-war London Erika had hardly seen Dr. Freud her mentor and friend. Her teacher and her *saviour*. In so many ways. Thanks to him she had been able to set up a small private practice in a small office in Camden Town near Gloria Mars' home, aided by his daughter Anna. That work was the only means of paying her rent, but she was yet to realize her own value as an analyst.

Then around six months ago Erika was approached by the director of the Tavistock clinic.

'We are very interested in the new psychology from Vienna. It offers something different and effective for our work with our shell-shocked soldiers'.

She nodded her agreement trying to hide her excitement.

They want me to work for them – I am so excited.

She kept those thoughts to herself though.

'And ...' she peered at him willing him to continue. This hesitation was unexpected. '.. there are foreign refugees. Survivors of these German prison camps we are hearing about who have managed to come here even now. The lucky ones, although they don't seem to recognize that.'

Erika thought that was a little harsh, but she nodded, meeting his eyes encouraging him to continue.

'They don't trust many of us even here - and their English is not always so good.'

His dark blue eyes watched her carefully. Erika was unsure what to say to him. He hadn't really asked or told her anything directly. But she knew what *she* wanted. She had to work with these refugees.

And I think that's what he wants too. She felt compelled to discover what had happened to these people – her people - and to her country.

CHAPTER 13: JUNE 1945

Thus, as the war in Europe came to an end, she began to work with highly damaged patients from across central Europe. Some had escaped in time as she had done. They felt scared, out of place and guilty. Survivor guilt. Others had managed to get away from the war itself to find a home in England. A few had arrived very soon after the conflict as displaced refugees. Many who had come to Britain wanted to be fighting but instead of that some were sent to internment camps. Germans. Austrians. Enemies. That's not how they felt. Almost every one of them had experienced great loss. But there was something more – far greater than bereavement. Something that maybe even a psychoanalyst could not touch. Neither then, nor across generations to reach me and my contemporaries.

It is around now that he, Max yet another dreamer, enters her life – I don't know, and I suspect neither did she – whether it was for the first time. He certainly dreamt about her. I know that because even now I have his dreams. Even now after they are both dead. But I have little doubt that she was a woman of integrity despite her connections to that evil man – the scared-face giant. Even women of integrity have to balance their psychic turmoil and she no longer had the luxury of regular guidance from her mentor. Nor did she have an obvious enemy to fight.

Erika took a deep breath and returned her mind to the present. Her morning agenda. Charlotte Stein, a relatively new patient, was waiting for Erika. Early again. She sat alone on a wooden bench, very still, staring ahead across the gloomy hallway, oblivious to the noises and the smells.

Sometimes Erika imagined that this melancholy scenario resembled a place where people queued awaiting a definitive sentence. *Of death?* She felt guilty but knew she had to leave Charlotte waiting. Timing, for both patient and analyst, was sacrosanct. The beginning and end of the fifty-minute sessions marked important boundaries which enabled the containment of the patient's problems and the analyst's energy. It also enabled the clinical staff to manage the limited consulting rooms. Charlotte would have to continue to wait until 8 am before her treatment session could begin.

Erika nodded a brief acknowledgement to her patient and almost immediately felt a deadness. Her legs and arms became too heavy to move. Her mental vitality faded noticeably until it was absent. She focused on this briefly while she entered her consulting room.

Was this feeling transmitted by the patient?

Or at least her memory of the patient from previous work. Erika felt her brow puckering with an unexpected anxiety followed by a return to a warm blandness to help her meet her patient.

This sense of deadness. What provokes it? Who?

This lifeless lack of emotion, that was replicated with almost all the refugee and survivor patients she saw, had continued to haunt Erika. She knew how important it was to identify and think about this feeling that she believed was transferred unconsciously from the patient to herself during the therapy. Erika's work was to help her patients disentangle themselves, their consciousness – their ego - from her own being. Then they could begin to work together on the patient's feelings and fears. To decide to whom a feeling belonged. Erika was forced to wonder how much of the feeling she herself owned. If only he were still here to help me.

She had longed to be with Dr. Freud again. To have supervision. To clarify her own emotions and desires. But it was too late. Far too late. He was gone. He had barely survived the move to Hampstead. She knew she could never replace him although her British supervisor was more than good enough.

It had been hard to think about Dr. Freud's death. This miracle man of the 20th Century. A man whose ideas would live forever even though he could not. Erika felt a strange relief that he had died as if from his own hand. Abusing his health with those cigars. Ignoring medical advice. He would not stop smoking. Even though his jaw and roof of his mouth had been removed and he had to battle with the prosthesis. The "monster". Anna his daughter had to help him insert it, remove it to clean and be there for him as he managed the pain of his disease and the instrument to put in his mouth to replace his own bone and tissue.

He had escaped the Nazis. Thanks to him, Erika too was in London. Physically safe. Mentally, coming close to being destroyed. It was what they had both left behind. The guilt, shame, fear. They had escaped death but then they had to *live* death. Every day. Sigmund Freud's death came soon. Erika's was not to do so. She was learning rapidly and becoming an acknowledged expert in her work with Holocaust survivors as they eventually became known

Was it possible that all those people had been so brutally murdered? Discarded by what was once a tolerant and sophisticated society? Could survivors risk returning home to Germany? Austria? Where was their home now?

Even the report of the liberation of that prison camp - Belsen - had not convinced everyone that what the journalist Richard Dimbleby had so eloquently described, was *humanly* possible. Some didn't believe what he was telling them. It might have been blatant propaganda despite the photos.

> Most of us now in the 21st Century have seen the images of the concentration camps and death camps many times. It had been so traumatic but as the years rolled by denial of the Holocaust has increased. Is that hatred of Jews? Disbelief that something so vile could have taken place? Or might it be a defence mechanism? Something to prevent us having to think it might happen again?
>
> I have dreamed about some of those who were put on trial for genocide after the war – sometimes as Erika's dreams and sometimes my own in retrospect. The evil ones themselves

didn't truly grasp what they were being made to watch during the start of the first Nuremberg trial when the perpetrators were shown the mechanisms and outcomes of their evil action. Inhumanity. Their own personal inhumanity and hatred. We all have the capacity to be inhuman, but most don't act it out. Most of us will stop. We may not even be able to play out such mercilessness in our phantasies. Maybe that is why denial of the Holocaust is growing? Another story for another time I guess.

The clock chimed the hour. Erika moved to open the door of her consulting room.

'Charlotte, please come in.'

Charlotte came through the door. She was thin, pale skinned. Colourless skin. Dark hair pinned on top of her head. No shine. Lifeless.

Charlotte slowly and methodically moved her body onto the waiting couch. She sat, sighing before lifting her legs with an effort akin to lifting an enormous dead wait.

Dead. That word again.

Then Charlotte twisted her whole being, slowly and painfully, as she succeeded in spreading herself over the full length of the couch. Erika felt a sense of relief combined with dread as she sat behind Charlotte's quiescent head. Erika wanted to stroke it. To soothe Charlotte. She would never do that of course. She could see her patient's eyes squeezed shut while her lips, tensed and tight, appeared as if she were submitting to an imminent attack.

Erika took a breath, relaxing and winding her mind up to be both open and focused. She smoothed her skirt, noting the piercing shriek as her hands moved over the surface of the material in the otherwise silent room.

Please don't hear that Charlotte.

She hadn't. Or at least it hadn't caught her attention. Erika could hear the chattering of the young women residents in the distance. It didn't appear to upset Charlotte who began to talk in a dull, staccato voice. She was French from Alsace-Lorraine and she spoke French and German alongside her improving English. She had been a teacher. Her family – parents, husband, siblings – had been transported east. She didn't know yet of their fate. Charlotte herself had been warned of the roundup of Jews in her neighbourhood by Christian friends. She had been rescued by the family of a work colleague who arranged her escape to London.

Most stories that reached Erika were split – about those who did and those who didn't escape the Nazis. Everyone she treated had had their world ripped apart. There were two worlds separated by death and deadness and like her patients Erika found herself caught between the two.

> There were others too who were trying to escape as the war came to an end. That scarred faced evil giant the boss of a friend of Erika's – another dreamer. This Nazi whose death she dreamed about long after it happened, thought he had escaped justice in the mountains of his native Austria. In their native Austria. But he was given away by his lover. By chance? Freud would not agree. The story is that he, that is Ernst Kaltenbrunner, one-time head of the Gestapo, and another man had been hiding in the mountains and as they were being arrested his mistress saw and called out his name. He had been arguing that he was someone else entirely. A Freudian slip.

CHAPTER 14: PAIN AND DEATH

Fifty minutes passed. Charlotte had told Erika of her pain, once again, but without any outward sign of it. No tears. No hesitation. It was as if she were talking about something banal like a visit to an elderly aunt or afternoon tea with friends. But Charlotte's blank words stabbed Erika through the heart. Just a matter-of-fact account. Deadness. For Erika the pain was tangible.

Charlotte stretched herself on the couch before slowly standing up.

> The use of the threadbare couch, a new initiative for British clinicians, was to help the patient express anything that came to mind however shameful or terrifying. Freud had believed that this was best accomplished if the analyst was unseen and the patient free of feelings of scrutiny. The patient was at liberty to speak about whatever came into their thoughts without censoring their speech as most of us do. The words, sentence structure and the ideas expressed were the key to elements of the unconscious. But you all probably know that by now.

Erika rose from her chair behind where Charlotte's head had been. Charlotte glanced towards Erika seemingly more relaxed, but remaining impassive.

'Thank you, Dr. Adler. I shall see you next week' and she headed out into the corridor to the dark-painted hallway which doubled as a makeshift reception area.

Erika had to move her files from the consulting room to make way for her colleague, John, whose patient was sitting outside waiting for him. Towards the back of the house was a small room that had once been a store cupboard but now held a desk, chair, a shelf that contained post and other information for the therapists as well as a small table lamp. She sat down there with her notes to check first whether any mail or reports had been left for her.

'Nothing special as usual. Thankfully!'

But then at the bottom of the usual cluster of papers was a message written in the large, carefree hand of the director: Erika started.

> Erika –Mr. Max Mayer – an old acquaintance of yours I believe wishes to see you. I suggested you would write to him. His address is 24 Banbury Avenue, Chalk Farm. Let me know if you need anything else.
> Yours H.C-P.
> PS – it is confirmed – we move to Beaumont Street in August. Pray the conflict will be over by then.

Erika sat staring at the note. She had absolutely no idea who this Mr. Mayer might be. But she had often thought that by moving to London she had wiped out so many memories. So many people. Names and faces. And with what had happened to her home – well there was nothing there and probably no-one there who was part of her past. Even her parents were many miles away in America – somewhere she had never been. She had talked at length to her supervising analyst, an English man she didn't really like, about this whenever she got the chance. These thoughts occasionally made her feel physically unable to balance – as if she had no legs.

> *Or at least no past. It is as if I landed here with skills and knowledge of what was happening in Europe but with no personal link to it.*

Erika put the note aside – she most certainly longed for the opportunity to work in the Tavi's new building – the current one was becoming unbearable.

Thoughts of this Max Mayer soon evaporated, at least

from her conscious mind. She was busy and beyond her work, everyday living was hard for everyone. For those who had escaped Europe there were so many burdens to carry. But this man was going to be the one who would haunt her. Change her. Seal her fate.

> And because of him I have to keep dreaming for both of them even now - long after their lives had ceased. It is important that no-one forgets and that this never happens again. Evil must be held to account even if we cannot prevent it.

And then something else changed. Erika had an invitation. To assist in assessing the mental states of important Nazi prisoners who were likely either to be put on trial or summarily executed. If there were to be a trial it would probably take place either in Berlin or Nuremberg – in the American Zone.

Reparation. Judgement. The chance to inform the world.

She would be free to write about her work and the clinic would allow her a sabbatical to do this. 'Could it make things better? For them? Me?' She asked herself.

She wondered what going to Germany might mean – half in joy and half in fear. And then she remembered something that she had been trying to recall and trying to repress. An image of a tall reddish-blond haired young man. They used to talk sometimes at the university. He made her laugh. But she had never got particularly close to him before any of this.

'I am sure he is this Max Mayer.'

CHAPTER 15: TALKING TO ERIKA

'There is a Mr. Mayer to see you'.

One of the annoying young women had poked her head into the office cupboard where Erika had been looking through the notes on her next patient. She was drinking a cup of weak tea without the tinned milk that her colleagues favoured. But without the lemon of her choice either.

Him.

Erika realized she was shaking. She had to hold onto the desk to remain standing. After a few moments she moved down the corridor toward the department's makeshift reception area. There she saw him.

Remain professional. Keep standing.

But she was still shaking. More so now. The thought of someone from her old life, her old home had become a terror to her. Everything she remembered of her life until a few years ago had disappeared. She knew that. But what was left was terrifying to her. In so many ways she couldn't bear to know. She felt as if a place of torment was all that was left. A burning pit. A Hell-hole. She experienced it physically. It actually hurt.

Then she saw him in the shadows of the dark entrance corridor. Max. She narrowed her eyes and stared.

'Yes, it is him.'

He looked fragile. Very tired. His gingery blond hair had faded to a dull straw colour. As she came nearer to him she saw that his blue eyes were bright in contrast to the dark skin beneath them.

'Mr. Mayer – Max?'

She moved quickly towards him. She was unsure whether to hold him in an embrace. She did – it was the only way she could remain upright. Otherwise she felt she would faint. He felt thin. He didn't want to let go. She withdrew from him which was difficult then she stood back to look at him. He didn't smile. He just stared at her.

'I have a patient to see now. I am free in about an hour. Can you wait?'

Erika realized: 'I'm speaking German. How strange it feels. But it is me.' She was stunned.

He nodded, which was all he was able to do.

It was hard to give her patient, an elderly German refugee who had left his family behind in Dresden, the attention he deserved, but Erika had been well trained. She knew how to listen closely.

After the man had left the consulting room, she stood up slowly. Collected her handbag and keys from the cupboard and returned to the small reception hall where Max was sitting motionless on the bench. She had decided to take him home with her.

A single man. An Austrian. I need to hear his story for my sake not his.

They walked from her office towards Belsize Park and from there southwards to Chalk Farm where Max had his lodgings. They hardly exchanged a word until then.

'My flat – a basement - around the corner from here – would you like to come there?'

Erika hesitated. She thought about her landlady, Gloria's, response to her arrival with this thin, depressed, blond man. She couldn't expect her to approve her taking him to her own room. Erika herself was unsure whether she really knew this silent man. Could trust him in any way? She decided to take him home anyway. They walked on for another twenty minutes.

Gloria, having heard Erika arriving poked her head around the door from the kitchen where she had been preparing her dinner. The sight of those two standing in the hallway surprised her as she had never known Erika to bring anyone home. She assumed he was a colleague and offered them a cup of tea which both Max and Erika accepted hastily.

'We would love one thank you. Gloria may I introduce you to a former colleague from Vienna – Max Mayer?'

Max looked at her gratefully. Gloria shook his hand, although looked quizzically at him thinking: 'Surely we are still at war?'

Shaking her head lightly she decided to think no more about it as the pair moved into the small dining room, each taking a chair. They sat opposite each other across a small dining table still in silence but one that had become normal and almost comfortable. Gloria brought them their tea and faded out of the room leaving their silent conversation behind her.

Max began to tell Erika more of his story.

CHAPTER 16: STORYTELLING

Erika had experienced a profound sense of calm. Joy even. She believed Max's story – reminding herself however that he was also telling her forcefully that he had been a double agent. He intended it for good – that he was not a Nazi. But if he had managed to maintain his position as a Nazi then what sort of man was he really?

I must remember that. Is it ever possible for someone like him to tell the truth? Does he recognize truth anymore?

'What did you do? Every day? Tell me how your life was?' Erika knew that this was curiosity not therapy. But he seemed more than willing to tell her. It was cleansing if nothing else.

'It was a mixture.' He paused looking at her. Meeting her eyes. Then he looked down and continued to talk. 'Office work. That involved – well much of it was everyday police work.'

Erika looked a little surprised.

'Well for example we might be called to investigate if someone was thought to be colluding with the enemy.'

He paused thinking of an example. 'So, one manufacturer of machine tools for instance. Well, he was selling much of his stock at an excessive profit – to private companies - withholding supplies that the government had wanted for the mobilization effort. So – that was one.'

Erika didn't choose to ask what had happened but got a

sense of that level of secret police work.

'Sometimes in factories – well shop floor union workers – maybe foreign agents -might interfere with workers' beliefs. Say they might – well suggest - that pay was being squeezed by Hitler himself in order to keep the workers in check.' Erika nodded again.

'Another time – well we discovered there were people – um perhaps hiding enemies of the Reich. Maybe Jews.' He looked down immediately. He had not planned to say that to her. She needed to know even so if she didn't already.

'And we were often sent as guards to camps for political dissidents and enemies – particularly once the war had started.'

She sighed. 'And what about Hans Gisevius and the other intelligence agents? What was their role in this? Did they help you?'

'I knew what was expected of me. It was important not to be exposed – I had to do things that a decent human did not have to do. I have nightmares. I dream of killing myself – in horrible ways. Setting fire to myself. Cutting my own throat. But I did what I could. Everything I could to stop this regime from destroying – well humanity. I don't know how to say anything more.'

Yes. He is right of course – at least about his dreams. And he is right about Hans Gisevius. He did not support the Nazi regime and Max had been recruited as an informer. The dreams are live even after so many years and thinking about what he has just said to Erika reminds me of a dream I had last night. I call it the Swiss dream – I had no idea why until I associated it with Gisevius who spent most of his time there – in Switzerland. In the dream I felt Max's terror. I was aware that the feeling belonged to Max because of the accompanying thoughts. Things such as I need to let Hans know. But I can't do it now – it's too risky. I can't blow my cover. The dream itself was symbolic not literal. I – or Max I should say – was driving a train. This train was unusual. It was most unlikely that it was something he could even have imagined in the early 1940s. I know the Nazis were good with trains – but this was silver, shiny and run by a hidden form of energy. Max was in the driving compartment along with the driver. They were racing along feeling good – accomplishing something important. Then his stomach gave a lurch his eyes literally screeched at me. I could see something bigger, faster, louder and terrifying heading towards him. But at the last minute his train managed to leave the tracks. It was fine. He relaxed. I have no idea what happened after that but clearly his dream ceased and resolved itself for him.

And after he told Erika about his fantasies about self-mutilation he cried. Sobbed. His body rocked and he didn't cease his crying for at least five minutes. Erika found herself alarmed. She thought she knew about pain, sorrow, guilt, regret but she had never seen anyone this deeply disturbed. At least not outside the consulting room.

When he had recovered, he told her that he had an example for her. One that had been important for Hans and his colleagues and that the images had never left him.

CHAPTER 17: MAX IN LONDON, 1945

'And that is how it happened.' He told her. 'You need to understand how it is that I am here.'

'I am listening. I am *hearing* you. I promise. So please explain a little more.'

Erika wished she hadn't expressed herself quite like that. It sounded pretentious even though she meant what she said. She heard what he was trying to tell her: *that I am not a Nazi. I have fought against them. Not everyone can see what I have done. Not everyone will believe me.*

Erika also realized that he was going to tell her more. Then he was going to ask for more. More understanding? But she felt herself on his side without any sense of knowing exactly why.

Max moved in his chair shifting the position of his legs. It made him realize that he had been fixed to the same spot for about an hour as he had related his story. He felt stiff, uncomfortable and strangely old. He knew his work was not finished yet, so he needed to go on. Telling her made him understand.

He continued his story as his fragmented thoughts returned to him.

He knew that he had to tell his full story to Dr. Erika Adler. The woman who had known Freud. Been his student. She was now at the famous Tavistock Clinic in London. Max needed her help but not solely because of his state of mind.

She was from Austria. He needed to uncover the torments he himself had gone through. He needed to have a chance to examine his own guilt. He needed to feel safe again. He needed to know that she could help him take revenge on the man who had killed one of his collaborators and friend. The man with the scarred face – his erstwhile boss at the Gestapo headquarters – Ernst Kaltenbrunner.

'There is little point in remaining alive if you couldn't live with yourself is there?' he told another colleague and mentor.

That man had managed Max's journey to London. Far away from those devastated capital cities. The one he had loved and felt at home – Vienna and the other one, Berlin, where he had conducted his work. His secret and dangerous work.

Max had known Erika – she had been part of his "set" at university, at least until those laws came into place. Even before that his parents had been unhappy about the background of several people he knew.

Will she remember me? I'm not sure I want her to. We were no longer able to spend time together because of her race. But now I need her. She is part of the plan.

An appointment had been made for his "assessment" to see whether he would be a suitable candidate for psychoanalytic therapy.

'You have to be patient ...'

'What do you mean?'

'Well, it's not like taking a tablet – and anyway there is no cure. Just a better knowledge of who you are and how you can be who you are better.'

Max nodded. It made very little sense but then he recalled that this so-called "Jewish" science was a bit like that. He had read a lot about Freud – although the books had had to be hidden. They were Jewish books and the penalties for owning them were harsh.

'And you have to be able to comb through your own

mind. To face yourself. To let the psychoanalyst interpret some of your feelings and return them to you with a meaning. To make you see yourself. Understand?'

He thought he did. He thought that would be the best way for him to go. There was a great deal he needed to talk about.

He arrived early on that sunny April morning it had not taken him long to walk to Hampstead. He looked up at the sky feeling sun on his face. It felt good and he believed then that this dreadful war might actually end.

Then what will happen to me? I doubt she will remember me. I wonder what I can say to her? Should I apologize? Can I apologize for what has happened to Austria?

He had a reasonable, although improving, grasp of English. A bit clumsy perhaps. There had been no reason to know it. Vienna and Berlin had been the centres of his cultural universe. But in the fleeting hours during which he had been able to arrange his escape to Switzerland, it was the only place he had ever wanted to go to. And his linguistic skills were improving – they had to.

For several years before and during the war, endless they seemed now, he couldn't live normally. He had forgotten what that had even meant. Those he loved and respected thought he was an avid Nazi and avoided him. His friends in his daily life had believed that too although they saw it in his favour. That was of course until they discovered what he was really doing.

'Then I had to run.'

He had done all he could to survive after that, but without the blessing and help of Hans Gisevius and his American contacts he wouldn't be here now. He would still be at the camp. He would still be a *guard* at that camp. He might have become a prisoner.

'And if Hans had not rescued me …. Maybe I would have thought myself guilty too.'

Many of us create personal stories – we have to do that in order to manage a sense of who we really are. None of us wants to see ourselves as lacking. We want to think of ourselves as good, decent people. Citizens of our homeland. Helpful friends and neighbours. The stories we tell ourselves do not necessarily, or even often, chime with the way others would see us. But those stories we tell ourselves – that we repeat and revise – they are essential for emotional survival. Even Hitler, a man who most agree now was an evil monster, could justify his beliefs and actions by seeing those he tried to wipe from the face of the world as enemies of Germany and the dregs of humanity. He came to see his murderous deeds as a necessary sacrifice for the sake of the Thousand Year Reich and the continued welfare of the Aryan race. If he hadn't believed that, then how could he have convinced a nation to collude in the disappearance and destruction of more than six million human beings?

Max had felt like killing himself so many times. His comrades had failed in their attempt to kill Hitler and stamp out the evil of his regime. Gisevius was free. But another, Wilhelm Canaris a former Admiral and head of the Intelligence Service – the Abwehr, had been arrested along with the other so-called conspirators. Max knew from his contacts in the Gestapo that Wilhelm and the others were being systematically beaten, starved and tortured mercilessly before they were murdered. By people Max had worked with and counted as companions.

By that man – the giant with the scars on his face.

'The people who tortured and murdered were my comrades. They think that killing Canaris and the others was justice. To gain revenge on these men – the decent men who could take no more of the tyrants. Some get a kick out of torture. I want to vomit every time I think about it.'

Max knew his grandfather might have been Jewish but that was rarely discussed.

'I can't recall how I was even aware of anything about that. That's not how we were raised.'

Max, despite this dubious heritage, was tall, thin, gingery-blond with pale blue eyes. He had also been physically fit and strong. Once.

'Not now. Not since I've been on the run.'

Like many of his contemporaries he had been the essence of what would become understood to be the Aryan dream. Whatever that is now it is lying in tatters. At the time he left home he had no understanding of any of this, other than he looked like many of his friends. But so did his father's father – the grandfather they would never discuss.

No-one ever made it clear. So many friends and acquaintances had Jewish backgrounds. The only ones he recognized were the religious ones. With their curls and hats. But Jewish people he knew were no different from anyone else.

'So what?'

But he did care about Erika. At least he may have done – who can tell now after everything that had happened to them. She is now a famous doctor. There was nothing strange about her. She was like every Austrian he knew in his home district. No strange religious practices. Well, no religious practices at all.

She herself had been almost too busy at the time to give him much thought, although he had hoped then that she had had warm feelings for him. Something he never forgot. That kept him going.

CHAPTER 18: PSYCHOANALYSIS AND CONFESSION

He found it difficult to look at her. He felt responsibility for all that had happened. But he was desperate for help. And *her* help in particular. Without it he might just as well kill himself. Given what he had seen. What he had done even though there had always been a higher purpose. Or so he chose to believe. Had he managed to save anyone's life? He had tried. Hans Gisevius, the spy who was his mentor, had reassured Max that he had given a great service to the people of Austria and Germany. To help defeat the Nazi regime. But it was very hard to see that now.

'I have worked with the intelligence services. Against Hitler.'

He looked up slowly trying to see her reaction, but he still couldn't meet her eyes. *She seems paralyzed. And so do I but I must go on. She has to believe me.*

I was more or less sent to Berlin – by my parents – but there was an agenda ….'

Erika looked at him: 'What do you mean?' She sounded stern. She immediately regretted her tone as he disintegrated before her eyes. She was being unprofessional. Freud would not have forgiven her.

Should I try to reassure him? I am finding this hard.

Max discerned a brief light of concern in her eyes which made it easier to continue even though he expected her to hate him even when she had heard his full story.

Erika began to imagine then what it was going to be like for her working with the Nazi prisoners awaiting their trial. She felt guilty but told herself that by listening to Max, a man she had had friendly connections with, in that very different time, she might learn something about those men. And about herself. And how to live alongside evil in other human beings.

'Please go on Max. There is something more you need me to know about – I can tell. What is it?'

He managed to meet her eyes this time.

'I have been told that you're going to Nuremberg.'

Erika was shocked: 'what do you mean?'

'The prisoners. Nazis. Trials.' He gasped as he said this. She was looking at him with hatred, at least that is what he imagined everyone felt about him.

'Hans Bernd Gisevius is my - well my boss. But my teacher too. I have been working for him. I told you he is to be a witness at the trial at Nuremberg – if they do decide to put the Nazi leaders on trial. '

Max gulped 'I was in the Gestapo. I was later a guard at …. At one of those camps. Near Munich. And I am here now because he, Hans, brought me to Switzerland and safety.' He hesitated 'And he knows about you – what you're going to be doing.'

She was stunned, unable to react. She stared at him.

Max looked down at his hands that were twisting under the table. He realized that he had been squeezing them so hard that his left hand was going to bruise.

'Not all of us managed to escape. Some very good men – much better and braver than me are being tortured. In Nazi prisons. They weren't killed until their pain had become unbearable. But I am free and …' he found himself about to cry. Tears escaped.

Erika watched. If it were any other patient, she might have felt pleased that they were getting in touch with something important inside. She could not understand her own feelings now. *And neither can he I'm guessing.*

'We need your help.'

She was taken aback with this statement it didn't fit with their conversation so far. It was more assertive. More confident as if he were back in his role as a spy against the regime. Suddenly she believed him.

'We? Tell me your story and I will think about what you are going to ask me. But I want to know first who you really are.'

Max smiled and wiped him face with his palms.

'I shall. But I need to begin from when it started.'

Erika nodded slowly thinking that that made sense of course but he was trying to convey a slightly different meaning. She was not happy about the smile.

CHAPTER 19: HIDDEN IN THE FILE, LONDON PRESENT DAY

Wilson tried to make sense of the unconscious elements in these people's stories. According to the notes he had made so far this man Max appeared conflicted. But it is almost a story about the beginning of love affair rather than that of a brutal Nazi or a traitor's confessions.

But the love story is not about Mary – Marion's grandmother. The love is between the psychoanalyst and Max. This woman Erika. Where does Mary come in?

Wilson sighed, took off his reading glasses, then closed the file leaving it on the desk in his study before glancing out of the picture window that overlooked the dark flowing river. Wilson sighed, running his fingers through his thinning, still wavy, greying hair. He couldn't work out why Marion should think the contents of the file to be of any particular significance – at least not any political significance nor of significance to her.

It was interesting though.

He left the room and began moving towards the drinks' cabinet in the living room – one that was also had a window looking onto the River Thames. He poured himself a medium sized glass of whisky. His body felt stiff and his back was aching. His eyes were tired. He took the whisky to the sofa, found the remote control and searched for the streamed drama-documentary of the Nuremberg trial. He was becoming obsessed with it he noted to himself.

The episode he turned to focused upon evidence provided by Hans Gisevius. This was evidence for the defence case for Hitler's finance minister – Hjalmar Schacht. Like many Germans he had been a supporter of the Nazis in the early 1930s.

And so had Gisevius – at least he worked for them.

As Minister of Economics when the party achieved power, Schacht had been active in the stockpiling of weapons but with Gisevius' support showing that Schacht was unaware of the true significance of this, he became one of the few to be acquitted by the international court.

Ignorance is no bloody excuse in my view.

Wilson shifted position taking another gulp of whisky before placing the now empty tumbler on the coffee table. His head slid back along the soft bulky cushions along the sofa as he drifted into a relaxed slumber. The television hummed quietly in the background. His mind was occupied with this man, Max, then the Jewish psychoanalyst from the Tavi and Gisevius. He didn't know much about Gisevius – at least not yet.

He may be the major clue to the identity of Max.

But Wilson did know something about the Tavi. He decided he would explore the archives. There has to be some information about the psychoanalysts who had been there when the new building opened even if it was just their names. There were accessible documents.

It is amazing what the mind is able to do when it turns itself off from sequential time and place and Wilson was now fast asleep in the time and place of the trial.

In my dream I can see him there. Feeling safer now. No more crossing the border to Switzerland in case they found him. His friends and allies from the Abwehr – those who tried to kill Hitler were dead. Tortured to death. He could see it as if he were with him. He could feel it. The pain was not like the kind you could imagine. Not just that it was more severe, although it was, but it was that there was no end. Pain usually signified that the sufferer could be helped – take a pain killer. Reduce inflammation. The thing causing the pain would stop. Heal. Feel better soon. No. This pain was intended to get worse. It didn't hurt in the same way. In some ways he could see that each of them prayed the pain would get worse because then they could see the end. They would be free. Forever. He knew it might have been his pain too. Thank God for that American. The man he worked for – Allen Dulles. It was Dulles who was going to help him testify against those men.

It's strange but I can't yet see his dreams. Not that one – obviously I can see his dreams. Gisevius. But this man – the one on the sofa. I know he has them. I can feel the vibration. But I haven't been able to share. I cannot know. But Max does. Max believes he might be discovered for who he really was even though he is no more.

Wilson awoke with a start, caught in the middle of a snore. He felt his neck. It was sore as if someone had tried to garotte him.

My windpipe!

He stretched and rubbed his neck and lifted his shoulders. He looked at his watch. It was only about 11.30. He turned off the television trying to recall where he had left the trial programme so he could take it up again the next day. It was giving him much food for thought. Not simply about Max, Erika, Mary and Marion. It was making him think about human nature and the instincts we have towards death, hatred, damage and blame. Justice almost didn't come into it.

PART 4: THE DANGERS

CHAPTER 20: A BRUSH WITH BRUTALITY, BERLIN 1941

Max arrived at the Reich Main Security Office on Prinz-Albrecht-Strasse his main place of work. It was 12th Night. There had been fewer Christmas decorations than usual that year. They were all but finished now leaving a bleak, colourless and bitterly cold day. The building added to the bleakness with its dark stonework, high opaque windows each adorned with the red and white background of the swastika flags.

Is it my imagination or are they looking washed out? Rather lifeless.

The sense of hope for a victorious Germany had evaporated despite Hitler's railing on to the contrary. The German incursion into the Soviet Union during the previous summer, when Stalin appeared to have yielded to the Wehrmacht, had been turned on its head a few weeks ago. Hitler had failed to grasp the force of a Russian winter. The 4th army had almost reached Moscow to scenes of triumph all around Berlin. But then the unthinkable happened – the German 4th Army was driven back, not by the Russians, but by the biting, freezing blizzards. Hitler had left his generals unprepared. What could they do? Their supply routes were cut off by the snow. Their soldiers needed much heavier clothing to protect them from the Russian winter. The evidence was all around them – soldiers collapsing in the snow. Limbs frozen. Feet and hands unable to move. Bodies – victims of nature.

Not only was Hitler a psychopath but he is a severe danger to his people. He took risks with the lives of his soldiers, but his answer was to blame the generals.

The phone rang on Max's desk. An unfamiliar voice requested, or rather instructed, him to go to the cells in the basement prepared to interrogate a prisoner. The caller did not identify himself and had put down the phone before Max could get his mind together enough to ask.

'This is strange. But, well …. It seems important. Genuine. You always had to be on your guard.'

He sat there for a moment staring at his desk. Moved some of the papers around. Unlocked the filing drawer next to the desk. Locked it again. Sighed and stood up arranging his uniform and patting his pockets. The Gestapo didn't often wear uniform but sometimes, when office bound, there was an unstated expectation. There was competition between the different groups based in the main security, the RMSO, building. Each wanted to maintain their identity,

Max ran a mental check on what he might expect from the interrogation to come. He had his gun firmly in its holster and his black jacket was pristine. He pulled on his peaked cap. He was a policeman.

'As I have no idea who wants me, I need to look the part.'

Max's heart sank. He knew he was in danger. Almost every day he risked betrayal, by friends, foes or himself. His regular life was among those who policed others' insurgent thoughts and deeds. But for him, his real role was to provide intelligence to Hans Gisevius. Against Hitler. Against the vicious regime that imprisoned and murdered ordinary German people. Just for speaking their mind.

Gisevius spent a great deal of time in Switzerland now. Max had been assured by him that Arthur Nebe, head of the criminal police division, the Kripo, another group based in this building, was "aware" of him. That hardly helped his mood. The Kripo had been incorporated into the SS. Nebe, in Max's opinion was a murderer and friend of that psycho Reinhard Heydrich – the boss of them all. It was Nebe who had led the murdering groups of the SS in the East. Burying the dead in the pits where they fell from the bullets. He was sent east regularly now.

So why would Gisevius trust both of our lives to someone like Nebe? There may be more to him than it appears. I bloody hope so.

Max left the office just as his office mate, a member of Nebe's criminal police department, entered. Joachim always presented himself as harmless. Benign. He wore his uniform badly – mostly because he was unable to fasten his buttons when he was sitting at his desk unless there was an emergency, such as a visit from Nebe or Heydrich. Max had seen the buttons explode from Joachim's enormous stomach at least twice over the Christmas period during which he had grown even fatter than usual. He also had stains of previously spilled food and drink spattering the collar of his jacket. Max didn't trust him.

But I never trust anyone now. Why the Hell did Hans bring me into this? Make me stay when he ....

Max didn't think he would really want to swap after all. He was at least at home in Berlin now – not hiding in Switzerland.

Joachim was eating already. A large chunk of black bread with a lump of bright yellow cheese perched on it was having problems getting into his mouth. But he didn't look happy.

It can't just be the cheese!

'*He's* down below.'

Max knew who Joachim meant and his stomach knotted. Reinhard Heydrich, the so-called 'Blond Beast'.

'Christ. It must have been his voice on the phone. What the Hell does he want?'

Joachim was speaking of their over-all boss. Second only to Heinrich Himmler. He was not often in Berlin these days as he had so many other responsibilities, so there had to be a very serious reason for his presence. And more worrying – his request for Max.

Max could barely remember how he had descended to the basement. He had been mindful of the noise of his footsteps on the carpeted corridor followed by their changing tone on the stone stairs. The elegance of the high-ceilinged halls and stairwell had barely etched themselves on his consciousness by the time he reached them.

Eventually he was down to the level of the large entrance hall. It was draped with swastika flags and hosted an enormous polished oak desk to the left of the main doorway and in front of a telephone switchboard. Standing at each corner of the hallway were SS guards and behind the table were two women identically and impeccably dressed in grey jackets with blond hair tied up in buns.

Max turned left at the bottom of the stairs. He was met by two SS men whom he recognized. They bowed slightly while all three exchanged 'Heil Hitler'. These men guarded those in the SD and Gestapo, who gathered intelligence, especially about German citizens who might find the means to oppose the regime. Then the sounds shifted. Louder somehow but with a dull echo. The space became smaller. More mysterious as they moved further down into the basement.

A heavy iron door was pushed open for Max to enter. Seated behind a desk was a thin, rather gangly man, probably tall judging by the length of his arms, with a long straight nose, a thin face and slightly receding, slicked down, flaxen hair.

Max gulped. He knew that this man had information on everyone in the building, which, however trivial could be the cause of a disappearance and "protective custody". Some colleagues joked that Heydrich collected gossip. But each scrap of information he held was potentially lethal. If an individual were in a position to enhance his intelligence portfolio, however, a temporary reprieve might kick in.

'Heil Hitler'. Max held the posture and waited for the response which came as a piercing glance. Heydrich leaned back on his chair, scratched the side of his nose and continued to take in this well-build tall blond Austrian man. Max clenched his stomach.

'Do sit down Herr Major'.

'Gruppenführer'. Max nodded, clicked his heals and bowed his head.

An SS guard standing behind Heydrich leapt forward to pull a chair towards Max.

That is a good start. Breathe. Breathe.

'I have been advised that you have skills.'

Max was little startled. He hoped his mouth had remained closed.

What does he mean for God's sake?

'You find the truth. I need your help with this'.

Max still slightly shocked became wary.

I need to be very careful now. Slow. Slow.

'There is a Jew in this building. He denies it. But I can tell. He is here illegally and as you are aware, he is an enemy of the Reich.'

Max nodded.

God knows what I'm nodding about. What on earth has this to do with me? Shit does he mean me? My grandfather?

But as these thoughts chilled their way through them the heavy office door opened, allowing two further SS guards to push their way into the room holding a young man between them by his arms. He was wearing the grey uniform of an SS officer with its tight black belt and shiny black boots. His hat was missing, his high collar was open, the insignia not there and his hair disheveled. Max thought the man had blood around his nose but couldn't be sure.

So not such a terrible roughing up then.

'Is this man familiar to you?'

The men who had brought him into the room pushed him away from them in Max's direction. The man staggered a little and then managed to stand to attention, raise his arm with 'Heil Hitler'.

Max had never seen him in his life and was relieved to tell Heydrich 'No – I do not know him'.

'Your name?' from one of the guards.

'Kellermann. **Standartenführer** Kellermann'.

'It has come to my notice Kellermann has spoken out against our Jewish policy. He claims that it is reasonable to allow Jewish businesses to suck the blood of Aryan ones and for Jews to teach in schools and corrupt our Aryan youth. He is upset that we have removed these vermin from such positions'.

For a man teased in childhood about the possibility of his own Jewish relatives it doesn't make sense that he wants to make a show of this. Or maybe that is the reason – once again proving his own credibility – his racial purity. Kellermann doesn't look like a Jew to me.

'I want you to reassure me Herr Major that you have no tolerance of those lying about their ancestry. I have been informed you have little patience for those who wish to contaminate our Aryan blood'.

Max swallowed as gently as he could.

'Yes Gruppenführer. Of course. That is the case'.

'And what would you do then if you found one such person had infiltrated your organization?'

Max had little time to think before: 'Well arrest this person and then ....'

Heydrich looked to one of the SS standing beside his chair and nodded towards his desk. The man bent down opened a drawer retrieving a hand-gun. He handed it to Heydrich. Heydrich held it towards Max and then in an instant aimed at Kellermann and shot him through the arm. Kellermann fell to the ground. Heydrich shot the other arm, the legs and then the heart. Max thought he would faint. Heydrich laughed. Then he turned to the SS men who had brought Kellerman in and nodded at them.

'Heil Hitler' they said in unison as they picked up the unfortunate man's body and dragged it from the room.

Max managed to remain seated, upright in his chair focusing on Heydrich behind his desk.

'Good. Good.'

Heydrich wiped the gun unnecessarily and returned it to its drawer.

'I have a mission for you Herr Major. You are just the kind of man I am looking for'.

Max waited with bated breath. He was still in shock.

Has this been a joke? The man is mad. What does he want with me?

'You are dismissed. I shall call on you soon'.

Max, making certain to follow all the correct formalities and pledges of loyalty left the room before being escorted up the stairway to the main street entrance by the guards who had brought him to the basement. They left him there. He then managed to ascend to his own office where he came face to face with Joachim who had another message for him.

'You are going to Munich' he smirked at Max.

'What? Why? When?

'Orders from the Beast. That's all I know. Oh – yes I forgot. Dachau'.

For a minute Max thought he was going to die on the spot. His heart pounded he felt dizzy. That was the place that political malcontents were imprisoned – along with other undesirables such as Jews, homosexuals, religious dissenters and those who were identified as work shy whatever that meant. Max had noted from the various documents that had crossed his desk over the past year or so that the death rate was growing there. His heart thumped and he could feel the perspiration leaking from his armpits and around his stiff uniformed collar.

He was vaguely aware of Joachim looking at him. Then Joachim launched into a loud guffaw.

'Herr Major! No. You didn't think?' he laughed again.

'You are to assist with intelligence gathering among the communists, Jews and other scum. You are to assist in the various important re-education actions. You are to train the guards in how to do this. Leaving tomorrow. I am to drive with you.'

'Drive?' Max's voice faded with the question.

'The trains are busy. You know that. There is no time to arrange for a separate carriage.' This time Joachim's face was stone hard. No hint of laughter – mocking or friendly.

Max who hadn't yet had a chance to sit down at his desk grabbed the back of his chair hoping that Joachim didn't notice that he needed assistance to remain on his feet. It was impossible to feign nonchalance, but Max hoped he looked less perturbed than he was feeling. The room was spinning as he shuffled round his chair and managed to sit down.

The transports. Taking people to the East.

He felt sick. He felt a fool. He breathed slowly while managing to remind himself that he had just managed to survive some time with Heydrich and watch as that man murdered an innocent colleague. For fun it appeared.

Max didn't want to give any further thought to how Joachim had all this information. But it did lie in the dark recesses of his mind. And, so did everything he found there once he had arrived in that black place in Bavaria. So near to his beloved Salzburg but so distant from civilization.

CHAPTER 21: DACHAU 1942

Max was transferred to his new role in the south via the front bench-seat of a large open-top Mercedes driven by a uniformed chauffeur who managed to make the drive smooth by avoiding most of the numerous random potholes as well as the dramatic bomb craters in the roads through and beyond the city. He was accompanied on his expedition by his corpulent colleague Joachim who lolled across the back of the car. Although he didn't actually take up that specific position until they had left Berlin some way behind.

No doubt like me he needs to be seen as conforming to our image as disciplined, loyal and reliable.

Max remained uncertain of whether he couldn't trust his soon to be former colleague. They had shared an office but not confidences and Hans, Max's mentor and enemy of Hitler's State, had never mention Joachim as someone on their side. Not like the way he kept talking about Arthur Nebe whom Gisevius obviously believed was to be trusted.

Am I being watched? Surely this journey doesn't require an escort? Does Heydrich not trust me? If not what am I doing here? Why me and why now?

He decided to feign some sleep that was hardly going to raise suspicion given they had left their office at 5.30 in the morning in order to miss traffic congestion. Mostly roads towards the south were quiet as Berliners wanted to avoid being caught up in crowds. There was an understandable reluctance as well to take account of the results of the overnight bombing. No-one wanted to think that the German nation might lose the war. Not even Max. It was not just the British who bombed that city killing so many and threatening the sense of impending German victory. The Soviets "the Ivans" were also making regular nightly attacks and everyone knew what would happen if they caused the downfall of the Reich. They were animals. Vicious animals and Max knew what Germany had done and was still doing to suspected communists and to Russians on the Eastern front.

The Germans had also penetrated Russia itself until around a year ago when Stalin "awoke" deciding then to retaliate with force. As far as Max knew Arthur Nebe himself, the man who was supposed to be aware of him and a friend and ally of Hans Gisevius was involved in massacres of Jews and others on Russian soil.

The car journey to Munich was long. Max was becoming hungry and tired. Joachim more so if you took account of his complaining and the sound of his stomach gurgling away as he lolled on the comfortable back seat. Max also realized that he was quite depressed and becoming more so the further they drove. Even though Germany was still winning the war, and Goebbels and his propaganda machine were talking of great victories, there was a strange feeling of uncertainty as they drove south. A sense that some of the towns and villages were too quiet. A little intimidated by this official car and the uniformed officers.

They don't like our uniforms. I've never seen that before. You wouldn't know but I think that some people are suspicious of us. What does that mean?

They continued to drive as the day wore on and Max tried to prevent himself drifting off to sleep. He had great admiration for their determined taciturn driver but was also slightly anxious that he too might succumb to slumber. But he didn't and by four p.m. they were heading towards the palace and park that bordered the camp near the town of Dachau.

When Max recalled his time there, and he did so far more often than he would have wanted, everything hit him in flashes. Fragments of memory – in dreams at night and intrusive thoughts while he was engaged in his ordinary everyday plans.

The smells – that may have been the worst. Smell of excrement and the smell of burning – but not cleansing as it might have been. The sounds of building – new blocks for the ever-increasing number of prisoners. The illnesses. The punishments for those whose work was deemed inadequate or for those who were surplus to requirements in one of many ways. Bodies – dead and alive - were routinely hanging from trees and boundary posts. Some were made to stand still and upright for hours on end until they dropped to the ground. They were generally shot after that. The Russians and Poles were brought to Dachau while Max was there – prisoners of war. Max knew that was not acceptable according to the weakly enforced international laws regarding conflict. But so much else was happening. Was it legal? Max wondered at what point death and torture became normal. He had witnessed death close hand. He had not tried to prevent it. He had never tried to prevent it. He had taken it for granted. Like some stage play. It had happened. He had watched.

But the sounds – they returned to him constantly. Particularly the occasional sounds of silence. Sounds of death. His own as well as all the real dead. But maybe more than anything. The children.

On the third day of his position at the Dachau camp, Max was introduced to the medical team. These people must never be forgiven. But could he himself ever be forgiven?

The experiments. The children. He couldn't even believe any of it himself now. Even though he repeated what he had seen. What he had accepted to himself. An act of cleansing? An act of self-blame and punishment? He didn't know.

Men, women and children were injected with the

infectious glands of female mosquitos to induce malaria. They were injected with typhus and other infectious diseases. They were subjected to freezing temperatures and then to heat – to help German troops fighting in Russia and the desert. Worst of all were the experiments on children – twins particularly. Attempts to join their bones, muscles and nerves. They died of course but not until they had suffered terribly.

No-one could ever forget that place and we all shared dreams about it. He did especially for many years – the rest of his life. His dreams were not like hers though. Hers were like mine. Probably based upon other people's representations. Survivor accounts. Films – like the one they showed those men during the trial. Historical stuff – the oldest concentration camp. The camp that went through changes, rebuilding, inmate characteristics – Poles, politicos, Jews, Russians. They were forced to work. They had little food. They died and were incinerated. They were gone forever.

'Not true' those men said. 'That didn't happen'. But even the fat one appeared shocked when he saw images in the courtroom.

Max's dreams were about being there. Memories etched irrevocably in his senses – smell, noise, fear, pain. And a shameful pride. His appearance. Uniform. The response of the commandant, the SS guards, the prisoners and Himmler. Being 'other' than those whose bodies were burnt, punished, hanged, flogged and smelled. He could know, by being there among those people, that he was not one of them. He was the elite.

He had been aware of that place for years before. He had feared it. He thought that it was like some hellish furnace – a place you didn't want to enter. And you didn't have to. It was in another country. Later though that country and his became one so there was more to fear. A danger that he might fall over the edge. Communists were sent there. Sometimes they returned. Jews were sent there – then they were sent away to the East. Or simply disappeared. Who knew? But he was better than that. Nothing like that could happen to him.

And as I continued to share those dreams, I learned more about him than anyone would wish to know about another human being. One who had mutual friends – even if they were not in the flesh. Our mutual acquaintances were all dead. Did he manage a moral reprieve via his work with Gisevius? Things might be different for him when he was awake.

It was a time of high anxiety for Max. Being there in Bavaria. Dachau – that small unassuming town with its typically Bavarian, medieval houses. With a palace and a park where families could relax and enjoy the greenery. And there was a stunning view across the town and the plain towards Munich. There was no enjoyment there for him. Just fear. Fear of the camp. Fear of being found out. Fear of Heydrich.

The face of the commandant, Piorkowski, came back to Max most nights for years after his return to Berlin and even after the executions of that man and his colleagues. Brown hair, brushed back, thinning with that heavy nose and constantly perplexed expression on his face. He was demanding of the prisoners and the guards including Max. It was as if the commandant had no idea why anyone might want to challenge him for what he was doing. And then of course what he did – feathering his own nest – but that has to be another story because Max had left by that time. Piorkowski had worked there in Dachau, before he became the man in charge, organizing the finances. He knew how to handle money. Max was warned, gently, to be wary but also instructed to keep a keen eye open. 'This man may not always have the best interests of the Reich upfront.'

As he attempted to sleep Max would suddenly find his heart racing and Piorkowski would be there – staring at him. Wondering what was going on. What had happened and why. After the Americans arrived Piorkowski and all the others from Dachau whom Max remembered were interned in Landsberg Prison before their death sentences were achieved and carried out.

Nothing they experienced was as cruel as they had perpetrated.

But events overtook both Piorkowski and Max long before that.

It was the summer of 1942. Max had been at Dachau since for nearly a year. He had been told that his contribution to the development of the dormitory blocks, the new crematoria and the training of the Gestapo and other guards had been exemplary. He was not proud. He wasn't ashamed either because for Max it was an ongoing dream. But then the news that no-one at the Reich Main Security Offices or the Gestapo itself had ever imagined. Heydrich was dead.

His just deserts?

Max now had more important things to do in Berlin and Arthur Nebe expedited his transfer to his former station and his work with the Kripo and then by the new definition he did so as a member of the Gestapo.

CHAPTER 22: THE MAN WITH THE SCARRED FACE, BERLIN, JANUARY 1943.

Joachim appeared disappointed to hear that Heinrich Himmler had decided to step aside from his role as acting head of the Reich Security Services in favour of Ernst Kaltenbrunner, known to be a bully. Not necessarily the brightest of the bunch either even though he had qualified as a lawyer. He was also known to drink to excess and killing anyone who became inconvenient.

'He's an Austrian by birth – you'll be pleased to know.'

'We're all of the same Aryan race' Max countered.

He was beginning to feel slightly more at home here in Berlin now. He knew what to say and do.

'And I know a great deal about him – so do you. The Lieutenant-General of Police has been a loyal member of the party for years. And I have seen him around the building – he has worked here among us for some time.'

'I know. I'm glad you are pleased.'

Joachim looked slightly relieved to have shared these views. Max couldn't fully grasp the true outlook of his colleague, who was almost a friend now.

'Kaltenbrunner's career is on the rise. We need to make sure he understands our loyalty to the Reich. Being a fellow Austrian won't be enough Max, will it?'

Both Joachim and Max were aware of Kaltenbrunner's reputation. He was ruthless and very cruel. In so many ways the ideal manager for the members of the Reich Security. But not necessarily a charismatic leader which made him a useful commodity to Himmler who was planning to grant a greater range of powers to this man.

Kaltenbrunner was rumoured to be visiting individual offices that day – to inspect the troops or at least the criminal police force, the Kripo as well as the Gestapo. While Max, and doubtless Joachim, put time into convincing themselves they were but senior law officers, doing regular work on behalf of the Government, they were also mindful of the many duties expected of them during war time. Prevent free speech particularly any criticism of the Leader or the Party, identify any Communists, Jews or other undesirables hiding from their intended fate. Max was well informed of the meaning of this. Dachau was difficult to shake from his mind – waking or asleep.

But life was different for him now. Easier. Better. Kinder even – although not that kind.

If we were so kind, we would be no better off than the others here in Berlin – Germany. Short of food. Supplies of most things limited now. Petrol. Most things. And there are the bombs. They were not supposed to happen. Not here anyway.

The Reich Main Security Office had been used to a regular supply of reasonably pleasant tasting coffee. The availability was less reliable since Max had returned from his work in Dachau. Apparently there had been a decree last summer that more attention had to be given to food and drink excesses among the general population. The Russians were blamed for stealing food from German mouths.

Were the Ivans somehow attacking supply chains? Surely coffee didn't come from the East?

Max was staring into space – far away from Berlin now. Far away in time and place. Unexpectedly and harshly the office door opened. Max's mind by then had wandered from philosophy towards getting one of the women typists to bring him a coffee. They were in an adjoining room, filing and typing for the most part. But always on the end of the internal telephone line and eager to please. He felt slightly confused as he hadn't finished organizing his thinking along those lines before this intrusion.

Two members of the SS in their best grey uniforms, bound by black belts with matching glistening black boots, entered the room. One held the door open. The other stood opposite his colleagues with his eyes straight ahead.

How often do I see this now? Eyes at attention. Not seeing. Maybe that is how it needs to be. The blind eye. That's what I do now. Since that place.

Neither SS man faced into the office but glared at each other – although of course they weren't glaring. They were blinding themselves to what was to come. Then a large, heavy-set man forced himself through the remaining space. It was hard to see how he achieved his entry. He was tall – taller than most people Max had met – a lot taller than Himmler for instance. He was also broad. Not fat. Just big. Altogether a terrifying vision. An unfriendly giant. He looked cruel.

All the men who had been working at their desks, including Max and Joachim, sprang to their feet. The SS men shouted Heil Hitler, making the appropriate salute, that was returned by the shaken inhabitants of the Kripo office. Kaltenbrunner too performed the salute. He moved forward, lumbering into the office and leaned against an empty desk. His brown hair was slicked back revealing a receding hairline that made his large face with the prominent nose and large ears appear even bigger. His face, as everyone had been forewarned, if they were ever to encounter him in person, was deeply scarred on the left side.

Do not stare. Was it from a fencing accident as those

around him claimed or had he had a motor vehicle accident while inebriated?

Theories abounded depending on politics and fear in equal measure. He was known to have a chilling and erratic temper so anyone who had any sense would comply with his wishes while attempting invisibility the remainder of the time.

His dreams from that night were different. I could feel now that he was no longer scared. No longer conflicted. He felt a connection. A closeness to the scarred man. His mind was like a roundabout in a fairground. He was on a goat, holding its horn tightly as the roundabout spun faster and faster. Kaltenbrunner was standing there, next to him with his hand stretched towards the goat. Reaching. Getting closer to Max, the policeman. The Austrian with his Jewish confidante – the psychoanalyst. He grasped the man's hand and pulled him closer. He kept spinning while in his peripheral vision he caught glimpses of Arthur Nebe, his insurance policy, of Joachim his colleague and even further away Hans Gisevius the man he was working for. His mentor. The double agent – just like he was meant to be. The spinning slowed. The man with the scars relaxed and stroked the goat. The men at the side were no longer visible and the dreamer awoke slowly to the sound of screaming.

CHAPTER 23: THINKING ABOUT THE PAST, LONDON 1945

'Not so very long, maybe a bit more than a year later, after I was posted to – to that place – Heydrich was dead. Murdered. Executed I should say. Wounded by Czech nationalists, he died soon after.'

Erika knew about that. Recriminations had been harsh, particularly the liquidation of the Czech town of Lidice. She knew that these people, the Nazi high command, were completely ruthless.

'I was then posted back to the RMSO. I was relieved. Very. Even though the occupants of our building saw far more of Heinrich Himmler after that. Rumour had it that Himmler was happy to have a greater hands-on control of our work - policing and security. Heydrich had been a powerful and overbearing figure. This, I have been told, had bothered Himmler who may have been pleased that now Heydrich was gone.'

Erika nodded - that made sense.

'But what about Heydrich's successor – Ernst Kaltenbrunner? He was an Austrian. A lawyer, wasn't he?'

'I was informed that Himmler didn't exactly trust him.'

'Oh?'

'Not that he wasn't loyal to Hitler and the Reich – no it was simply to make sure his actions complied with policy. Kaltenbrunner is no Heydrich that's for certain. In so many different ways – not as efficient and not as ruthless. Or at least not so much of a psychopath. Kaltenbrunner remains a dedicated – no - better to say fanatical Nazi, antisemite and self-regarding sadist.'

'Which may have bothered Himmler?'

'Yes and no of course – he wasn't a threat to Himmler – he didn't want to outrank him – far from it. But I believe that Himmler considered that he needed to be kept up to speed.'

Despite these misgivings from the top, Ernst Kaltenbrunner, as head of Himmler's Security Headquarters, was Max's boss in the Gestapo. He was absolutely loyal – he had been in the Austrian SS providing security for Nazi party members at the beginning. Max felt that his time with the Gestapo, especially when on duty at Dachau, had shifted his own moral compass. As he became more deeply involved in his primary work, outside morals, outside beliefs were becoming increasingly distant. He knew that Arthur Nebe, the head of the criminal police force – the Kripo - had been providing some cover and security for him.

But it was difficult to see how Nebe, who had been involved in executions of Jews in the East, could be a friend of Hans and his colleagues.

'They were not in any sense saviours of the Jewish people but at least ultimately they were firmly against the Nazi rule of Germany and the murder of innocents – and that eventually included Jewish people.'

Erika thought how important it must be for Max to believe that. She did know that that wasn't quite as straightforward as Max was hoping.

Or trying to persuade me?

'They – the Nazis - executed Nebe. Said he was part of the plot against Hitler. So maybe he wasn't quite the monster ....'

'He wasn't a saint either.' Erika interrupted him. Max agreed but wondered how or what she knew.

Kaltenbrunner! This man is whitewashing him. Don't you know what he did? It was Kaltenbrunner who dragged Sophie Scholl and the White Rose group of Munich students in front of the "People's Court" before having her head axed from her body. He arranged this for her brother Hans, Christoph Probst and so many more. What had they done wrong? They protested against a speech given by a gauleiter of Hitler's. 1943. They were tired of the regime and the war. Kaltenbrunner was possibly frightened that the students might be heard and others might 'get it'. Do you think so? Or was Kaltenbrunner as dumb as Gilbert and others have argued? To me, looking back, he resembled Lurch the servant in TV series about a family of monsters. Lurch was slow, ponderous, ugly .... And did the writer and production team have anyone in mind? The TV series was broadcast only twenty years after Kaltenbrunner's execution. Maybe this creature we all laughed at was meant to be him – a truly awful monster.

While Kaltenbrunner was organizing his savage reprisals against free speech in Munich he met Admiral Wilhelm Canaris there. This reasonably decent man – there are conditions to be added to his description – who was then head of naval and armed forces intelligence – the Abwehr. I've been told that Canaris didn't really know which way to turn. He had supported the Nazi rise to power, but gradually by 1943 he had doubts. That did take some time didn't it? But Canaris kept many of his doubts to himself. He didn't realize that his colleagues and those from the Reich Main Security Office – particularly his recent acquaintance, **Ernst** *Kaltenbrunner could sense his ambivalence. But they fed off commitment – they didn't appreciate being starved of absolute allegiance. As the monster grew in his leader's estimation Canaris' dithering became increasingly easy to intuit. Don't forget – dreams can be shared! None of us has complete privacy.*

Max could not help but ponder how a woman living in London, a psychotherapist, could have even heard of Arthur Nebe if he himself hadn't told her who he was? The news of Heydrich's murder and the recriminations had been world news. But Nebe? Despite noting this doubt, he was relieved to be having this conversation with someone who was neither in the Party nor the Abwehr. Someone whose stake in Europe was as an innocent citizen – neither a double agent nor a Nazi. And with no checkered history.

Max had thought very little about any office politics after Heydrich.

'Life didn't appear so dangerous then. I had no interest in thinking about how far Kaltenbrunner had power. What I did find out though – from that oaf Joachim – that Heydrich, following the murder of Kellerman in front of my eyes, appointed me, along with others he had deemed suitable – that is ruthless and without pity, to police prisoners and the guards, including the SS, at Dachau.'

'That sounds to me as if you had been elevated to a high position.

'It was awful. Yes. But also, it was not always easy to contact Hans Gisevius or other trusted colleagues, especially during that Dachau service. I cannot express to you just how disturbing it was to work there. It was even more disturbing to imagine that a bastard like Heydrich had identified me as being someone he could trust. To be like him.'

'But at least he didn't kill *you*.'

'I wish he had done sometimes. So often I think about that. Sending me there to that camp – it was like he was punishing me. Not just because of the violent, brutal and obscene cruelty inflicted on inmates. But that there I became hardened to everyday life in Dachau. I could not avoid being part of the terror of the system.'

Erika could think of nothing to say, so simply looked at him. Partly willing Max to continue although uncertain that she wanted to hear any more. He chose to remain silent. At least for a time.

> *There was a baby. I saw it. Heard it. He dreamed of a little brown haired English girl. I was very surprised, but he went through what happened time after time. As if she might change events by dreaming about them. Or maybe he wanted to relive events. It was unclear – to him. He went deeper and deeper into his mind – conscious and unconscious. Still, he didn't really know and still he did know he was never going to see her or her mother again.*

Erika, sensing some of Max's conflicting thoughts, reminded him that she was to go to Nuremberg. She was going to meet some of those men – Kaltenbrunner, Hans Frank, Speer, Goering. She felt sick with excitement and dread. Max regarded her quizzically.

'Maybe I can help you. Give you information. What you could look out for. Before you go?'

CHAPTER 24: DOUBLE LIVES - LONDON, PRESENT DAY

Wilson needed a break. He was becoming too immersed in the double lives that certain of the protagonists were leading. But in some ways he was unsure which ones were doing so. Max – apparently his colleague Marion's grandfather, was clearly in a difficult position and highly conflicted if you believed his story. His father had had contacts in Berlin and had sent Max there, and as far as Wilson could tell, Max was to work as a double agent – Gestapo and Kripo in everyday life while also an informer to the American intelligence networks, via Gisevius, in his duplicitous other existence. Although which one was duplicitous in this case? It certainly appeared that working for American intelligence – or at least for Gisevius, had been planned for Max by his father.

On the other hand what had Max achieved for his Allied masters by 1943? He seemed to have worried about his police work in Berlin. He had stayed in his so-called training role at the Dachau terror camp for as long as that monster Heydrich had wanted him to do so. Then he seemed to fall into Himmler's and then Kaltenbrunner's arms at the Reich Main Security Office after Heydrich's death. No-one there – with the possible exception of Joachim and maybe Arthur Nebe - had been in the least surprised that he was doing his job as well as any of his bosses had wanted him to do. Max was a perfect member of the Gestapo and a perfect Nazi.

Wilson scratched his head. He stood up stiffly pushing against the cushions on his comfortable sofa which had become his favourite spot for reading Marion's files. He moved slowly towards the picture window. It was dark – the clocks had been returned to Greenwich Mean Time as October was fading into winter. Wilson looked at his watch – 11.30 – no wonder I'm tired. He stretched and stared out towards the river, via his image in the window glass. He could see the lights of Chelsea Bridge over the River Thames and the occasional sparkling from the moored barges swaying in the water.

Wilson was due to have lunch and catch up with Marion the next day when they were both seeing students and patients at the Tavi. So far Wilson hadn't discovered any details about Mary the grandmother. Why was she there in Germany? What exactly had been her relationship to Max and then of course there was a baby – Marion's mother.

If he was to get more concrete information on Marion's murdered grandmother Wilson needed a bit more direction from Marion. He now had to admit to himself that he didn't really know what he was looking for.

He had managed to work out that Max had been lucky. Gisevius had made sure that Max could reach London in relative safety as the war in Europe was coming to an end. He had been treated – at least by the CIA - as if he were a bona fide undercover agent whose loyalties were with Gisevius and the western Allies – against the Reich.

If he's not what they thought he was – they would have taken some kind of action. Revenge? Interrogation?

Then there was Erika. She appeared to be the heroine of the story so far. A clinician trained by Sigmund Freud himself. Freud looks to have thought very well of her. She herself had been highly successful even without him after his death. She did more than find her feet. And it looked to him as if there was a great deal more to her career than seeing patients. She was going to be an official of some sort at the Nuremberg trial.

I have to admit I am intrigued. I shall keep the next part of her story until I am more focused.

But still he couldn't work out what he was looking for. What Marion had wanted him to do with all this fascinating information? Was she simply whetting his appetite so that he would chase up the secret files about her grandparents? Something she couldn't do. Then it was time to turn in for the night.

I think I am wanting to please Marion – to show her I am knowledgeable, smart – that she was right to approach me. But what I really need to consider is why me? and how did she actually discover things about me?

CHAPTER 25: LUNCH WITH MARION, PRESENT DAY

It was late October, and despite his very part-time status, Wilson found himself looking forward to the Christmas break. He couldn't recall having had that feeling since starting at the Tavi. Was it because other matters, such as discovering the truth about Marion's family or watching television had become more attractive than the former energising impact of students and the patients undergoing psychoanalysis? He sighed deciding it was something to think about. For now he needed just to get on with things.

'Let's go to that nice little Turkish café on Finchley Road' Marion's head had appeared half-way up Wilson's open office door. The sun had started shining. He had seen its sharp light and contrasting black shadows against the statue of Freud's head. He realized that he felt hungry and as he was in minimal pain he acknowledged her suggestion with a smile.

'Just give me five minutes. Come in. Come in Marion – I really won't be too long now.'

He swept the pile of student papers into the file drawer on his desk and locked it. He would arrange the details and marks later in the afternoon but he wanted to be sure that they were out of reach for any prying eyes.

Not James. He wouldn't interfere. Some of the admin staff take pity on students and try to give them a heads up about their marks before their tutorials.

'I deliberately have left your box file at home. It's safter there.'

Marion nodded. She didn't appear particularly concerned. He thought that to be a little strange as confidentiality had been one of his priorities and he assumed it to be hers too. He took a breath and heaved himself up onto his feet, grabbed for his walking stick and headed towards the door.

He locked the office and the two of them walked down the long corridor to the stairwell. Wilson was rather bemused as there was a strange silence between them. He couldn't think of any comments that might break it or be welcome. Marion herself looked as if she had little desire to engage in polite conversation in spite of earlier smiles. They both nodded to Nick the porter on duty at the desk in the surprisingly unprepossessing entrance hall before heading across the road towards Maresfield Gardens, Freud's former home and famous consulting room. Then on to Finchley Road, the latter typically clogged by traffic crawling in both directions – one cluster heading north towards Brent Cross and the M1 motorway while the other had central London in its sights.

Finchley Road was at a slightly lower altitude than Maresfield Gardens. That meant descending a slope that was something he usually needed to think about. Wilson walked down the slight incline with his right-hand hovering over the central handrail just in case he might stumble but was relieved to find himself and his spine strong enough on that day to make the descent unaided. Hence his mood lightened.

The café in question, where they were planning lunch, lay just to the right on reaching the main road. A small table in the window bay was being wiped by the waitress as they arrived. They pulled out a chair each and the waitress returned immediately with the menus and a smile.

'Take your time. Call me when you're ready to order.'

'Two coffees first please' Marion requested. 'Double

espressos.'

A little surprised, Wilson grinned. He would have made that choice himself but he expected to make his own requests.

What a strange woman she is. But I must remember that I am an old man – a 'pensioner', 'grandad' – and if it weren't for the Tavi I would be consigned to the pile of the disregarded. Or at least a member of the group that needed to be told what is best for them - but yes, double espresso is simply that – good for me.

They both studied the menu, giving their choices to the waitress as their coffees arrived.

'So?' suggested Wilson.

Marion took a deep breath.

'I know you well enough to realize you're reading the documents and giving them most of your attention. You are, aren't you?'

He smiled and nodded taking a swig of the hot coffee.

'And you need to know now what I have to understand from everything written there. My grandmother Mary was murdered – but there is no evidence that the death was investigated. Please read what is in the file and see if you can find any clues as to how we …'

He noted the inclusive sense in that word "we".

'…. Can find out whether justice has been done and if not … well how it might be so now.'

'Marion so far I haven't seen a great deal of reference to Mary – maybe we should talk more when I have finished reading?'

He stared giving her the opportunity to respond. She seemed grateful as she smiled turning slightly pink before taking up her story.

'I know – but I want your assessment of the file. I want to discover how Mary and this man who is apparently my grandfather – Max became connected. And then whether or not Max was truly a double agent or actually a Nazi who betrayed, or at least helped to betray, those who fought Hitler.'

'I see.' Wilson looked at Marion who seemed agitated

and animated. 'And Mary? Your grandmother – do we want to discover anything more about ...'

She cut across him. 'I think you know a great deal about Nazi history and Nazi organizations – I have read one or two things you wrote 20 years ago.'

It was his turn to blush slightly. Yes, after Hanna's death and his varying discomforts with associates of his own secret service handlers, he had attempted to discover their true loyalties – especially Jacques and the new man (or at least he was at the time) Gabriel. However that was in secret.

Following recovery from Hanna's death, managing to live with his injuries, along with the need to wind down his clinical practice at the time, he had turned further towards his academic interests in human relations.

My book – she has read my book about Nazis in West Germany. That's all it is – that's why she approached me.

The Nazi past, and at the time as Hanna had known, the Nazi present in West Germany, had consumed him for several years. Then came a resurgence of his health, strength and clinical work and the blessing of his post at the Tavi.

He hesitated before taking the conversation further but knew he had to have more information from her. 'What about Mary? Do you want to know who she was really working for?'

Marion looked angry and about to interrupt.

He continued.

'To do her justice – to discover the truth – if it's possible – I don't really know now – but you must expect anything – it could be a number of things. The truth about her death could be for so many different – maybe conflicting reasons ...' He let his voice drift away to allow her to think.

Their food arrived at that point.

Most timely.

He unwrapped his fork from the folded napkin and dived into his baked aubergine but was increasingly perplexed as to what this woman across the table from him wanted.

How did I get into this? I am swimming in golden syrup – sadly only metaphorically. But I am intrigued and will continue to follow up the stories if nothing else.

PART 5: BEFORE THE TRIAL

CHAPTER 26: ERIKA AND THE JOURNEY TO HELL (AUGUST, 1945)

She was to travel to Munich on a RAF plane the next day. This was her first time in an aircraft of any kind. She was anxious as well as mesmerized by everything that was happening to her. A stressful combination. Although Erika had never actually set foot in Germany since the war, she had passed through that country during the longest and saddest journey of her life. It was when she left Austria to begin her new, safe, life as an immigrant in London. Mirroring the Freud family passage, she had travelled on the transcontinental Orient Express leaving Vienna for Paris and then on the boat train to London. It had seemed as if that journey would never end, but it was one she knew was to save her life. This new journey, the one she was to make in the morning, would be different. It would be fast – about five hours on the plane she had been told. She was to act as a witness to the devastation of Europe and the start of reparations and justice.

The RAF driver called for her the following morning. Erika was surprised to learn that her flight would take off from a small aerodrome in Essex – Southend-on-Sea. It sounded rather exotic, although actually proved itself to have been misnamed – the town was beside a muddy river estuary which the driver skirted shortly before reaching the awaiting plane.

The plane was larger than she had expected. Her visions of planes clustered around Lancasters, Spitfires and Messerschmitts. This RAF transport was large enough for 10 passengers and the pilot, but Erika was the only civilian passenger on this flight although she shared it with two young RAF men who appeared to have tasks to perform – such as navigation and technical assistance - rather than being merely passengers. She felt a strange mixture of importance, guilt and terror.

Is this really a British plane? Am I being kidnapped?

She made herself think more clearly about her situation. It occurred to her that she was likely to be the only Austrian, albeit a British national now, who was not a lawyer or in the military, heading for the Nuremberg Palace of Justice with its prison and court systems. So consequential security demanded she be separated from anyone else travelling from Britain for their sakes and hers. She was right of course.

Afterwards Erika couldn't decide whether it had been her paranoia or the mechanics of the flight itself that had caused her alarm.

Soon after the scary takeoff, one of the young RAF men handed her a plastic cup containing weak tea. It was perched on a saucer, so she assumed this was something of a luxury. She was grateful anyway, as she was thirsty. No sooner had she lifted the cup from its saucer by the handle the plane lurched, and bounced, moving rapidly upwards and then down again equally swiftly. The tea splattered from the cup landing across her lap. It was hot. She was disappointed, but more so she was shocked. Actually, she was terrified - not by the burning tea but the action of the plane. The young man was slightly apologetic.

'I'm sorry. It does this quite often – we met a passing cloud I expect.'

'Oh' she managed, using a handkerchief to brush the tea from her skirt rather pointlessly.

'Should be plain sailing from now on though.' He chuckled, mostly to himself. 'The weather across the Continent is quite settled this afternoon. And we won't be long now.'

He had a nice smile and brought her another cup of tea and a napkin. This drink was a success. She would have liked to have talked some more to the young officer, but it was clear that idle chatter was taboo. Pleasant nods and smiles would have to do.

Is it routine or my accent? Are they avoiding me?

But then a strange sensation in her stomach, made her grip the arm rest.

'Here we are!' her companion indicated that she might wish to look out of the window. She did so with some apprehension. They were descending. The plane was losing altitude but in a regular controlled motion this time. Below she could see rounded green hills on one side and distant mountains that looked snow-capped on the other.

'Hold on to your hats!' the young officer who had given the tea called out. His companion remained tight lipped although regarded Erika with a brief smile. The pilot whooped with delight: 'Here we come you bastards!'

Erika wondered whether the silent officer thought she herself might be one of those bastards. She was too anxious and excited to care at that point, but it did give her pause for thought later. She wasn't British and her accent would sound like those whose cities they were heading towards.

The descent continued to make her stomach lurch. The plane jerked as it landed on an air strip near to what looked-like a built-up area. She attempted to face out of the window to watch their landing, but her eyes were squeezed tight shut.

As they released their seat belts, two American military men in khaki uniforms and matching metal helmets materialized as the door of the aircraft opened. Bavaria was in the occupied American zone. One of the RAF officers handed Erika and her cases over to the Americans who poured over her travel documents and politely asked her what was in her cases and the reason she was in Munich. She explained as best she could, observing that the soldiers were alert to her accent. She felt embarrassed wanting to explain but then anger began to rise in her.

'We're keeping an eye on this lady sergeant' the friendlier RAF officer told one of the Americans.

'We're waiting for some more Brits to arrive – we're looking after them all for now.'

'Make sure they all go through our security checks before you take them away.' The American, pointing to a building at the edge of the airfield, was brusque but left Erika in the hands of the RAF.

As she clambered down the two steps of the extended exit ladder onto the rutted tarmac, Erika could smell smoke. She found herself shrouded in a haze of yellow dust that hit her throat making her choke. Her eyes began to water. She blinked and wiped the tears away with her hand before she was able to see anything around her.

The scene that did eventually meet her eyes was dreadful. The yellow dust swirled around the airstrip where a bunch of other small aircraft were parked randomly. The landing strip had evidently been bombed heavily. She judged that their pilot must have been highly skilled or very lucky to have achieved their safe landing and avoid collapsing into one of these vast open wounds on the tarmac. In the near distance Erika could just see the ruins of the city of Munich, wrapped in a dusty haze.

An enormous military-style jeep was slowly making its way between the potholes towards them. Erika was then ushered into the jeep while the RAF men loaded her cases and bade her farewell.

'I thought you said there are others?'

'Later – I wanted him out of our hair ma'am. Goodbye

and good luck now. I expect our paths may cross once again over the coming weeks.'

With that the two men departed, although the pilot remained on board to wait for more passengers, presumably going back to Britain.

Erika's attention was captured then by a British army corporal who was leaning against the front of the jeep smoking a cigarette. In the excitement she hadn't noticed him or given a thought to who was driving the vehicle.

'I shall be driving you to Nuremberg. But first I shall need to take your passport and other papers to the immigration desk. You have to come too of course.'

She nodded silently and somberly following him across the pitted air strip. The immigration building was a hut with brick walls, corrugated iron acting as the roof. It must have been hastily pulled together from what may once have been a storage room. Consequently, it was rather hot inside. They joined a small queue of men mostly wearing army uniform and nearly all smoking sharp-smelling cigarettes that did nothing to improve the immediate environment.

The corporal held out his hand towards Erika who handed over her papers. A gruff American soldier in khaki helmet and uniform eventually peered at them and grunted. Erika had been issued a British passport a year after she had arrived in London, but it did not prevent the American official from staring at her with overt distaste as he handed it back to her.

'Adler?'

'That's right.' She remained tight lipped as she hastened to place the precious document safely in her handbag.

'What kind of name is that?'

Erika hesitated – should she say Austrian? That would upset this rude man. On the other hand, without this man and his fellows, Germany might have succeeded in murdering every Jew in Europe.

'Jewish,' she growled at him staring into his eyes.

He nodded 'Go ahead ma'am. Both of you now.'

And waving a large blunt hand to sweep them aside, he turned to a group of men in American army uniform – the ubiquitous khaki clothing, metal hat and strong cigarette.

Erika remained angry and humiliated by the immigration official's comments. Her companion, the driver looked slightly sheepish but probably felt relieved that nothing had arisen to disrupt the journey.

'May I suggest we refresh ourselves – wash and so on. The trip north to Nuremberg will take around 3 or 4 hours – it depends on the state of the road and checkpoints along the way.'

'Thank you – that would be good.'

'Don't worry about them. The Americans are trying to make up for their late entry by overzealous security now we have won.'

Erika smiled.

They then headed towards the back of the immigration building where they took turns to use a battered, grubby toilet. The good thing was that the wash basin did have clean running water and greasy soap.

'Now for the journey I have a flask of tea for us and there is an American base we might stop at about 3 hours away if nature calls. I believe there is some lunch here too in this basket.'

He opened it revealing some rough looking bread rolls, some filled with processed pink meat and others with bright yellow cheese.

Erika sighed. The driver took up his position in the jeep, Erika sat behind the driver. She wanted to have some sleep if she could.

The journey began through Munich as the driver headed towards the road leading north. The city had been bombed heavily. They passed churches, civic buildings and what were even yet homes, none of which had remained fully intact. Windows were dislodged, mostly smashed, and absent but some had endured, clinging to their shattered frames deciding whether or not to let go their hold and fall onto the street. Everywhere small groups of civilians, mainly women, milled around as if they had important places to go or specific sights to see. Erika guessed they were seeking information about food supplies or trying to get other basic provisions for their families.

'Don't worry about this lot ma'am' her driver turned to look at her.

Help – watch the road!

'Remember who they are – although of course we need to show compassion.'

'They are hungry and scared I expect. But it does all look so awful doesn't it – like a strange Hell. London is terrible – but somehow this seems more desperate.'

He nodded and this time without turning around: 'You need to wait until we arrive in Nuremberg.'

Nearby each group of German civilians they drove past, were at least three or four American soldiers, their rifles handy in case of trouble. It wasn't clear what these beleaguered-looking individuals might do to warrant this level of vigilance, but it made sense that a strong guard remained in the area in case of insurgency. There were few men or children visible that afternoon and Erika wondered where they might be. There were no schools, and most men were likely to be unemployed. Eventually it became obvious though – German men and some older children were scattered through the broken city in work gangs clearing rubble with armed Americans looking on.

What worried Erika the most were the signs of the all too recent past. The cast iron figures of eagles, swastikas, statues as well as many tattered red and black flags that still fluttered in the dusty breeze, crying out "defeat". But they were still chilling. Erika wondered how Salzburg and Vienna looked now.

The dust was relentless, made worse by their army

vehicle chugging through these sad street scenes on this warm, dry afternoon. Erika felt desperate to put Munich behind her although judging by the driver's warning, she wasn't expecting anything in Nuremberg to improve her mood.

From leaving the city they joined the road northwards to Nuremberg in the heart of Bavaria. The A9, the motorway built by the Nazi regime, was surprisingly in-tact in contrast to everything else they had seen up to now. As the jeep motored along she rested her head against the back of the seat. Erika felt herself getting drowsy.

> She dreamed. I dreamed. I was flying above the jeep, sometimes hiding behind the rounded hills, dipping into the rivers and streams, scaling the tops of the tress in the woods and forests, and watching the snow-capped mountains retreat. That is a feeling of intense power. As Austria had retreated. We could both see a sleeping woman with a man driving. I could watch the numerous work details, German men, digging and clearing the space for this roadway - about 10 years earlier. This tarmac and the bridges ensured Hitler's popularity.

"No - he wasn't going to take us to war – he is creating employment. He is helping us getting from one place to another fast. He is unifying the great German people. Making us take our place in the world. Helping our race prosper and survive."

The population of Franconia could from then on profitably transport produce from their farms lying to the west of Nuremberg, rapidly southwards to the city of Munich, near that small town of Dachau, where many people died and where Max spent some time, only about 4 years ago. He was training guards to make sure the prisoners were worked to death. If that didn't kill them – well there were other means and other places. That hardly mattered did it? Not now the German people were able to travel far north to Berlin to visit the seat of government for the Thousand Year Reich. "We shall be great again."

Soon Erika woke up, stretched herself and rubbed her neck. The driver, a corporal whose name was Bill shared out the bread, meat and cheese on the move. There was no need to stop even for a comfort break. Rivers, hills and trees had been left behind. They were reaching the outskirts of Nuremberg, veering away from Autobahn 9 to the east of the city. The outline of the castle could be seen in the distance while the jeep circled what must have been a large park area around the periphery.

'It would have been a pleasant place to take walks at one time don't you think?' Bill ventured.

'You mean before Hitler?'

'Yes naturally. But more - before the carnage.'

Erika had liked Bill so far but his response made her feel uncomfortable. She imagined this would not be the last time she had that experience.

'So whose fault was it? Should the Allies have left the Nazis to get on with it? Provide a wonderful life for the Aryan people?'

'I know. I know. You don't need to tell me. I was on active service.'

'I'm sorry. I didn't mean …'

'I know ma'am. I hate these people – maybe like you do.'

They both decided to end that conversation. Now though, as Erika could see, the former recreational grass spaces had been turned to mud and rubble. Bombs had left enormous troughs across the expanse of the park, most of which were full of rainwater and rubbish. Many of the trees had been blasted, scorched or chopped down – perhaps for firewood. As they came nearer to the remaining buildings themselves, Erika witnessed the details of this devastation. It was hard to find any building that had all four walls standing. Windows had been broken and blown away – far worse than Munich Erika thought. Perhaps because the scale was smaller.

'The citizens of Nuremberg must be desperate' she thought, although she wondered whether she actually cared. And then suffered a pang of guilt This was the seat of the laws that had victimized the Jews of Germany and Austria –

the Nuremberg Laws - that removed people from their jobs and their livelihoods marking the beginning of what would eventually become the Final Solution.

> But all of that had come to an inglorious halt now. It had not been prevented. Millions had been tortured and died. None of us knew exactly how many as yet. None of us could understand exactly what had happened. And none of us grasped how it was enabled – allowed to happen.

This city of Nuremberg was also the place that the Nazi party had held its massive rallies where Hitler was lauded, his speeches cheered, and many of the people that Erika was soon to meet, had stood among the swastikas, Eagles and other Nazi icons raising their arms to the population who responded with matching salutes and shouts. It was here that Albert Speer had designed the auditoria for these displays of hatred. Massive structures fit for the Emperors of Rome.

It was not difficult to be shocked, despite this knowledge of recent history, by the desperate plight of the citizens. As with Munich, the American service men were plentiful here too, ensuring control over the multitude – men, children and women who hovered outside their bombed-out dwellings looking. Just looking as if they were stunned. As if what was going on was completely unexpected, exceptionally perplexing with nothing to do with them.

'You should see the old part of town' Bill told her. 'I can drive you around this evening if you wish – most people do want to see for themselves.'

He waited for an answer. Erika nodded quietly. She too was in shock, although wondered what she had expected. The defeated enemy. Why wouldn't there be evidence of the conquest?

'And soon we shall be passing the place where Hitler stood commanding the rallies here in Nuremberg. It is nothing special now. The Americans have seen to that.' And he gave a snort.

Erika's thoughts until her arrival in Germany had been focused on the bombing raids over London. The sirens wailing. The bombs hitting or missing their targets – either outcome would be shattering. She would sometimes have lain in bed, listening to the terrifying noise trying to guess what it meant – a house, a church, the docks, a factory? They all had their own particular sound as they gave up their life-force to the violent onslaught. The loss of people's homes.

There were other things that were hard to believe and almost impossible to imagine. The atrocities committed by the Nazis against the Jews, Gypsies, disabled and homosexual people as well as communists all across occupied Europe. The things Max had told her about. Until you saw Germany for yourself, in this raw state, you could never quite understand that the enemy had suffered too. She didn't really want to know. She dreaded that one day she might have to return to see what had happened to Austria.

'Nearly there now.'

Bill interrupted her thoughts. They were in what must have once been a middle-class residential district. Erika could see that the bombed-out houses would have been substantial three story detached homes with decent sized front gardens. The house they had pulled up before was double fronted. The entrance door was wooden, appearing unharmed. But both ground floor windows were boarded up with one of the windows on the middle level secured by a rope tied from inside leaving a gap on one side between the glass and the brickwork. No lights were visible from outside.

Bill knocked, pushed at the door and entered carrying Erika's luggage. A small German woman came from somewhere towards the back of the house.

'I'll see you later ma'am.'

Giving a nod and smile to Bill, Erika followed the woman to a room on the first floor toward the back of the house. The stairs creaked mercilessly.

'They are safe Miss. Don't worry. Here is your room. I shall meet you in the morning for your breakfast. The front door is not locked. We are lucky to have it.'

Erika was surprised to hear the woman give a brief laugh.

'I have prepared some bread and cheese for your supper. And then a cup of tea. I'll show you the dining room.'

Erika descended the stairs behind the woman into a bleak ground-floor room. It was one that had boarded up windows. There was a table – long enough to seat six people at least. The woman turned on a dim lamp placed on the centre of the table. Erika, realizing that she was hungry now, ate her sandwiches and drank the weak tea the woman brought her.

'My name is Erika by the way' she said.

'You're from here?' the woman looked startled.

'I am Ursula' the woman told her quickly trying to cover up her question. Erika thought that Ursula had stepped beyond the permitted boundaries. But as she had been pleasant towards her, Erika volunteered 'I am from Salzburg but ..... well I have been living in England for a great many years now.'

It was apparent now that the issue of her voice and seemingly local accent was going to be something she had to consider.

After eating Erika went to her bedroom. It was large with a high ceiling featuring an oversized dusty chandelier. It was as if this room alone might boast that it had escaped any bombing. However its very survival served as a reminder of its downfall. She discovered the bathroom and sat on the bed to unpack. But just then Bill arrived to take her on the promised tour of Nuremberg.

This time Erika sat beside him as they drove up a steep slope to a flat area of ground where they could park. He leapt out of the jeep, and held her door open.

'We'll begin with the castle grounds where we can look down upon the bombed churches and the medieval old town.'

Erika considered that his glee was a little too candid, but given his war experiences she understood. Then she silently berated herself.

They deserved what they got.

The moved towards a stone wall where total devastation was clearly visible in the late summer evening light.

Driving from the hostel, to the castle and beyond, they had taken in more of the sight of the city itself. Tired looking women were standing or sitting outside their ruined homes. Sometimes young children were playing among the rubble even though it was becoming dark. But it was hatred Erika saw in all their stares as they motored slowly past. This conflict was not over yet. Erika was convinced that the smoke and dust still rising from the carnage were the mists of Hell itself.

It was about ten o'clock when Erika eventually went to bed. Despite the summer heat her room had a dank atmosphere accompanied with a characteristic smell of mould. She looked around her. Her suitcases were still neatly placed neatly at the foot of her reasonably sturdy looking single bed. She opened a case choosing a warm full-length flannel nightie – in fact the only one she had brought with her.

It might be rather warm, but I am not sure I want my skin next to the bedding.

She undressed and pulled the blankets up. There was no sheet, making her doubly grateful for her nightdress. She was uncomfortable but appreciated that she did not have to share her room. She wasn't certain of the arrangements that had been made for anyone else in the lodgings but right now she didn't care.

CHAPTER 27: THE PRISONERS ARRIVE, NUREMBERG, AUGUST, 1945.

Erika flinched. It was morning. All too soon. She had dozed off again trying to ignore the persistent screaming and clanging of her alarm clock. The dust mites were visible through the gaps in the fraying curtains. She stretched and remembered with a sense of gloom and hopelessness where she was and why. Then she sat up in bed suddenly. Shivering. The shrill ringing had evoked images. Ones she would rather have avoided. Men. Old mostly. At least a little older than she was. More than twenty of them.

But today it begins.

Erika climbed from the bed. Choosing her wardrobe was hard. She didn't really have much choice given the size of the luggage allowance. But she eventually decided upon a formal dark blue striped jacket with small shoulder pads and a matching skirt that reached three inches below her knees. She had packed a number of blouses and two more skirts so she should manage to keep up the appearances she wanted. She then tied her dark hair into a pleat.

This look combines power and invisibility – that's just what I need.

Her image in the mirror gave her the confidence for the

task ahead.

Erika was treated to a reasonably appetizing breakfast of hard-boiled eggs and bread, served by Ursula the lady from the previous evening. There was no butter, nor any margarine, for which Erika was grateful, at least about the latter, as it typically tasted disgusting. The weak tea with tinned milk wasn't too pleasing either, but she had become used to it in London and drank it gratefully.

She had little idea of what was expected of her except that she had to visit the Palace of Justice, where she was to be based, to have her papers checked once again by the Americans. Bill had informed her the previous evenings that the building was in a bad state of repair although better than much of the surrounding area. Erika had been told that renovations were continuing on the damaged roof along with repairs to the Court rooms. She was interested to see everything that was going on for herself. She was also to be shown the adjacent prison – a depressing thought but she knew that it was an area she had to become familiar with in the following months.

She made her way to the Palace of Justice. Bill had indicated the route and she had rehearsed it too using the street map the Americans had issued when she had registered. There was a disclaimer that the roads shown in print were not necessarily passable, but she reckoned she had grasped the general direction she needed to take. She had become used to the desolate scenes of people and property even after such a short time. Her walk lasted about forty minutes leaving her plenty of time to look around her. As she approached the area of the court buildings she saw and heard the American guards. There were amassed at the main entrance and along the front of the main building in wide jeeps, with troops sitting at the open space at the back, rifles razed, helmets on. There were also a series of small tanks, with troops similarly placed. The tanks were khaki like the uniforms each with a large white star on the front.

Everyone was waiting and there was a muted buzz of anticipation in the atmosphere.

The prisoners were due to arrive.

Shortly a series of army prison vans steered slowly down the road. These men who had caused so much destruction, were arriving here - at the Nuremberg Palace of Justice. She had learned that most of them had been held in a prison camp in Luxembourg – Camp Ashcan - that had once been a hotel. How strange that must have been. She had seen the official photographs of several of them – the more infamous ones such as Rudolph Hess, Albert Speer, Julius Streicher and Hermann Goering of course. Now she could see them in the flesh. She was less sure that she would recognize Hans Frank or Ernst Kaltenbrunner, nor did she know whether they would be coming with this convoy.

More military police and army officers were arriving at the building alongside the Palace of Justice with these men. These were men chosen to represent the evil of the Nazi regime to the world. But there were many more.

All-pervading security kept both onlookers and officials away from the court entrance. It was hot. The kind of heat that you rarely experienced in London where there was always some relief. A breeze. A passing cloud.

But not here in this Hell hole.

Erika had stood with the crowd watching and listening. It was dreamlike. Sounds. You could feel the sounds – weirdly as they were floating away. Strange silent sounds. Sounds of the crowd watching – holding their breath against that severe summer heat and disbelief.

These were those men. They were so small. So unkempt.

Hermann Goering was the man that attracted the most interest from the observers that morning. From her knowledge of his former appearance, he looked diminished. Much thinner. Weak.

Good. He has suffered from his imprisonment.

But Erika had other concerns – those she would be

working with. One in particular who had escaped capture until recently, but he was here now – Ernst Kaltenbrunner – head of Hitler's security services. Max Mayer's former boss. There were things she needed to discover from him.

Others of that evil regime had escaped capture. Hitler. Goebbels. Dead by their own hands. Complete cowards. And Himmler – killed himself after trying unsuccessfully to ally himself with the British. But there were men who were still being pursued – at least she prayed that they were. Eichmann – where was he? Bormann? Erika stared again towards the arriving captives. Blond, pinch-faced Ribbentrop – the man who thought he could do deals with the Soviets and the British.

That's him. Yes.

Robert Ley – the union leader. He was overweight, gazing at the witnesses to his capture with a sneer. He had also thought he had escaped. His boss – the debonair Albert Speer calmly good-looking – at least in comparison with his fellow prisoners. Doenitz, Keitel and Jodl the military men. Then to her surprise she recognized Hans Frank – murderer of Jews and Poles with his dark, receding hairline and the smell under his nose. He was just like the photographs she had seen before the war. The last one she recognized was that overbearing, bald, heavy man Julius Streicher. The primary school teacher. The pornographer. The so-called journalist madly obsessed with Jews.

Their arrival at the Palace of Justice, even though it was so welcome, had been almost unbearable to witness. Imagine animals being unloaded from those army lorries to be locked up until their trial. Almost certainly these men were to experience their last ever days of freedom and life. Imagine other men, women and children also being unloaded from endless streams of cattle trucks. Tired, hungry, thirsty, unwashed, confused and scared. These men here, now, were also tired and poorly dressed. Some in old, ill-fitting suits and some in equally shabby German military uniforms.

Were they scared? Were they confused?

She knew she would be one of the few to find this out. Soon. They were here. In Bavaria. And the world intended that their millions of victims would achieve some kind of justice from what was to follow.

Erika knew, even then, that justice would not be a simple process. Churchill had wanted the Nazi leaders, these men, shot. Summarily. Stalin similarly wanted his pound of flesh and pint of blood. He had wanted all Nazis to be executed without the nonsense of a trial. Roosevelt had not seemed to care about the mass murder of European and Russian Jews, Gypsies or the disabled. He had been reluctant to come to the aid of Churchill or any of the rest of Europe at first. It was so distant from all he cared about. But Roosevelt is no more – Truman is in charge.

Eventually these three powers, along with the French, had agreed to hold a trial to show the world that justice was possible. Not just for the millions of victims of Hitler's war but also for those who supported him. The victors were to be seen to be fair but they were also to be seen as victorious. Those men arriving to face the judges had ravaged the world. Her world. The world of many across Europe. Evil was an inadequate description.

But what else could you say?

She knew a lot about most of them. Those vile followers and henchmen of Adolf Hitler.

Their Fürher. If he were really their leader, they would all have followed suit and killed themselves by now. What a coward. And Himmler and Goebbels too. Disgusting people.

Murderers who knew they were guilty. Ultimately, they could not face themselves. Or at least could not face their accusers. And Goebbels even feared that his children should know the truth. So, he killed all of them too.

Should I think good riddance? They were innocent children weren't they? Erika couldn't feel sure about that.

But one other man's child had been spared. Gudrun

THE BROKEN COUCH

Himmler. Her father had taken cyanide after his capture. It was well known that she and her mother declared his innocence of any crime. They mourned him openly. Few shared their opinion. But Gudrun – she still thought that what Heinrich Himmler had achieved was praiseworthy. And she planned to inform the world. Erika had heard that she was to be one of the witnesses at the trial.

Erika was to speak to these prisoners. Some of what she was to do required appearing relatively informal although naturally all information gleaned was to be coordinated with the rest of the mental health team and fed back to the military and civilian men in charge. And, thus, to the lawyers. Both sides presumably.

She was both appalled and excited. She had read all there was currently available on each of the prisoners. She hadn't heard of them all – not in any detail. The army leaders. The politicians. Not many outside of Nazi Germany knew their names. But she did know of the most notorious defendants such as Julius Streicher, the schoolteacher whose hateful newspaper, *Der Stürmer*, produced rampant anti-Semitic articles and caricatures. She knew of Rudolf Hess – he had had treatment at the Tavistock Clinic following his arrest in Scotland. Goering and Speer – some time favourites of Hitler.

> *I can feel her confusion as she looks at these men. Her dreams are scary. She is worried that Max – she still calls him 'her 'Max' but I think she may know more than she is prepared to really know. She isn't certain where to start. All these men. A stew of evil stirring around soon to be in their prison cells. She wants to know how to begin. Where to begin. What it will be like. Can she punish them all? Can she carry out revenge? She wakes every twenty minutes and her dreams confuse me. I wish I didn't have to share them. I was not there. I don't know what it is like to think about facing them. Looking into their eyes. Finding out what they think without feeling forced to violence. Thankfully she is awake now. I can retreat.*

One man who interested her, clinically, was Hans Frank. He had been head, of what Hitler identified as, the 'General Government' of occupied Poland. As such he had overseen the round up and murder of Slavic and Jewish people living in the east many of whom had been transported there and herded into death camps.

Frank wrote prolific diaries which Erika expected to provide some insight into the mind of evil. The man who had murdered so many in Poland had become a staunch Catholic once his reign had ended, writing of his repentance for those crimes. It had to be the behaviour of a madman. Something akin to a document of evil and deathbed conversion. At least she hoped he was mad.

'Can I bear to meet this creature face-to-face? Do I really want to be near such a man? Such men?'

Erika recalled one particular line of Frank's early diary:

> 'One way or another – I shall tell you quite openly – the Jews must be finished off'.

Erika replayed those words over and over. Frank even decried the criticisms of 'measures' against the Jews within the Reich. The Jews had to die – but away from Germany. They must disappear. German blood should not be spilled to enable even one Jew to survive.

This man had been a lawyer. Can we expect justice enough to punish him? But then so had he – Kaltenbrunner. Nazi lawyers.

Erika suddenly knew she had to meet them. Confront them – all of them. Then she shuddered – what kind of person puts ideas like that in writing as Frank has done? Worse – what kind of culture had they created that made it possible to think that and to state it publicly?

She was to be an assistant interpreter for the American Colonel Andrus and the British Major Neave who would be serving the indictments to each man in the morning, which would mean entering their cells. She wanted to do this but feared how she would respond. She could not afford to be removed from this work. She had to keep her head. There were things she needed to know over and beyond the needs of Andrus and Neave. She had to meet Goering. She had to meet Streicher. She had to meet Speer. Speer had been captured along with Doenitz and the others who had tried to establish a government after Hitler. And, of course, Hans Frank. But Kaltenbrunner too. He was important. His former absence had haunted her, but he had been captured in May in Austria but was now safely in Nuremberg with the others.

In the meantime, she was forced to wait until her other professional colleagues - Dr. Kelley the prison psychiatrist but especially the man who had recommended her to the prison authorities, Dr Gustave Gilbert, arrived to start work.

CHAPTER 28: OCTOBER -THE PALACE OF JUSTICE

The following day Erika awoke with more energy. Today her work was going to begin. Ursula produced a breakfast which she ate slowly finding it to be more enjoyable than the previous day. She was eager to get to the Palace of Justice to meet her future colleagues and discover exactly what she was to be doing, and more so – how. She walked as fast as she could along the pitted roadway which wasn't too difficult, provided she kept her eyes on the ground scanning for potholes or other hazards. Lacking the opportunity to engage any more with her environment, although not wanting to think in too much detail about the days ahead, a dream leapt into her mind.

> *She had been in a large building and was desperate to arrive in an office on the top floor but each time she climbed a set of stairs, intended to take her to the next level, an obstacle occurred. Once or twice the staircases were absent. Another time she was able to ascend, but she was forced to squeeze herself between railings that appeared to close up as she moved nearer her destination. But she did get there. A woman. Young. Perhaps in her early twenties was sitting alone in the middle of the room on a chair behind a small, empty desk. Erika tried to reach out to hug her but somehow the desk was in the way or else she found herself outside the room and trying to climb up towards it once again. Then she heard that noise again. One she recognized. But from where? A distant banging. Was it a door blowing in the wind? She then thought she could hear a cry. A scream. A woman's voice.*
>
> *She believed she had kept this one to herself – why would she not? But in fact I had felt, heard and seen it all too. It made my hair stand on end. What do you think it all meant? I shivered.*

As Erika recalled the dream, she became increasingly

convinced that she had not been alone among those images and sounds. Not simply her sense of the night but a sense of sharing. Someone had intervened – joined her – that was what she felt – in that dream state.

Don't be ridiculous! Your imagination is playing tricks.

Erica pulled herself back to the moment. She was supposed to be able to make sense of dreams. That was her job. Relate them to unconscious desires. What she seemed to be doing now though was making those visions more obscure. Tying knots around what she should be able to, at least, begin to interpret.

Come back to the work at hand!

She had been told that Burton Andrus, the American army officer, had been appointed governor of the prison where the Nazis were to be held. Someone told her he had been in charge at Camp Ashcan too, so he ought to be well up on their states of mind and behaviours. However, she had been led to believe he was not really that kind of person – more likely he focused on rules and structures.

The prison itself was situated adjacent to the Nuremberg Palace of Justice.

Andrus' reputation suggested he would impose a strict military regime, pay attention to detail, show little sense of humour and expect women to know their place. Most women at the prison and Courthouse were there to carry out secretarial duties including, she had been informed, some English women who worked for the British Government and were to live in her hostel. Erika was well aware that she was likely to be the only woman with a distinctive professional role with significant access to the prisoners. How was she to manage this man Andrus?

That needs to be the least of my concerns right now.

Nuremberg, like the rest of Germany was in ruins as she had witnessed on the tour of the city. The wreckage was physical and emotional. There was nothing left that resembled a national infrastructure – not even the Courtroom. The military tribunal comprised the four victorious nations – France, Great Britain, the USA and the Soviet Union.

Strange bedfellows now the war has ended.

Erika thought about the sense of helplessness and frustration that failed systems imparted on the people who had previously taken them for granted.

What was Germany now? How will it manage to survive what it had done? And do I care – or do I want my own revenge?

The newspapers and radio broadcasts were all foreign. No-one cared about the Germans.

Was this payback? Did all those people truly deserve what was happening to them?

Erika was clear that the men coming before the court deserved everything that might be heaped upon them. And more. They were here now. Most of them anyway. She had seen them arrive in those armoured cars. During those several months at Camp Ashcan, the converted hotel in Luxembourg where almost all of the high-ranking Nazi prisoners had been held, they had undergone an initial round of interrogation. Crucial evidence for their trials. And evidence that might be available to Erika and her clinical colleagues. Max had asked whether she might let him have some information. She felt unsure what to do about that.

I need to wait and see what it will all be like.

The military tanks remained in place guarding the outside the Palace of Justice just as they had been since the first prisoners' arrival. As required, Erika joined the queue along with general staff, guards coming on duty, soldiers, lawyers, administrators, translators and even the judges to gain entrance to the buildings. Once through the doors she made her way along the familiar corridor past the doors to courtrooms, noting the noisy activity around Courtroom 600 while it was being prepared for the forthcoming trial. It seemed that none of the existing justice chambers had been large enough to hold the defendants, press, cameras and the legal teams expected for this trial. This one wasn't going to be particularly roomy either but it would do.

The military policeman outside Andrus' office looked surprised.

'I am here to meet Coronel Andrus and Major Neave.'

The MP scrutinized her papers, stared at her some more, handed them back and nodded her into the outer office.

She breathed a full complement of air into her lungs and passed through the door that he opened. Instead of the anticipated anteroom where she expected to await orders and meet her colleagues, Erika found herself pushing her way through a group of noisy men – at least two in uniform, one in priestly garb and two others whom she gradually recognized as Neave and Andrus. They were entering from the office door at the far end of the lobby. Andrus was, in part, as she had been led to expect. Military bearing. Precise. In his mid 50s she guessed. Formal with highly polished shoes and neat uniform. He was tall, taking up lots of space like so many from north America. Healthy and well-fed despite the conflict-ridden hunger in Europe.

Neave was different. Much younger than Andrus for a start and less confident. On fact rather shy. Haunted. Dark brown hair. Rather nondescript despite a full mouth and long thin nose. But even so, good looking in a British way that she recognized now from her adopted home. No-one paid her any attention at first. They all appeared preoccupied with their own conversations. There was a table at the centre stacked with files and she made her way between the men towards it. She wanted to appear to know what she was doing.

It's a face-saving skill! Some files bound with a thick ribbon, others in soft cardboard folders and a pile of boxes stacked at one end of the table with, she guessed, further files. She put out her hand towards one of the folders.

'And you are?' boomed an American accented voice. A soldier.

'Dr. Adler.' The words were spoken by Neave, the

Englishman. Erika looked at him with surprise and nodded. He smiled and put his hand forward to shake hers. He looked about her age.

'We've been expecting you.' He hesitated 'but I thought you were to be a man! I apologize – I can see you are not'. Erika noticed a slight blush and was uncertain how to react.

Best do it with humour.

She smiled, meeting his eyes, and immediately turned to Andrus with her hand ready to shake his. She then wondered if she had snubbed Neave and grabbed his hand again immediately feeling embarrassed and slightly clumsy.

Pull yourself together.

Neave smiled 'I am looking forward to our working together. It won't be for a few days yet I'm sorry to say. I am still doing some investigations with the Krupp family – their role in armaments and so on.'

Erika knew about the Krupps of Essen and their factories but not a great deal more. She hoped to get to know this man better and to learn about his investigations.

'So we meet properly in a few days' he nodded and smiled once again. Erika sensed an aggravated impatience escaping from Andrus.

'I'll show you around the complex here. And then you can read some of the existing files. I am expecting you to add significantly to the information we have about the prisoners here in Nuremberg.'

It's as if he is a bit competitive – jealous even of Neave.

CHAPTER 29: NEAR GARTENSTRASSE

Exhausted from that first strange day, but alert with the excitement, Erika walked back to her lodgings along the rutted road. It was around eight p.m., a dark clear night. She made her way past the bombed-out houses and blocks of apartments that were to become familiar to her during the months that followed. She thought she ought to be feeling the cold more intensely. That morning she had been more focused upon establishing a professional appearance than dressing for the weather. The adrenaline that had kept her fired up throughout the day, had prevented her body from becoming chilled even now. Everything was racing inside her generating a fire. There was no further capacity for feeling the impact of anything outside.

Erika found it difficult to imagine how the women who hovered on each side of the road, along what were once pavements and even front yards, were able to live normal lives among these ruins. They seemed to materialize from the still-smoking debris of their homes to talk to their neighbours and manage their children, many of whom were playing in the desolate bomb-damaged streets most of the day. No schools right now. Erika was curious rather than sympathetic attempting to work out how far she should feel guilty about such feelings. She couldn't quite decide.

The morning walk to work at the Palace of Justice had taken her about forty minutes. She remembered because she had wanted to ensure that she was always going to be punctual. She realized now, as she made her way back to her lodgings though, that she had been walking for almost an hour. Even allowing for her tiredness and the dark, she had to accept that she was adrift in this strange city. Her predicament reminded her of the German fairy tale about Hansel and Gretel – the siblings who had become lost in the forest after the trail of breadcrumbs they had laid down to find their way home had been eaten by birds. The route to her lodgings looked completely different from the trip to work.

Hardly a surprise but ... where the hell am I? I thought the journey was more or less straight from A to B.

The landmarks she had noted earlier that day did not look the same despite her effort to remember them. And now it was dark. She realized that she would have to ask one of those women, the bitter, tired ones living amongst the rubble of their homes, directions to Gartenstrasse. From there she knew how to recognize their lodgings which were on a short road off it.

'Excuse me madam?'

A woman, probably in her forties, judging by the age of the two early teenage boys she had been shouting at, stared at her. Her blond hair was mixed with grey and tied in a loose ponytail with what on closer inspection looked like a shoelace. She wore a grey and white dress, neat but old and what must once have been a scarf was tied around her waste in lieu of an apron.

'You're from Bavaria?' the woman almost smiled at her.

Erika was stunned – that wasn't what she had expected to hear. The woman presented a mixture of joy and puzzlement.

Perhaps it was unusual to see a local person wearing such good clothes and looking so healthy and neat.

Erika knew that Germans, particularly in the south, always talked about their State (or *Land*) rather than Germany as a whole. And a Bavarian accent was closer to Austrian than to other German language dialects.

Erika decided that she should respond politely but officiously because asking for directions while claiming local origins might still be dangerous. Nothing felt safe in Nuremberg.

The woman, who told Erika that her name was Helga pointed towards the direction that Erika should take reassuring her that she would arrive in ten minutes.

'But please can you help me madam. My children. Your countrymen ...'

Helga looked down at her feet.

'Food. There is nothing here – nowhere to buy food. We rely on farmers, but they don't arrive here often. Please.'

'I shall try. Tomorrow? Will you be here?'

Helga nodded and Erika nodded back to her.

'What is your name?' Erika told her and smiled. Later she reflected on their meeting. How strange it was – the woman was an enemy. She lived in a country, and a particular part of a country, that had wanted people like Erika dead. Or at least to be removed. But during their encounter they treated each other like human beings – the one poor and hopeless. The other compassionate – at least at the time.

When Erika discovered that she had been given the correct directions, she felt obliged to try to help Helga and her family.

I wonder whether she would have thought to help anyone like me. Huh! You're better than that. Help the bloody woman.

Erika turned off Gartenstrasse heading for the dimly lit house that was now familiar. It was one of the few still intact –her temporary, she hoped, home. Exhausted she put the key in the door. That proved unnecessary. The door opened from the pressure of the key in the lock.

Ursula, her landlady, surfaced immediately to inform her that she was to be joined that evening by three English women who were also going to be working at the court buildings.

'They will be here by supper time I am told.'

Erika nodded feeling a little disturbed as already she had a routine that was now apparently going to be disrupted. She had no desire to meet anyone else who might want to take up her time or challenge her legitimacy.

I still feel like an imposter. Coming here has made me a little confused – am I Austrian? Am I British? And how is it going to be living and working among those who wanted me dead?

CHAPTER 30: THE ENGLISH WOMEN

The three women from London disembarked finding themselves on the pitted tarmac of the airstrip near Munich. They stared at their new surroundings as if being there was something they had not anticipated. An unexpected surprise. They didn't have to stand there for long before two men clad in familiar RAF uniform greeted them while another, presumably more junior colleague, made a pile of their luggage ready to be transported to their lodgings.

They were led towards the building to be registered in Bavaria by the American occupying military force. The new arrivals were listed with the American immigration authorities as secretaries working for the British War Office. Their role? to assist the military and civilian authorities with evidence gathering for the trial in the Court to be established in Nuremberg. It was assumed by the Americans that their duties would be light. Evidence was all around visible to any casual observer.

After leaving the immigration building, they were guided towards a military jeep by another RAF officer who drove them from the landing strip at Munich, north to Nuremberg and to the lodgings where Erika was billeted. The jeep dropped them at the hostel at around six p.m. shortly after Erika had returned from her day at the Palace of Justice.

Ursula, waited in the hallway as the three women pushed open the door depositing their luggage and looking around them. Once again, they appeared to be surprised at being where they were.

Erika joined Ursula in the hallway catching their horrified glances as the new arrivals looked around them taking in more detail. The oldest and it appeared, the leader of the small group held out a well-shaped, soft be-ringed right hand to both Erika and Ursula. Erika judged her to be around forty years old.

'My name is Catherine.'

Ursula, avoiding the handshake, quickly volunteered to make them some tea. She hurried to her own quarters at the back of the house and the kitchen. Erika thought this retreat was rather too hasty as she hadn't waited to be introduced to the remaining two guests, although she understood Ursula might be embarrassed as well as overwhelmed by the presence of these carefully dressed and clearly well-fed women.

Catherine had, what Erika guessed to be, a perpetual look of anxiety and attention to everything she had not yet done. Her brown hair was short and neatly permed, with a side parting held by a silver hair clip. Her dark pleated skirt, by contrast, was flattened in some places so that along with the badly knitted jumper, she reminded Erika of the women who had been tutors at the medical school in Vienna. For them, dressing fashionably was a sign of intellectual deficiency while the underlying quality of their clothing indicated their social status. Erika thought that Catherine's clothing was more likely to have been faded because of the impact of the war than an attempt at a superior academic image.

'You must be Dr. Adler – the doctor of madness?' Catherine offered a patronizing smile. 'We are to be staying here, with you, at the same lodgings. Away from the men of course.'

She chuckled slightly as her eyes searched for Erika's reaction. Erika smiled back at what she chose to take as a joke, while curious as to how this woman knew anything about her given that she herself had had no previous information about these new arrivals other than they were English. And even then Ursula had been the source.

The woman continued. 'My name as I said is Catherine – Catherine Barton and ...' grabbing one of the other women with her left hand 'let me introduce my colleagues. First, Mary Hart.'

Mary a formal-looking woman, a few years Catherine's junior, near to Erika's age, wore a fitted dress of green, draped by a fur stole, with a matching feathered hat over her smooth, tucked-under fair hair. She appeared as if she were on her way to a reception or cocktail party. She offered a shy smile slightly at odds with her powdered face and bright red lipstick. Mary directed her relaxed limp hand towards Erika who took it graciously.

Mary. No shortage of clothing for her.

Catherine continued: 'And now Sylvia Ricks.'

Sylvia's dark fringe reached below her eyebrows, encouraging Erika to rub her own eyes.

It must be such a nuisance. It must be irritating!

Sylvia had made no obvious attempt to apply make-up and her grey skirt and jacket were unremarkable. She moved forward to shake hands vigorously with Erika.

'My father is a psychiatrist. I didn't know women did that kind of thing.' And she giggled. Erika smiled.

Another attempt at humour?

'Erika. We are looking forward to getting to know you better.'

Catherine's attempt to relax everyone was working despite obvious differences between each of them as well as between these English women and Erika herself.

'And I too am pleased to know you all. We'll be lodging together for quite some time I should imagine.'

'It might be fun.' Mary suggested although Erika would take a lot more convincing either that it would be fun or that she would share an appreciation of pleasure with her new companions.

None of the women wanted to go to bed early even though they had felt so tired after their journey. They all realized now that they were being offered accommodation considered the height of luxury. Instead of heading for their rooms they went into the living room that Erika had not seen before then. It proved to be a dark, unhappy and rather chilly place containing four aging armchairs and a coffee table placed in front of an unlit stove, the latter enclosed by a large, ornate fireplace that had deep cracks across the surround. There was a blackened oak dresser along the opposite wall that was lopsided. Erika guessed that a bomb had shaken up the floorboards that creaked and had various sized splintered gaps between several of them, which Ursula their landlady had attempted to hide with an old threadbare carpet. There were no pictures on the wall. Neither was there a chandelier, simply a standard lamp with a ragged light shade and low voltage bulb that occasionally buzzed threatening to expire. It didn't though at least while they were living there.

'I have some liquor' Sylvia volunteered. 'Whisky. Will anyone join me for a glass?'

All four women nodded in unison. Erika considered it was likely to be the only occasion when they might all agree on something but found herself smiling happily as Sylvia triumphantly discovered four large, although rather dusty, tumblers in the oak dresser. Their conversation focused upon their impressions of Munich and Nuremberg and the destruction of both cities. How pretty Nuremberg's old town must have been. The castle. The river and those bridges. Erika's thoughts were about the people. The people who had begun this nightmare and were, perhaps, beginning to pay the price. She hoped they were but felt slightly guilty although didn't want to make her thoughts known to these English women who would never be able to understand.

Sylvia told Erika that they needed to register their presence in the American zone at the Grand Hotel that morning asking her what she knew about it.

'Well, I don't know a great deal but I can tell you that the hotel was one of the few buildings that was more or less in one piece. The Americans had done some necessary repairs, including decent lighting.'

'Really?' asked Mary 'they have done work on the buildings already?'

'More than that' Erika tried to provide a competing patronizing smile. 'Local military gossip has it that the bars in the hotel are all well stocked and frequented by troops during the evenings. And friends of troops of course.'

'Maybe we might go out there one evening?' Sylvia suggested. The responses were unenthusiastic.

'So, what do we have to look forward to?' Mary asked Catherine. Erika found it slightly odd that she hadn't been officially briefed while assuming her companion had been.

'After we are scrutinized by the American authorities, which might take forever – although I hope not....'

'I don't think I like the Americans' Sylvia offered to the group.

Catherine pressed on. 'Then we have two days orientation to learn about the rules and the details of the forthcoming events involving the prisoners, the relationships between the civilian delegates, lawyers and service personnel from the countries involved.'

'Sounds simple' Mary laughed in a flirtatious way that once again puzzled Erika who was attempting to assess their relationships and hierarchy while wondering if they were not actually a collective, but a coincidental assortment of women with similar missions.

I need to be wary of this lot.

'To cut our story short, so Dr. Adler knows what we are about ...' Catherine looked sternly at each of her compatriots. 'We are each attached to the British delegation connected to the forthcoming trial. I am selected to liaise with the French and the Russians while Mary and Sylvia here' she pointed to her colleagues in turn 'they are to attend to relationships with the Americans. Unfortunate for you then Mary?'

It seemed a bit unwarranted to Erika, but she didn't give the details or their individual preferences much thought as nothing about her lodging companions' work impacted upon her.

CHAPTER 31: NIGHT

As Erika and her three British companions sat together over their night-cap she recognized that she would need to be careful how she behaved and talked around them. They all seemed to like to gossip and were keen to mention names familiar to her, including Colonel Andrus and Airey Neave.

Erika had a feeling that Catherine at least was trying to make Erika think they were all doing comparable work and expected similar relationships with some of the key personnel. Erika had had enough recent experience to be careful before trusting anyone attempting to get close to her.

But Max? Have I discounted deceit there?

'This must have been one of the hostels that escaped some of the bombing. It has a kitchen. The walls and roof are still intact' Catherine ventured looking around the room, surveying the ceiling and the furniture as if she had never entered such a squalid house in her life before.

The conversation has reached a point where we either go deeper and get to know each other or leave it at the polite English style. I would like to know more about them before any more informality, but I think but it's not up to me.

Then from out of the blue: 'Can you tell us what *you* are actually going to be doing? If it's not hush-hush that is.' Catherine asked Erika bluntly and it seemed, forcefully. Erika appreciated her direct approach having been conscious that they had all wanted to ask her but hadn't known how to do so.

'Well, I have been asked to help with translation for the prisoners, lawyers too but more so make a psychiatric assessment of some of the key prisoners and ensure they are fit to stand trial.'

Mary looked at her blankly. Despite the long evening, and the longer journey that had preceded it, her make-up was still impeccable. Erika got the sense that Mary was doubtful of her story but couldn't decide why.

Sylvia giggled.

'Do you think you can?'

'What do you mean?'

'Well assess what these people are really like. Do you know what they have done?'

'Some of it. Yes, I do know.'

'Do you think it's true?' from Mary.

Erika froze in horror and looked at Mary for a long moment wondering whether all the middle class, privileged English women had similar thoughts. Erika lowered her head and stared into the strong anonymous spirit she had been drinking.

Strange women. Do they understand what they are going to see and hear? Surely even after all we have been told they have a sense of evil – this place – Nuremberg, reeks of it.

She hoped they couldn't read her thoughts as they may well be her main social companions during the coming months.

The people I can relax with. Maybe!

She smiled discretely. No-one could guess when the Court would be ready to sit or how long the trial itself might last.

Catherine gave the impression of being annoyed. She looked embarrassed making Erika feel slightly reassured.

'It will be hard for you. You in particular. I know.'

'Do you mean because I am Jewish?'

Mary and Sylvia stared.

'Jewish?' asked Mary. 'I thought that you were .... Well, I don't know. One like these people – the ones here. I've not met too many Jews before.'

'I'm here solely as a professional psychiatrist. I came

from Austria – my family have done for several generations. *I am Austrian.*'

Erika spat this last part out only realizing how angry she was when she heard and felt the power of her speech. She breathed in.

'So, I know the German language. But, of course, my background has relevance.'

Erika was getting tired. Her head hurt and she made her excuse to go to bed. 'It's going to be an early start tomorrow don't you think. Good night.'

It was soon time for everyone to retire to their bedrooms if they were to manage themselves effectively when they faced the unique, but different, tasks that lay ahead of each them. The next few days would prove to be testing times for all four women - Catherine, Mary, Sylvia and Erika - in different ways. They were all keen to discover what their lives were to be like here in the godforsaken city.

Erika stood up as slowly as she could, yawning and smiling at the three other women. She didn't want to be offensive. But more so she didn't desire to be a curio. She bade them good night and left them to any lingering thoughts and chatter.

While trying to get to sleep she wondered how to begin the exciting, formidable task that awaited her. It was daunting.

What were they going to be like? The evil men. The lawyers. The American soldiers.

The names of the men she was to meet – prisoners and staff – were familiar to her. Max himself had given her a few rather gentle – maybe too gentle – instructions and information.

Talk to Hans Frank – find out if he really is a reformed man. Don't trust anything he says. Get Ernst Kaltenbrunner to understand what he had done – but don't believe a word he might offer in mitigation. He is evil and a liar. Don't get too involved with either Streicher or Hess. Try to see whether

Speer will spill the beans on some of his colleagues.

She wasn't sure that she would stick to his rules. Streicher himself was not particularly interesting although the impact his disgusting publication – *Der Stürmer* was. It had been so popular and influential during the Nazi regime – it had sold many copies, but the readership was far larger than that. It had been left in cafes, stations, doctors' reception rooms – it had successfully penetrated the psyche of the German speaking nations.

Rudolph Hess though was a different matter. After his flight to Scotland, he had spent some time being assessed at the Tavi. It would be interesting to discover what he was actually like – mad? Was he? Trying to make a peace deal? Maybe she could make sense of him. Whatever he might argue Hess had signed off on the Nuremberg Laws that had effectively made Jewish people illegitimate.

Speer, in spite of his close relationship to Hitler and the rest of the Nazi leadership, was likely to tell a different story – a traitor to his former cause but potentially a useful source of information to the Allies. Which side of the moral coin did his predicted reactions fall upon? Erika was interested to meet him – one of the more intelligent prisoners and one of the least predictable.

And then of course Hermann Goering.

'He will charm you. Please don't talk to him – he will convince you that the German people were blameless, and the Nazi Party was the saviour of their souls. The more Erika thought about it and recalled Max's face with its intense expression as he told her these things, the more she wondered why he had found it so important. Surely he knew they were all – each and every one of them - repellent to her? But she imagined he also knew that she was supposed to try at least to be impartial when face-to-face with them. They needed to be fit for their trial. If they were intimidated in advance, then it was possible that the trial might be invalidated. That must not happen.

Erika had imagined that Albert Speer might be the one to pull the wool over the eyes of the prosecution and more importantly the world, rather than Goering. Speer was known to be very bright, charming – not like Goering but charming in that he could judge the mood and style of whomever he was talking to. It had been mooted among her colleagues at the Tavi who knew what she was going to Germany to accomplish, that Speer might be able to wangle his way out of anything.

Her thoughts and attempt to sleep that night were interrupted by a scream. It was distant. The noise disturbed her even so. It sounded as if an animal was being slaughtered. High-pitched and sustained. This scream was followed by what sounded like far-off banging – *a door hanging off its hinges in the wind?* That was common to almost all the doors she had passed through.

She lay quietly alert for about half an hour, half expecting more noise. But there was nothing. She considered then that it had probably come from someone along the street. Maybe neighbours were fighting over possessions discovered in the rubble? There was a curfew but there was also madness and the Americans could not hope to shut everything down. Erika's mind was far from in tune with what would be sensible – that was to get to sleep.

It's not dark enough. Why?

She became aware that someone had taken away the bedside lamp that had been there the previous night. Without thinking she had left the overhead light on when she got into bed. She groaned inwardly, heaving herself out of bed to search for the light switch. She was unsurprised to discover it next to the door into the room. She hesitated as she reached to turn off the switch. She had heard another noise – it sounded like a series of muffled thumps. They sounded as if they were coming from inside the house. She leaned into the bedroom door. She noticed that her heart was thumping and that she was scared. The feeling was terribly familiar to her although it had not surfaced for some time.

Am I scared of the Germans still? They are defeated. Don't be silly.

Rebuking herself did not alleviate her anxieties but her heart did calm a little. She listened carefully, still pressed against the door. She heard nothing now. Reluctantly she opened her bedroom door to the hallway in darkness and a piercing silence.

Thank goodness – I must be mistaken. I really don't want to deal with anything more tonight.

She switched off the overhead light, returned to her bed and fell asleep immediately.

By six a.m. Erika awoke managing to be the first to use the shared bathroom, intending to be early for breakfast. It was partly excitement about the coming day alongside a minor concern about the English women getting in her way as she dressed and collected her thoughts. She had to begin work even though at the moment it simply amounted to reading existing files.

She was disappointed when she arrived in the dining room to discover that Catherine and Sylvia were sitting at the table receiving their eggs and tea from Ursula. Erika had wanted to relax and think through what she needed to do with no desire for inane chatter at that time of the morning.

They all bade each other good morning and Erika, smiling at Ursula, took her place at the dining table.

'When will Mary be coming down?' Sylvia inquired of Catherine.

'Oh, I think she is very tired. She knows where to come so she'll join us when she feels ready.'

Erika wasn't overly worried about these women's plans but given their recent arrival in this unfamiliar city she noted Catherine's lack of concern with a little surprise.

Erika decided to mention Helga to her hostess.

'Ursula – a local woman was helpful to me on the way home last evening. She asked if I might bring her some food for her children – and herself no doubt. What would be the best way to do that? Naturally I will buy it – but where?'

'Leave it to me Miss. I shall buy some bread, meat, cheese for you to take to her. Um but I shall err need some money now. Is that alright?'

'Of course.' Ursula told Erika how much her gift to Helga and her family would cost. Erika took some dollars from her handbag. Ursula looked happy.

Shortly after that Erika headed off for the Palace of Justice. Andrus had made sure that she had access to several important files which she was determined to get to grips with before Airey Neave returned from an assignment in Essen, so that they could collaborate. The main thing she knew they were to do was to serve the indictments. Her preliminary job was to translate but more importantly make an initial assessment of each prisoner's health status.

She found that daunting, although reminded herself how much she was looking forward to engaging with the task ahead.

Is that immoral? I want to see those men suffer – that can never be enough. But I also want to explore their minds.

She also liked him – Major Neave. From a brief meeting she envisaged him to be sympathetic, intelligent with an unusual amount of emotional depth.

Not the typical Englishman. Nor the typical soldier.

She anticipated that he would make an excellent colleague and she was eager to learn from him as well as from Major Andrus who appeared to be the opposite of Neave. It was going to be exciting.

CHAPTER 32: MARY

Erika felt much more relaxed when she left the Palace of Justice that evening. It was almost as difficult getting security clearance when she left as when she had arrived for work. She understood why. Documents needed to be kept private and secure. No information about or from any of the prisoners to the outside world was to be taken beyond the confines of the prison and Court.

Erika made her way to her lodgings, this time thinking ahead and recalling the details of her route. Although the streets were relatively empty, she hoped to see Helga and tell her about the food. She was proud of herself as she recognized exactly where they had met and consequently knew Helga would not be too hard to find the next evening. In many ways Erika was pleased not to have to face anyone this evening. She was rather distracted as well as being energized by the excitement and real significance of what was to happen over the coming months. In 40 minutes, the time she had noted her journey had taken, she was in the street where her lodgings were. She sighed.

Although the food is not the greatest, I am looking forward to dinner and an early night. I have heard that Airey Neave may have returned, and we can start the important work.

She approached the rather depressing entrance to her temporary home. She didn't expect to have to use her key. The door opened as she had anticipated with a strong push, but a surprise was waiting for her. Two men in American army uniforms stood in the hallway. Erika could hear the muffled

English voices of Catherine and Sylvia. Erika nodded to the men and smiled a good evening.

'Just a minute ma'am.'

'Hello. May I help you?' she considered that a typical English response.

'Can I see your papers please ma'am?' It wasn't really a request. The soldier had thrust himself towards her barring her way to move down the hallway.

'For sure' and she shuffled around in her handbag – one that was now fully used to being searched. 'Her you are. May I ask what is going on here?'

'Are you German?' the second soldier butted in.

'Austrian – soon to be a naturalized English woman. A former refugee.'

He stepped back and the first soldier returned her papers, nodded to his colleague and allowed her to pass them. She headed to join the English women she could hear talking in the living room

Two of them were sitting in the shadows of the vintage chandelier. Their heads shot up in unison as Erika entered. The shaken expressions they shared softened as they recognized their visitor, and both stood. Catherine reached Erika first pulling her down onto the poorly stuffed sofa. Sylvia sat down. Erika was puzzled.

'Mary is dead.' Catherine told her. Sylvia whose face was now in the dim light had been crying. Catherine was still managing her stiff upper lip.

'What?'

'Murdered. Last night. Early this morning. I don't know – they're looking into it.' Catherine gestured towards the hallway and Erika guessed she referred to the Americans. Sylvia wiped her hand over her face nodding.

'She had been stabbed. More than once. And I think – kicked or beaten up. I overheard the Americans talking. We weren't allowed to see her. She's still up there – her bedroom. One floor above yours.'

Erika imagined, probably wrongly, that Sylvia was launching an attack.

My fault? I had no idea where her bedroom was.

She then thought she was being churlish.

'Who found her?'

'She didn't come down to breakfast. We thought maybe she had woken early and gone for a walk. Or something. Then we heard someone running – jumping more like it – down the stairs. It was the maid. She found her on the floor by her bed. That's all we know.'

Catherine was giving lots of detail – almost like a defence.

Erika toyed with the idea.

Why am I suspicious of her? Erika couldn't decide but she couldn't shake the feeling that something wasn't right.

'I heard some noise.' Erika spoke slowly staring at Catherine as she did so. 'I was lying in bed. A scream. Thumping ....'

'Didn't you do something?' Catherine sounded angry.

Another one casting blame.

'I did – I went out into the hallway. I listened. It was dark and silent. Undisturbed. I went back to my room. The window doesn't fit well. I listened at the window thinking it must have been coming from somewhere out in the street. Again dark. Still. Quiet. I then went to bed.'

All three women looked at each other, then continued to sit silently as if thinking about the answer to an academic problem.

'Who do you think would do this terrible thing?' Erika put to them.

'It has to be some of those dreadful creatures haunting the streets – families blaming us for what *they* did. They are the ones who caused these problems. We're here to help them sort themselves out. Don't they know that?'

Sylvia screaming her response almost broke down in tears. Erika leaned towards her and touched her arm.

'I'm not so sure. But let's hope the Americans can do

something. As far as I know there have been no attacks on individuals by the Germans here in Nuremberg. Resentment. Begging even ..'

She recalled Helga and wondered when she could take the food to her.

'But I think any protests are more public. And – well – I'm unsure but I suspect that a quiet murder ...'

'What is that if I may ask?' Catherine's tone resembled what Erika guessed was the one she used when reprimanding a junior office worker.

'What I mean is – and please bear with me I am rather shocked by what has happened .....'

Catherine nodded and looked down – a version of an apology probably.

'What I mean is that there was no – well *display* – that's the word I am looking for. From what you've told me it doesn't seem to be political in the sense that well – just that. No-one will know it's happened other than those of us most affected. Until the trial – if there is one. Mary's death only means something to us and the people who did it. And. I hope, to those investigating. Do you see what I mean – if the Germans wanted to make a point about people like us being here, eating their food or whatever ills they believe we are casting – well this murder. Mary's death would not be what they would choose. Do you see?'

Catherine sighed and Sylvia nodded between tearless sobs.

'What has happened then? Why Mary? And who?' Catherine looked thoughtful as if she were contemplating answers to her questions. Erika fleetingly pondered whether this woman, ostensibly the head of the group of the three English women, knew more than she claimed.

Because I have no real idea why any of them are.

There was a loud series of taps on the living room door, which Erika had left half open, and an American man in army uniform with the regulation crew cut to his dark blond hair, brown trousers with a darker buttoned brown jacket secured with a brown belt, came in. He was typically polite and formal standing just inside the room, more or less to attention. Erika guessed he was a middle-ranking officer, possibly connected to the intelligence services.

'Ma'am' directed towards Catherine 'just to let you know my men have examined the body. Your friend – that is. We are taking her to the nearest hospital for a postmortem. But I can confirm that she was stabbed to death with a sharp instrument. A very long blade. But there were marks on her legs and her torso that look as if they were inflicted before she died. Bruises. Possibly burns. We will know more after the post-mortem.'

'Thank you' Catherine gasped. She appeared visibly stunned by the news.

'I hope I've not said too much Ma'am. But one of my colleagues will be in touch soon. Thank you.'

And with that he left the living room and the three women who remained there sat in silence.

A respectful and puzzled silence Erika concluded.

CHAPTER 33: HELGA

Erika was surprised at how shaken Mary's death had left her. Her *murder*. She had no desire to eat, she was feeling nauseous. The thought of food caused her stomach to clamp tightly. That made her remember the debt to Helga and her children. Making her way into the kitchen to seek out Ursula, Erika became was half aware of Sylvia and Catherine in the dining room talking to each other in urgent tones. They sounded as if they were making important plans or decisions rather than shocked or saddened as might be expected.

Erika's mind was elsewhere at the time though and this half-remembered thought didn't resurface until the following morning. She called out to Ursula who appeared to be expecting her.

'Miss Adler – I have what you asked for. Please come with me.'

Ursula appeared from the kitchen with a large straw basket.

'You managed to find food for that family along the road?'

'Yes. And I have money to return to you – it was not so expensive.'

Erika was puzzled but refused the money noticing Ursula's gratitude without surprise.

She is almost as poverty stricken as everyone else in this city.

'I shall try to find this lady now so I might be a little late for supper. Would you mind?'

Ursula smiled and nodded. Erika decided that a short

walk and some time on her own might restore some of her appetite and avoid embarrassment if she joined the two remaining English women.

Helga was easily discovered sitting on some crushed concrete steps that must once have led to a dwelling of some kind. She was wearing the same grey dress as she had previously, but she looked less relaxed than Erika remembered. She was wringing her hands.

I can't imagine anyone relaxing here and now anyway.

'Excuse me? Helga?' She looked up and gave Erika a kind smile that turned into a more vigorous one when she noticed the basket.

'You have brought us food?' Her voice was shrill. Helga stood up and ran towards Erika. She then lunged towards her and hugged her. It was a strange experience for them both as they came apart and stared. Then they both laughed.

'I hope you will find some things to enjoy.' Erika felt the words were clumsy but in her obvious delight Helga was unlikely to notice and Erika felt the warm glow that we all experience when making a welcome gift. Erika knew that this woman might have hated Jews. She might have betrayed people. But she was part of a defeated community. A community that was starving and she was trying to care for her sons.

'Please sit with me for a moment? I want to thank you – and want to ask you who you are? You speak like us but you're with Americans.'

Erika sighed. 'I live in England. I am becoming an English citizen but was born in Salzburg ....'

'Ah. You are so near to your real home. So why ...?'

Erika noted Helga draw back slightly. She must have realized – at least something if not the full details of Erika's identity.

'I need to return to my lodgings now. I work in the morning.'

'You are involved the trial – the court case?'

Erika nodded.

'Americans have been near Gartenstrasse all today. Do you know why?'

Erika hesitated. 'I think a woman – an English woman has been killed. Maybe murdered.'

Helga was silent but looked up and stared into Erika's eyes. She realized that this woman may not be exactly as she appeared – perhaps not a simple housewife and mother. Nothing sinister but maybe she had had a professional role in the German war effort. Perhaps she had been an office worker – a manager, something a little bit out of the ordinary.

'The woman in green? With fur? Very smartly dressed?'

Erika was confused. Should she acknowledge that Helga had it correct – in detail? As far as Erika knew Helga lived about ten minutes-walk away from their lodgings. There was no reason for her to link Mary – and anyway how had she even set eyes on Mary – with Erika? OK – Mary was English. Erika was working with the English in Nuremberg. But it was a very long shot. Unusually accurate. It didn't make any sense. Helga had merely been in the right place at the right time for Erika to ask for directions. Erika's brain flicked through an imaginary index – but nothing appeared to link her with events at either the lodgings or the Palace of Justice.

Unless of course she was involved with local Nazis? I really don't want to know and I need not see her again. Debt cleared.

Helga then grabbed Erika's hands and held them tightly.

'She was not what you believed. Be careful. See what you can find.'

And with that remark Helga gave Erika a brief hug and went along the road a little way and into a ruined building that may have once been her home.

Erika stood for a moment looking after her. She was stunned. Erika moved to walk back to the lodgings. Before she had gone very far, she heard heavy footsteps and turning saw a young man, perhaps in his early twenties, passing her along the pitted road. He dropped scrunched up ball of paper that landed not far in front of her, turned, looked at it, looked at Erika and strode on keeping up his pace. She stopped to pick it up staring out into the direction the young man had been heading. But he was no longer anywhere to be seen. The paper as she unfurled it was thin - a single sheet. She put it inside her jacket, looking around to see whether anyone else might take issue or claim it. But there was no-one. She headed for her lodgings wondering what on earth had just happened. More so what was going to happen and what message had the local Germans sent her.

Erika realized that she was hungry. A strange response, she thought as she pushed open the front door to the lodgings.

'Ah Erika – we thought you had gone AWOL!' Catherine exclaimed. She and Sylvia were making their way towards the dining room.

'AWOL?'

'Oh my dear – my apologies! It means absent without leave.' Catherine was laughing at her, but Erika didn't feel particularly offended. Rather she was slightly irritated that Sylvia and Catherine had not yet eaten their supper and the three of them would spend time in the dining room together.

PART 6: CONNECTIONS TO THE FUTURE'S PAST

CHAPTER 34: A DIARY, LONDON PRESENT DAY

Wilson knew he had to find a firm connection between Max and Mary if he were to tell Marion anything of value to her. And he had possibly to seek out a connection between Max and Mary's death – or at least try to discover Max's response – emotional and practical. And, if he could, he should try to discover whether Mary's murder, for clearly it was a murder, had actually been fully investigated. Somehow, he doubted it. He guessed that the mistake the intelligence services made at that point was allowing her death to be discovered.

If any of this is true. I am getting a strange feeling about this.

He kept returning to the thought that this murder had taken place before the trial had started. It even occurred before the English women had established themselves effectively in their different purposes for being in post-war Nuremberg. It was clear from everything he knew now, why Erika was there. She had a valid role to play working with the prisoners – assessing their mental state and attempting to discover relevant information about the Nazi machine. And she was fluent in the language. The other three women, superficially, claiming more prosaic intentions than Erika presented, were a mystery for that very reason.

He was lounging on his sofa, his neck and back propped

up with soft cushions, while papers from Marion's file lay spread out next to him. His legs were stretched onto the footstool that he had recently retrieved from a corner of the room. Generally, his body felt calm and pain-free. This suited his demeanor while he puzzled-out the hidden meanings behind everything he was reading.

He wondered whether he should be paying more attention than he had been to Max. His story appeared to be a sympathetic as well as a dangerous one. Mary's reason for being in Nuremberg and her sad death, more or less on arrival, appeared to be the anomaly. She looked to be so insignificant. He scratched his head and gazed up to the ceiling.

So, Max may or may not be a double agent. Working for Gisevius? Working for Kaltenbrunner and friends? All sides? Which is it? I know how to discover all I need to about him, I think. Maybe not from this file but there are many other records as I know from the postwar German authorities and their efficient filing systems.

But Mary. I need to become a lot better informed and take this more seriously now. I'm reaching something of a log jam. How do I overcome this?

It's still unclear why Max and Mary met let alone how they became Susan's parents – maybe finding the answer to that will help me to go further.

Gisevius may have introduced them – he had seemed to know her – or someone called Mary. But was that by chance? And when and how did Max die? I am assuming he is dead – perhaps he is not.

He pondered giving up for the evening and watching something on Netflix – he had a long list to catch up on. But that would not really help him achieve even a minor goal as he was due to have lunch with Marion at the Tavi two days later.

'Ok. A glass of the amber nectar then fresh energy into this puzzle.'

He stretched, rose and headed to the drinks' cabinet.

And why not?

He took his whisky back to the sofa but this time sat up attempting greater focus on the main task. He decided he need a clear list of what was needed.

Firstly, check the Secret Intelligence Service, MI6, records for information about Max and Mary.

If they'll let me. There can't be much that is secret now – or what? Maybe. Were they British spies? Double agents and if so where was their primary allegiance?

Wilson wanted to be able to reassure Marion that both of her grandparents were working for the Allies but so far, evidence was lacking. In either direction.

I need to make contact with Jacques – or Manfrit as he is also known – my former handler for MI6.

Wilson wondered whether Jacques was still around. He had once told Wilson that you could never retire from espionage. That made some kind of sense.

But he meant me too!

He shivered as he thought of getting in touch with Jacques. He could never forget everything that had happened since they had last worked together. Wilson's wife Hanna was murdered under Jacques watch and there were also Wilson's own injuries.

But the one thing for sure – Jacques would know what to do.

He made a note – it just said. 'Contact J.'

The second thing needing doing was to follow up anything about the everyday activities of the Gestapo under Kaltenbrunner. Some things would be mundane. Other inquires would focus on associated post-war German activities – particularly any evidence related to the life and times of Hans Gisevius and Allen Dulles the American intelligence agent, head of the CIA based in Switzerland during the war.

Was Max Mayer working for them as he claimed?

Gisevius' credentials as serving the interests of the

allies had been rubber stamped eventually, particularly because of his support for the plot against Hitler. But others? Friends and colleagues of Gisevius, in the German intelligence service – the Abwehr - and those working with the police in the Reich Main Security Office such as Arthur Nebe had been tortured before being murdered by Kaltenbrunner.

But Max had escaped a similar fate. He had been in London at the time.

The details need careful checking. Did he count for anything at all? Was he a fantasist – more to the point is Marion?

He erased that thought. At least then.

And I need to discover everything I can about Mary – and I suspect her two companions as well – Catherine and Sylvia. Did they work for the British SIS? The Nazis? Were they innocent bystanders or did they murder Mary? If so why?

The answer to these questions would broaden the overall quest towards a number of possibilities. Wilson drained his glass, headed for the decanter and poured another drink. Then he straightened the papers into a pile placing them on the floor next to his wonderfully comfortable sofa and tuned into Netflix.

Now I have a working plan I can relax for a few hours.

He planned to have the beginnings of an answer to Marion's questions in two days' time.

CHAPTER 35: 'CONTACTING J', LONDON PRESENT DAY.

It was going to be the most difficult, or at least the most painful, part of his investigation – getting in touch with Jacques. That was partly why it was first thing to do on Wilson's list. He knew that if he could get Jacques on board the evidence would fall into his lap with ease. And there might well be a great deal of it.

Who knows? I might get all the answers I need in one fell swoop.

Contacting Jacques was easy in the practical sense. There was a telephone number – updated many times over the years and now including a mobile number. Then a code word, another number – also mobile and then hang up and wait.

The call came back to him at midnight. Wilson was watching a French police drama series that he had enjoyed. He unthinkingly switched it off. The actors all had fascinating faces – unusual – ugly even - but riveting. He had never enjoyed watching the typical film star looks. He was engrossed in the end game following a series of perverse and bloody murders. But the phone call brought him back to earth.

'How are you? What is the name you need?'

'Alphonse is chasing after Oedipus.'

'Wilson Coffey! My dear friend – what a pleasure to hear from you.'

Wilson gulped 'Hello Jacques. How are you? Where are you?'

'Around and about. What may I do for you after all these years?' and before he could answer: 'The trattoria behind Waterloo Station. Lunch at 12.30 tomorrow.'

And then the call went dead. Wilson felt every limb tense along with his back that had begun to ache fiercely. His head pounded and was beginning to hurt even though he had been thoroughly relaxed only a few minutes earlier. He let out a long breath and stared ahead of him at the blank television screen.

The last time he and Jacques had dined at that particular venue he had been young – or at least middle aged. Nearly thirty years ago. *Benni's Trattoria!* He hadn't felt so young at the time though because he had been reliant on a wheelchair. Now he managed without and all the pain he had had now was less than it had been then. What he needed from Jacques now was not personal. It was for Marion. As for Wilson himself, he was merely fact-finding – a special challenge without emotion. Or so he thought.

It was difficult to sleep that night – memories enveloped him as he made plans for his meeting. He wanted to protect himself from memories that were painful.

But they are not related to Jacques – well not directly.

His thoughts about what to ask Jacques were like butter melting across his brain. Ideas softening, flowing in all directions, meaninglessly and out of control. He could no longer recall why he had needed to see Jacques. What possible benefit there might be for either of them?

In the meantime, he had opened a container that might have been better kept locked. He wondered whether he had been trying to impress Marion with his contacts. Then he remembered that Marion herself had told him – almost charged him – with her knowledge of his earlier, secret and terrifying life. He was courting danger and was unclear why.

What does Marion gain by discovering the true identities of her grandparents? Well curiosity served maybe. Perhaps she has always wanted to know more about her past – popular genealogy? But is there more to it? I should have been more careful. Is it just that I am old and useless trying to regain a sense of worth by doing all this intelligence agent stuff again? Trying to find Hanna out there somewhere?

He didn't expect to sleep well, so threw another small glass of whisky down his throat before settling down for the night. He needed to rest but didn't want to oversleep. He had to keep a cool head for his lunch date.

A snore caught in his throat as he woke just in time to turn off the alarm. His swift action was followed by the dulcet tones of a well-known journalist on the early morning radio broadcast. It was difficult to concentrate on any news items, but he managed to discover that so far there were no traffic hold-ups between Battersea and Waterloo Station although he knew that the situation was fluid, so might well deteriorate at any time over the next three hours.

What are you even thinking about traffic for? Get yourself sorted – make a clear list of what you want and need and get this day over with.

His iPhone beeped with a text message and his heart throbbed against his chest as he realized that this was going to be his physical and mental state for the day.

He relaxed slightly. It was a message from Marion reminding him of their meeting the next day. He thought that was slightly odd though – she knew he was going to be in his office at the Tavi. More to the point – he'd never had a "reminder" of that sort and she had no idea – at least not from him, when he was going to put any of his search plans into action.

He had a shower, dressed, took his breakfast and then sat with a pen and blank pad making notes – ones he hoped were indecipherable to anyone else – with his queries for Jacques. One thing he needed to know, which might be beyond their present conversation, was about the role of the CIA based in Switzerland. That information might help to determine how far Max really did work with Gisevius or whether he used him to keep his Nazi masters happy, Kaltenbrunner in particular. It was the failed July plot against Hitler that might be the key. Gisevius managed to escape but his colleagues Canaris, Nebe and most of the others were found guilty in Hitler's "People's Court", before being slowly tortured and murdered by Kaltenbrunner.

Did Max have a role in that – one way or another? And what might Jacques be able to tell him about Mary – Marion's grandmother? Something kept creeping into his thoughts about Mary. Was she real? Was she Marion's grandmother? And why did there appear to be no connection in what he had been reading so far, of Mary's relationship, on any level, with Max?

Admittedly at least 100 pages remained among the contents of the box file that he had yet to consider. He was used to giving similar effort to this type of puzzle and even enjoyed it. The events between the 1930s, the plots against Hitler's leadership and the executions of the Nuremberg defendants in 1946 were reasonably well documented as well as being the stuff of television documentary and drama. But the "bit players" were invariably absent from the well-rehearsed evidence.

Wilson knew the way to the trattoria but was aware that parking would be more complicated today than it had been all those years ago when he had met Jacques there for dinner. Wilson had recently mastered the art of paying for parking with his mobile which instilled a degree of confidence. All he had to do was find a space.

His new car, a Porsche Cayenne, was in the underground garage. He descended in the lift, no longer having to concern himself with managing a wheelchair. He remained amazed at how he had once regained his life using aids for the disabled.

He would not have the strength to do that now. Ironically, he no longer needed such skills. He drove out of the garage, taking the exit at the roundabout by Battersea Park along Nine Elms Lane towards the South Bank and a half-step back into his former life.

CHAPTER 36: TAKEN

Parking proved to be easy, leaving Wilson rather smug. He swung his legs from the car grabbing the walking-stick that he still needed to support his weight during that type of maneuver. The day was warm, sunny and cloudless – weather that matched his reinvigorated mood. He almost whistled as he walked to the back of the railway station towards the busy, but often overlooked, area of shops, cafes and small restaurants that lay under the shadow of Waterloo.

Ahead of him he saw that *Benni's Trattoria*, even now, claimed the name but the display above the restaurant had been updated. It now looked to be a glamorous, upmarket, hidden gem. Wilson smiled to himself, in one way relieved not to be revisiting a distressing time in his life, although a sadness remained that he couldn't do so. But he acknowledged that things had moved on and today was to be a very different time for both him and Jacques.

He checked his watch to find he was about fifteen minutes early. Peering through the window he didn't see Jacques or anyone obviously waiting for a companion, so he looked at the menu in the window – familiar dishes with inflated prices.

That will be fine for us.

He decided to take a brief walk around the area to see if he recognized anything from the old days or whether there was something new to attract a future visit.

I wonder why I never come here socially? I think I know.

He recognized the theatre as well as a few pubs that were once shabby and now transformed to 21st Century standards. He noticed one that had a rather interesting off-license attached wondering they might charge for a litre of Drambuie – a popular alternative to whisky in his one-man household. He realized that once again he had sighed. He asked himself what he was doing here – waiting for Jacques he told himself.

But what made me get to this point? Is it for Marion? Is it so I find a purpose? Am I retracing the past?

He felt agitated and more than a little confused over his own motives. He thought back over the time since Marion had railroaded him – and yes - he believed now that that is what she had done. He had been flattered but maybe more so – he had been intrigued by the story and accepted a challenge.

Maybe life had become a little too predictable?

He was as happy as he had been for many years.

I wonder why?

The pain in his lower back became intense as he sauntered aimlessly moving away from the off-license window, lost in his anxious thoughts, unexpectedly wishing he had stayed home – away from here. Even away from the Tavi and all the work he was doing there and the people who had a call on his time – especially Marion. It was a strange feeling – he almost hated her. He then felt guilty and stupid. He caught himself in one more sigh remembering once again that he had a good life. It was fun, interesting and of value.

Then there was a stab of pain in his lower back as if an electric shock had passed through him, but unlike the normal pattern – when his physiotherapist did something of the kind that was healing – this was damaging. His nerve endings were on fire and his spine ached. He became dizzy seeing bright lights as his head absorbed a heavy blow that felt and even sounded like an explosion. Whatever was going on was happening from behind him, in broad daylight in a quiet street where he had believed himself to be more or less alone.

He became a little light-headed. He couldn't breathe freely. His mind questioned the connection between his spine and lungs as a strong hand pulled his right arm back causing his walking-stick to clatter helplessly onto the pavement. The pain in his shoulder from the tugging on his arm intensified as another man standing on his left side, demanded:

'Don't make a fuss. Look as if we are all together and you won't get hurt.'

His arm was jerked back again, as if for good measure. They had come out of nowhere.

Spies! At least two of them! The one who hurts and the one who gives orders. What the hell is going on?

'My stick please.'

He couldn't believe the sound of his voice – calm, matter of fact maybe a slightly exaggerated Scottish accent. He had never lost his accent completely and people he spoke to could always place it, but he had not been to Scotland for many years. That was a sudden awareness. His family were either dead or scattered across the south of England.

But now he heard himself talking as if he were meeting a couple of old, rather formal, friends from whom he needed a small favour – the return of his walking-stick.

Wilson glanced to his left to examine a man of late middle age, possibly early 50s, wearing an unfashionable black beret pulled rather low across his brow, a burgundy coloured, tight-fitting corduroy jacket along with blue jeans. This man stared straight ahead towards the window of the off-license – not looking directly at Wilson. But they could see the others' reflections. Wilson continued to stare into the window to catch a glimpse of the other man who was on his right – the one whom he hoped would stop pulling his arm and return his stick.

The man on his left, who had spoken was a stranger. There was nothing familiar about this man's voice. He might have been German, or perhaps Dutch. There was a slight accent to that effect. Wilson watched the man who, like him, continued to stare at their reflections in the window.

Not East European and not French or Italian. That is a

certainty.

The other man clamping his arm, whom he believed to be the one who had hit him, had remained silent throughout. He did bend to collect the stick from the pavement, although he had not yet given it to Wilson whose arm was in no position to grasp it anyway. This man didn't speak. His reflection was slightly obscured by the light shining onto the display. He was tall, taller than either Wilson or the Black-Beret man. The image suggested him to be thin with light blond hair, perhaps heading towards grey. Unlike his partner the silent man was wearing a dull grey business suit – or as far as Wilson could tell.

Courting obscurity.

'Please let go of my arm, give me my stick – I need it otherwise I could faint – that would draw attention. Then tell me what you both want. I can't believe I have anything of interest. I am a semi-retired psychiatrist.'

The dull man on the right, given the name "blondie" by Wilson replied in a soft but commanding tone.

'Surely you remember me Dr. Coffey?' A bland middle-class English accent – a southerner. Self-confident but not of the ruling class.

Wilson jerked his head towards the speaker discovering as he did that his right arm had been freed, although it still hurt him. The stick was handed to him with a smile.

Gabriel. The man I saw with Jacques – the last time we met – 7 years ago.

'Gabriel?'

'In one. How do you do once again Dr. Coffey?'

'And what about you? What's your name?' Wilson had turned towards Black-Beret. The man looked rather sulkily at his captive.

'There's no need for you to know that.'

'Let's have that lunch you came for,' Gabriel said, physically pushing Wilson back towards Benni's creating a superficial air of jolly friendship.

'And I am guessing now that Jacques will not be joining us?'

'He's like you – semi-retired. Mostly mopping up data from old files – still on that *Werwolf* trail of course. As are we – and I am led to believe – are you.'

Wilson could well believe that about Jacques, which is why he had been the first person Wilson chose to approach. They had worked together – or he believed that they had – identifying and seeking out Nazis who had escaped from East Germany to work in high positions in West Germany, the UK and USA in particular. Towards the end of their work Wilson had been unsure whether Jacques was working wholeheartedly for the Secret Intelligence Service – their employer MI6 - or whether Jacques himself had really been connected to *Werwolf* – or at least elements of it. To be clearing up information from old, pre-computer files might be because he wanted to find the last of their breed or to ensure his own tracks were covered. Perhaps both. It was often difficult to know.

The three men reached Benni's almost immediately. Black-Beret held the door open for the other two. Wilson, half turning back, noted that he had quickly closed the door behind them while looking through the glass at the street, presumably ensuring they had not been followed. The precinct outside the restaurant was quiet – it was slightly too early for most local office workers to be out shopping or taking lunch.

The trattoria held about 12 tables, each set for four diners. Until Wilson and his companions arrived only one other table was occupied by four women probably connected to the South West London University that was ten minutes-walk away. They appeared to be having an animated business lunch-meeting. One looked up as the men entered but her interest soon waned as she returned her attention to her companions.

Gabriel greeted the young female waiter, clearly not

Benni who had been Wilson's host the last time he had eaten there, and with her assistance Gabriel selected a table away from the window under the shadow of the drinks bar. Wilson engineered his own place with his back to the bar facing the door. From there he could protect his back and watch the street. He rested his stick on the chair next to him hinting that it was to be the empty one. His escorts complied without question making him slightly uneasy. He rationalized that they were in a restaurant and none of them was likely to make a run for it or a fuss. He began to relax and as the waitress gave them a welcoming smile along with the food and the wine menus. He started to ponder what he might achieve for his own ends from this small gathering. He reminded himself of the reasons he had wanted to speak to Jacques. His questions were about Mary, Max and Gisevius and his networks but he had intended, and still would, begin with relatively small matters before escalation and specific questions about MI6 and its activities concerning the high-profile Nazi prisoners.

Black-Beret and Gabriel were both intently scrutinizing their menus. Wilson thought he should do the same. He asked Gabriel if he himself had planned to choose the wine – Gabriel smirked before nodding.

'Red and strong in a generic sense if you please?' Wilson requested. Black-Beret looked at him and then at Gabriel before agreeing. The waitress seemed to know that a decision on their wine was imminent as she glided towards them taking the order and the wine menus promising to return for their food choices, which she did.

Wilson opted for lasagna which was his favourite dish and a repeat order from his distant dinner with Jacques. The others had more complicated tastes but soon all was settled.

As they drank the wine Wilson anticipated the awkward silence which he filled by taking his notebook and pen from his jacket pocket. He looked at the two men in anticipation. He planned to derive some benefit from this meeting and gain the information that he wanted, or at least get what these men were capable of telling him. He was angry about the attack and still had some pain in his back, head and arm. He was not going to leave empty handed. He decided to take control.

'It's now time for you to tell me what the hell is going on.' His two assailants stared at him.

'You've physically attacked me. You've usurped a meeting planned with an old friend and colleague. I've met you once Gabriel – and we met as colleagues – on the same side. At least that is what I had been led to believe. Now – who knows? But I do want to know. So, tell me. Now.'

Wilson felt that he had said exactly what he had intended and in the tone he had desired. There had to be a reason for them taking the trouble to meet him and if they didn't trust his motives – well there was nothing that had taken place yet to enlighten them either way. He himself was certainly in the dark.

The waitress arrived carrying two plates – one for Black-Beret and one for Gabriel. She smiled at Wilson.

'I shall be back immediately with your dish sir.' And she departed towards the kitchen.

The men's silence was excused by their preparing to eat – unfolding napkins, gathering their cutlery. Wilson gave each in turn a hard stare that he had to admit was to little avail.

'You're wasting time – yours and mine.'

Gabriel took a forkful of something that looked like a large prawn which he put into his mouth before taking it out to remove the shell. Wilson almost giggled.

Surely the bloody man knew how to eat the dish he ordered!

'Not prepared exactly to my taste' Gabriel muttered watching Black-Beret who seemed to know exactly how to manage his own plate of sea food.

Wilson sighed as the lasagna arrived in front of him. He placed his elbows on the table, even though his hunger was stimulated by the smell and appearance of his favourite dish.

'Come on guys – what on earth is this about?'

Gabriel sighed, put down his fork while Wilson lifted with its first delicious mouthful.

CHAPTER 37: LUNCH

'Tell us what you wanted from Jacques?' was Gabriel's opening gambit.

'Ok – I shall. It's quite simple and no great secret. I have a colleague – a friend – well almost – at the Tavistock Clinic.'

Wilson looked at each of the men who seemed to be more focused on their food at that time.

'Well, she wanted to find out about her grandparents – they met in the 1940s and were both – I think and so does she, involved in some way with the Nazi prisoners in the first Nuremberg trial. The lead guys – Goering, Hess and so on. With me so far?'

He was getting a little annoyed that his food was unnecessarily being neglected while his companions were eating theirs.

Both men nodded and Gabriel asked 'who were these people – the grandparents? Have you got their names?'

'Well yes I do.'

He took a few mouthfuls of lasagna and some wine. The other two had stopped eating and were staring at him. He had a brief sense of power over the company that was touched with slight irritation caused by the smell of seafood.

It's masking the smell of lasagna!

'I merely wanted to find out what Jacques might be able to discover from any of your archives. The mother was English and the man, apparently worked for the CIA via Hans Gisevius – you know who that is I take it?'

Black-Beret was the first to acknowledge this. Wilson became wary. So far Black-Beret had acted as the hard-man, the accomplice - the thug. Wilson now began to wonder whether in fact Gabriel, the one who attacked him, might be the "gofer" and what the significance of this man with the – now he confirmed to himself - German accent actually might be.

'I was wondering who you worked for?' Wilson stared at Black-Beret who stared back. Wilson now saw him more clearly – in the detail that he had overlooked before. He had sharp features – a pointed nose, small white teeth, a chin with an almost imperceptible blond goatee beard. His bright blue eyes gave the impression of being tiny little lights boring into Wilson's own.

A cliché member of the Aryan race. Hardly any Germans I knew resembled that so-called ideal but here is a prototype.

'We need to hear what you have found out and to tell you to stop what you are doing.'

Wilson snorted, and nearly choked on the sip of wine he had just taken.

'Grow up man – I'm doing a favour for a friend who wants to know who her grandfather was. Her grandparents didn't marry. Didn't stay together for very long – well not long enough to look after her mother. He mother died recently of old age. My friend is curious. End of story.'

Black-Beret and Gabriel looked at each other. The waitress hovered and removed their plates. Wilson clung to his – there were a few mouthfuls left. She looked embarrassed.

'It's Ok – I am finding this delicious – I won't be long.'

He noticed that here was something of a buzz around the restaurant now – chat, laughter and the clash of cutlery on plates. All the tables had become full and almost all the customers were eating.

We must have been here, getting nowhere, longer than I thought.

'I can give you what you need if you tell me more about the woman.'

Wilson sat bolt upright shocked that Black-Beret was conceding to his requests.

'As I understand it the grandmother was called Mary.'

That was enough. Wait to see what he comes up with.

Wilson noted that Gabriel had remained silent for some time. He felt rather proud of himself – there were some skills like observation that he had not yet lost. He might achieve something.

'Why you?'

'What do you mean?'

'I mean why did this woman approach you? You may be a nice guy. A clever guy. A man with very little to do in his old age ....'

Wilson winced a little bit at that – he had given that idea some consideration for himself attempting to dismiss it.

'There seems to be no reason to approach you in particular unless you have been indiscreet about your past work' Black-Beret hesitated slightly - 'for us.'

'Absolutely not.'

'Well then she knows something that you don't – about you. About us. We want to know how and what. You need to find out otherwise, as you are well aware, measures will be taken.'

Wilson had given all of those issues a great deal of thought. He had been appalled when Marion almost jokingly had referred to his intelligence work. But she had been so relaxed and so confident ... He chastised himself silently. He hadn't explicitly admitted to anything, but he had gone ahead trying to help her. He had temporarily blown his cover, probably because he didn't believe he actually had any cover to blow. But he did know that spies were always spies and never free. He felt himself begin to panic. To sweat and with much effort he prevented his hands from shaking.

'What the hell is going on? I seem to be caught up in something here. What?'

Gabriel reached over the table and touch Wilson's

wrists.

Too gently. I think I'm in trouble. But why?

'Look, there's nothing to worry about. We're all on the same side. It's simply that your call to Jacques alerted us – maybe something about *Werwolf* – or old Nazis. We don't know. I know you're to be trusted. But as you are too well aware Nazis worked for the West during the 50s – even in some cases up until 20 years or so ago and *Werwolf* remains committed to restoring the Thousand Year Reich.'

Wilson looked puzzled by this. Despite his recent addiction to the Nuremberg trial being portrayed on screen as well as in Marion's dossier, it seemed a far cry from the organization that Himmler had built to restore Nazi power where and when they could.

'We are building up a picture of who, when, where and what these former Nazis did. That's all, I promise you Wilson. Nothing for you personally to worry about but do please tell us what you know about this woman and her grandparents.'

Now Wilson couldn't face the remnants of his lasagna, which until now he had been closely guarding from the waitress. He felt slightly sick, so was pleased when the waitress homed in on his plate before delivering another two bottles of the red wine they had been drinking.

I must have missed this being ordered. They are getting the better of me.

'So now please' Black-Beret had taken over from Gabriel and was a lot less friendly, albeit polite 'what is this colleague called?'

What harm would it do to tell him? He might approach her. But I've already said it was a colleague. So ..

'Ok. Her name is Marion Morgan – Dr. – you know where she works. She's a psychoanalyst.'

Black-Beret and Gabriel looked at each other.

'The grandmother's name?' Black-Beret again.

'Mary. I told you. Mary Hart.'

'Grandfather?'

'Max. Max Mayer. I believe he was Austrian. That's about all I know except that he is supposed to have worked for the CIA – or at least with Gisevius and Dulles and that is what I wanted to talk to Jacques about – and now I am asking you. What do you know about this couple? Might this man Max, the grandfather, have been working alongside the CIA in Switzerland?'

Once again Gabriel and Black-Beret exchanged looks. They were now on to the third bottle of wine. Wilson berated himself for failing to notice that he too had shared the first two which had inexplicably disappeared.

Do they know anything about Mary and Max? Do they know that she was murdered? Is this what it's about? Who killed Mary and why? And – oh my God – is Marion really concerned over family or is she one of this lot? If so – whose side?

Wilson tried to consider the contents of the file – well more of a story – that Marion had passed to him, although with a certain amount of difficulty due to wine and this unexpected pseudo interrogation.

If the file on Max et al was so precious – why let me take it away – out of her sight? It is fascinating reading but ..."

Wilson picked up a full glass of wine and sipped at it to aid thinking. He noted that his companions had quietened down, and it was likely that they were watching him carefully. Perhaps they thought he was considering a confession of sorts. He had no idea what they might want from him that he hadn't already told them.

What on earth are the issues here?

He wanted to think through what the file had revealed before offering any further information. He guessed he wouldn't be able to go home until something more might be presented to them. There was a strong possibility that they themselves were to be prevented from going home empty handed after interviewing him.

He thought about what he had been reading.

Firstly, that as a young man Max Mayer had been

recruited by Gisevius to work against the Nazis, and it was possible that Max's father had set up their initial meeting. That might suggest his family was anti-Nazi.

That secondly, Max had worked for the Gestapo under Heydrich, had spent time "training" guards at Dachau and eventually worked closely – or more probably – with - Kaltenbrunner. Therefore, Max was most definitely well aware of the Nazis' policies for rampant imprisonment and extermination of undesirable elements – Jews, Slavs, gays and Communists. The question was, did he use this knowledge to the benefit of the Allies or was he simply the person he appeared to be – Gestapo? He may or may not have been a committed anti-Semite like most of his colleagues but on the other hand he may not have been a double agent either. Maybe Max was a bog-standard, plodding member of the Gestapo who cared for little beyond getting through the day? He decided that was unlikely.

Thirdly – Max was able to be in London – or so it appeared from the file – shortly before the end of the war in Europe. He had linked up with a woman – possibly an old friend – a psychoanalyst. Dr. Adler who had been trained by Freud and came to London as a refugee from Hitler's Austria because of her mentor and his family. The story appears to show Max's upset about all he had seen and been through. He would have had assistance to be in London at that time, but which side helped him – CIA or Nazi collaborators?

Fourthly – Erika Adler is interesting in this chronicle. She knew Mary – or had met her and knew about the murder. So far Wilson had found very little evidence about Max and Mary together except for that time before or at the start of war, when he met her at Gisevius' house. But what was an English woman doing in Berlin at that time? Who was she working for?

Erika Adler again, as a fifth point in Wilson's list, knew the officials at Nuremberg before, during and after the trials - Andrus and Neave as well as her fellow professionals Drs.

Goldensohn, Kelley and Gilbert. She had unfettered contact with all the prisoners as did the others. Is that why Max pursued Dr. Adler? Was he attempting to remove traces of his past?

I've still not finished reading all of this so don't know anything further about her ideas and what she had actually done. In every case, except for Erika Adler – it is unclear who any of them – Gisevius, Max or Mary - are working for although of course Gisevius has been identified by history as a good guy – at least by the end.

What he did know now was he had to read the remainder of the file, find the information he sought on Gisevius, the failed attempt on Hitler's life and the Abwehr – the German intelligence agents who had been tortured and brutally murdered. And then Kaltenbrunner's role. After which he might be able to make sense of Marion's grandparents – if indeed they were. And now he had to add to his list – who is Marion actually working for? Just for her own interest? And what did Gabriel and Black-Beret want from him?

He had to find a way of getting rid of those two – he knew he was physically unable to make a run for it. They knew where he lived anyway as MI6 had more or less "housed" him there in Battersea.

'We need to come to a deal, don't we?'

Black-Beret looked up from the task of pouring himself more wine and waving to the waitress for yet another bottle.

'What makes you think you have anything to give us?' Black-Beret stated blandly.

'Well, here we are. Having lunch – delicious if I may say and thank you. I take it you – or your organization plans to pay the bill?'

Gabriel nodded and smiled at the humour. Black-Beret grunted.

'We have reached an impasse – stale-mate. Don't you think? I want to go home now but you have both acted as if

I had something you wanted and I'm not free to leave. You need me to stop – well clearly you want me to refrain from following up on the Mary and Max story, don't you?'

'Not necessarily' Gabriel intervened just as Black-Beret looked as if he were going in for the kill, destroying Wilson's take on the situation. Black-Beret scowled at Gabriel. Wilson looked at Gabriel in anticipation.

'Tell me what you want' Gabriel asked Wilson.

'What I came here to do – to see whether you – or your organization that is - can help me uncover the background and allegiance of this man Max Mayer. I also want to know more about Gisevius and Dulles – but that is something that is reasonably well documented – I can probably do for myself. So, what do you want from me?'

Black-Beret behaved as if he were out of the conversation – rather like a young child who was impatiently waiting for his parents to finish their meals so he might leave and do things he thought were more fun. He looked down at the tablecloth scraping an unused fork round in a circle pretending not to be taking part in the "grown-up" negotiations.

'I want to know all you can tell me – or discover about this Dr. Marion Morgan. Why she is interested in Mayer? Why she claims this woman, Mary Hart as her grandmother. Because I can assure you even now that she is not. Neither is Max Mayer her grandfather.'

It was Wilson's turn to stare at the tablecloth puckering it between his fingers while he attempted to analyze what was required now.

'There's no point in asking why you yourselves care about this? What value the information from so long ago might have for you or for her? I can imagine why a granddaughter who never met her grandparents, and whose mother can't remember them – or even know if she met her own father, the grandfather in this tale, might want to know more. But surely the grandparents are both long dead?'

He avoided the issue of Mary's murder. At that point Black-Beret stopped fiddling with the fork, straightened up and for the first time smiled in Wilson's direction.

'I think you are nearly there now. We – and by "we" I am talking about the British – we want to know who Marion Morgan is working for. We need to find the truth – not about her grandparents – we already know they are not. But a British woman, known as Mary, was murdered in Nuremberg late 1945. Who was *she* working for?'

Wilson interrupted. He was quite animated by this time.

'But now – why so many years later? These people are dead. What would anyone have to gain by getting me to find out about a dead Austrian – who may have once been a Nazi and an English woman who may have been a sympathizer – or not?'

'This woman had information that might implicate – let us say some right-wing descendants or disciples more to the point - of Nazi war criminals who did not face justice.'

'As you know I am semi-retired – read "washed-up" for that ....'

'Not at all man' Gabriel cut in. Wilson nodded with a faint smile.

Well that makes me feel better – not! OK it does a little.

'Thank you, Gabriel I appreciate the support, but apart from my psychological abilities I am a has-been as an agent. You have to agree!'

Black-Beret scowled. 'There are people here and in Germany, even now, who believe that the Third Reich was unjustly demonized and destroyed. You may have heard of some of them – they call themselves *Werwolf.*'

'Okay – no need for sarcasm' Gabriel confronted Black-Beret, but Wilson knew from experience, that was now flooding back to him almost washing him away, that a faux dispute could be enacted in order to relax the suspect, tempting him on board. It also confirmed that he had not seen the last of these two.

They knew about his role in seeking out members of *Werwolf*, his long-time past connection to the East German secret police including his late wife Hanna. But Marion also appeared to know about this. Wilson had never revealed his work with MI6 to anyone outside the organization – at least the organization as he had understood it. He communicated only with people approved by Jacques. But who can really tell who anyone might be?

So, there must have been some kind of breach – a leak. At <u>that</u> time – over the years since the Berlin Wall fell and Hanna died – or more recently? If in the present-day then, why?

He really had been out of the spying game for years. About six or seven years ago he had met Gabriel for the first and only previous time when he had been called to identify the body of a man whom he had understood had been working with MI6 seeking out former Nazis and their allies. But anyway, that was such a long time after his work for them had ended.

But does that work ever end?

He felt weary. 'Okay – I'll do some digging into this – try to see what Marion Morgan is up to – if anything. I can't imagine she is though'.

As he heard himself talking, he experienced a prickly feeling along the back of his neck progressing to the left side of his head and face. He wondered whether he was about to have a stroke – he had certainly felt stressed of late. He ran through the clinical signs in his head, dismissed them just as he recalled that slight uneasiness following her text reminding him that they were due to meet.

'In the meantime, I would like access to any files you might have on – let me think – Hans Gisevius and Allen Dulles – you must have been keeping tabs on the CIA's involvement with German resistance to Hitler?'

Silence and blank looks from his companions. He noticed the almost full bottle of red wine, poured himself some and waved the bottle at the other two. Black-Beret snatched the bottle and poured himself a glass, Gabriel demurred remaining stony-faced and stared at Wilson.

'I would need to be kept informed about any information you were to provide for Morgan.'

'Agreed. I have to admit that I am intrigued by the background to that first Nuremberg trial - defendants and witnesses. The psychology of it I mean. And – well the documents Marion Morgan gave me are fascinating – insights into the mind of some of the defendants. Not a great deal that's not already in the public domain though – it's a story. I've read much of it – no obvious secrets or details about her grandparents.'

'Except for those two – Mary and Max. That needs to be your focus. That's what she is wanting to know more about.' Gabriel smiled slightly. Wilson thought they were beginning to have an agreement.

'Right' he drained his glass 'you let me come into your HQ to see any relevant files, I'll continue meeting Marion Morgan and reading on through the information she has provided. And then – I guess we shall meet at least once again? And in the meantime I shall report back to you. Just let me know how.'

'I'll get someone to inform you and provide access to files. You will be contacted about Morgan.'

Then Black-Beret moved to pay the bill. Gabriel grabbed Wilson's hand, squeezing hard – almost a gesture of fondness.

'Be careful driving home old man – you're a bit over the limit. We can get a taxi – not far to go.'

With that Gabriel joined Black-Beret as they both left the trattoria and Wilson stood, monitored his ability to stand without falling or pulling the tablecloth and decided that he too should hail a taxi to take him home.

PART 7: TRIAL, JUDGEMENT AND JUSTICE

CHAPTER 38: THE INDICTMENTS

There was a general sense of nervousness even from the American Andrus, although he had known the prisoners well before they arrived in Nuremberg – as he had been the commandant at 'Camp Ashcan'. For Erika the nervousness extended to the investigation by the Americans into Mary Hart's death. For a while she had worried, *most selfishly*, she scolded herself, that it would impede her work at the Palace of Justice but strangely that wasn't the case. She also felt that someone had begun to watch over her, to make sure her part in history wasn't blocked. That her work was vital, and it was imperative that she was the person to do it. She needed justice for herself and everyone who had been so cruelly murdered and made to suffer. That would never be fully achieved but she wanted her contribution to count.

And even some local Germans might not be exactly as they seem to be.

Major Airey Neave, a barrister, soldier and escaped prisoner of war, had the overall responsibility for delivering the indictments to the prisoners as well as assisting them in identifying their defence lawyers.

Was he nervous too? Is he my guardian angel?

Erika felt quite sure she could trust him and decided to share her strange encounter with Helga and the man with him. She found him in the room at the Palace of Justice that served as an office and store for prisoners' files and other equipment to aid the prison staff, military and prosecutors.

Over recent days she had become reasonably accustomed to the office itself and dealing with security in the Palace which was impressive. It made her feel safe. More so over the previous few days she was gradually become familiar with the detailed evidence against the men who had recently ruled Germany and murdered millions.

Neave greeted Erika warmly.

He has an aura of calm with self-effacement – rare in Englishmen of his class.

'Do you know I am feeling that I am just about to go on stage to sing at the Royal Opera House in London?' He smiled at her during the few seconds his remarks registered with her.

She smiled 'because of delivering the indictments?'

He nodded.

'A moment to be written in history.'

She paused and looked at him thinking how ordinary he looked and how kind. 'And don't forget you are a lawyer – and a hero! You will conquer your nerves – and help the rest of us do so!'

He blushed, turned away and grabbed a folder that was lying on the table at the corner of the room to distract himself.

'Major Neave ... may I call you by your name – Christian name? Airey. You are a hero – I know about the things you have gone through. But you are also a man of the law. And a good person .....'

He turned towards her again and mimicked a hurt look.

'You are making me feel guilty – or at least terrified that I might let people down. I do accept that I need to do what has to be done. I will do my duty. I have to see justice is done and I more than appreciate the support you and the others are giving me. I am grateful.'

'Airey, something very strange happened to me. May I tell you?'

He looked curious, gave her a warm smile and looking around him nodded.

'It is simply – but not really simple …well. To cut a long story short – I was given this. By a young German. About the English woman Mary Hart. She was murdered. In my lodgings'.

He looked at her calmly and nodded.

At that point Andrus came into the office accompanied by a priest and two military police officers. Erika wondered whether it might be a little too early for the visit of a priest catching herself before she smiled. Andrus, wearing his polished helmet in full uniform had his military stick firmly under his arm. His appearance and demeanor contrasted sharply with Airey Neave although, as she thought about the pair of them, Erika recognized their individual power and authority.

Essential for what they – and we – are about to do.

Neave began: 'The indictments are to be read to each prisoner – I'll summarize now to remind us all. Count 1 – the conspiracy with Hitler to commit the other three counts. They are Count 2 crimes against peace – planning an aggressive war, Count 3 war crimes – the violation of laws and customs of war, killing of hostages and ill-treatment of civilians and prisoners of war and Count 4 crimes against humanity – murder, extermination, persecution.

He will know about Count 3 first-hand – the poor man. Tortured when a prisoner of war.

Andrus spoke to the other men in the room, nodded to Neave and Erika and the group left the office as the Military Police officer on guard locked the door behind them. Everyone now, except for Erika, seemed to be holding a bulky folder. For a brief moment they all stood in the corridor appearing to be at a loss when Neave took command.

'Him first. Let's go. Dr. Adler please stay close to me as I shall need your help with interpretation'. She nodded, as did Andrus, although Erika had already sensed that Neave's command of German was impressive. The party moved down the corridor towards the prison wing escorted by two MPs one leading the way. Erika glanced round and saw another behind them. As they entered the prison corridor, she noticed a guard in front of each cell. Erika realized the 'him' Neave had chosen to start the process was Hermann Goering. Perhaps the most famous of the defendants. Certainly, Goering was the most high-ranking as the man left over after the other leaders had made their cowardly escapes. Hitler, Goebbels and Himmler – dead by their own hands. Eichmann and Bormann disappeared.

Presumably - South America. Maybe - nearer to home. No-one knows.

Many of the others – less well known - were here. In Nuremberg.

Goering had been in charge of Hitler's armed forces and one-time head of the Reichstag, the German parliament. She shuddered. She noticed that Neave, too, needed to take a deep breath and brace himself as the guard unlocked the cell door. Andrus, with distinctive military vigour, strode into the cell as the door swung open. Neave was next and stood next to him with Erika and the others close behind including the soldiers carrying the main documents. The room was full. She felt cold.

Goering attempted to mirror Andrus' bearing as he rose, unsteadily, from his chair.

So - this is the real monster?

He cast a pathetic figure. His grey uniform, at one time representing the full might of the Nazi regime, and the full bulk of his oversized body now hung loosely on his still large but shrunken frame.

He must have been very fat before he was imprisoned. Neave later suggested that Goering's face had appeared brownish orange – a bit like an actor whose complexion had been infected with years of using stage make-up. What struck Erika though was the corruption. Corruption of his shrunken body and his cruel, mocking face. Most of all his debauchery. His face appeared to Erika as that of a pig – small eyes, wide lips that looked as if they would devour anything that they came in contact with.

But here I am in the presence of gross evil. This is what it looks like. This is maybe where it ends.

The small, over-crowded cell, which she later confirmed was the template for the other cells, contained a steel framed bed fastened to the floor, a table with photographs – in this case of Goering's wife and daughter. There was a toilet and washbowl. All the bars and hooks had been removed from the walls and ceiling. She was told that the chair was taken away each night to prevent suicides. Erika's mind was no longer in the place she intended - as psychological assistant and interpreter.

Keep hold. Keep calm.

Neave was addressing Goering now. There was not much need for her linguistic services as they spoke mostly in English, leaving her free to watch the bizarre charade being played out. Goering had changed his demeanor from the frail, shocked detainee to an important, sought-after party host. As Neave read and handed him the indictment this monster seemed to fade before her eyes.

'Hermann Wilhelm Goering?' Neave asked that man. Erika shivered, not for the first time. Hearing that name. Being there in his presence.

Goering gestured towards his bunk and replied to Neave in a bizarrely jovial manner suggesting he, Neave, was a guest. A friend come to visit. Erika noticed Neave almost shaking.

He is holding his own, but he sees what I do. Corruption. Evil. Cruelty.

She began to admire this man Neave. He continued despite Goering's attempt to snare him in some form of camaraderie.

'I am Major Neave, the officer appointed by the International Military Tribunal to serve you a copy of the indictment in which you are named as defendant. This is Dr. Erika Adler, to assist translation. She is also a psychiatrist'.

She heard an imperceptible disapproving 'tssch' that they all chose to ignore. Erika felt she was floating above this scene taking place in front of her. Neave seemed to be on automatic pilot as he went on to explain how Goering was entitled to conduct his own defence or to have a lawyer. A silence fell.

'So, it has come' that man said.

Had he acknowledged that he was here? That he was to be judged?

Erika suddenly fell victim to an almost unnerving tiredness. She was unlikely to be the only one thankful to leave his cell.

> I can't bear too much more of this. My sleeping has turned into a series of short nightmares waking up my trembling sweating body. I tried to move away – not share what he was dreaming but I was unable to travel far from the horrors that had insinuated themselves in my brain. I was walking along those corridors – with Neave, with Erika, with Andrus. The military police, who should have provided safety. But they only added to my fears. The priest a symbol of death. My thoughts and dreams could turn at any point to include me in the shared agonies of the prison. You see it was not just what these men had done – the thought of what a civilized country had allowed and encouraged – it was the horror, the fear in <u>their</u> brains as we went round and round. Into their cells, past their cells and into their minds.
>
> Although I knew that this opportunity to be present in the dream-lives of those evil men, and accompany the people who worked to ensure justice could be delivered, was a privilege in so many ways – it was also, more so, a profound torture. So naturally I continued to try to sleep. That is how I could feel it all. But I find myself drawn into the mind of those murderers and it hurts. They are scared. But there is also that experience of ultimate power. The power to choose who would die and who might live.
>
> And it was then I knew that these were his dreams – Airey Neave – not Erika's. This is what was happening in his mind. You couldn't tell. But I did know that he had a past too – he had been captured and tortured by them. He was there to seek justice.

Neave handed the file on Goering to the military police officer and was duly handed the next one. Erika didn't recall everyone they visited that day. But some she could never forget. The people who still remained with her long after they were dead. Hans Frank, Julius Streicher and Ernst Kaltenbrunner. Neither could she forget Rudolph Hess who never experienced freedom again and Albert Speer, Hitler's favourite who turned against him at the trial to save his own life.

Erika had been interested to meet Hans Frank. Another

Austrian. A lawyer. Hitler's personal lawyer and Governor General of Poland. A Jew-hater.

Neave had told her: 'I had spent days on foot in Poland after my escape from prison. I saw and can never forget the savage repression of the Poles by the Nazis. Especially the Jews. And often old men and women. And as we now all know – most Polish Jews were sent to extermination camps. Murdered. Tortured.'

He had been so moved by telling her this that she had wanted to comfort him. He wasn't weak. He was honest and strong. A man with courage and moral strength so far above those whose cells they entered.

Hans Frank had produced far too many diaries. She had read most of them over the previous days where described his thoughts and experiences. It was hard to understand that this man would sit in his cell now, once he had enacted and fulfilled his evil intentions, reading the Bible telling all who would listen about his conversion to Catholicism and apparent remorse. This former Nazi lawyer firmly intended to use these skills to attract sympathy in court.

Like so many of them he had sought and failed to achieve the coward's way out slitting his wrists and stabbing himself in the throat. Now he wanted to atone.

When they entered his cell, his character was exposed to them. His eyes were dark and narrow, his nose long and his mouth small although his lips were full. His black hair was sparse, pushed back over his head. He was looking pale. His left hand, where he had tried to slit his wrist was covered with a woolen glove. Neave told her later that he had cut a nerve, leaving his hand paralyzed.

'I can see us now for what we all were. Goering – meekly being exercised by his guards – former President of the Reichstag. It is grotesque. Here we are in our cells. The toilet is visible through the spy holes. We are like ordinary criminals. God's wrath is more to be feared.'

Erika stared at him. Neave allowed him to continue.

Both watched and listened as Hans Frank, the Butcher of Poland blamed Hitler, and those he called Hitler's diabolical "men of action" Himmler and Bormann for what had happened– Himmler having killed himself, the latter being free somewhere in the world.

Hans Frank also caused me a great deal of distress because he was an avid dreamer, but his dreams were not restorative. His dreams were explicit. He loved to talk of them in a romantic way – telling the psychologists their content as if they were evidence of his repentance. But the anger the violent hatred, tinged with fear predominated. His aspirations transcended his lonely cell – he often used the word 'transcended'. I believe he thought it increased the image of his spirituality and holy life. A monk whose experience was beyond the mundane. Frank had actually reported some of his dream content to the American psychologist Gustave Gilbert knowing that it would be written down as part of Gilbert's assessment of his fitness for trial. Did he think Gilbert might choose to help him because of his dreams? Did he think this might save himself? He is more of a fool than he himself believed he was. Gilbert's rating of his IQ was 130 – that suggests he wasn't the most intelligent lawyer that Hitler could have chosen for his own purposes!

I digress – a bit of emotional relief. This creature told Gilbert that his dreams took him above the world – the sea, mountains, sky – a life unbound. He admitted to nocturnal emissions after emotional release. This is making me sick. I need to change tack.

In his conscious life he espoused his liberation and spiritual renewal – that he continued to claim had provided him with moral peace. Perhaps I shall think some more after I understand what Gilbert thinks. But he's yet to arrive.

The team had moved on. Neave told Erika later that he had been surprised when he first set eyes on Julius Streicher.

'I had no desire to meet this disgusting, corrupt man. A beast if anyone ever was!'

But when they entered his cell, there he was. Short, stocky with a very hairy chest. Erika confirmed later that she saw a peculiar light in his eyes – a light of darkness.

'He had the look of a sex predator – which is exactly what he is. And it wasn't the first time he had been in prison – although previously it was because he beat and whipped a young boy prisoner – that was when he was on an official visit. And do you know what he said?' Neave asked. But suddenly he looked as if he wanted to change the subject but by then Erika, the priest, the military police and even Andrus were staring at him waiting to hear.

'Dr. Adler. Forgive me. I am ashamed of what I am going to say but … well Streicher declared that his actions had given him an orgasm.'

> The silence that followed led me into his dream – I'm talking about Airey Neave's dream. He was sweating. He was tossing and turning. We all did that during these times - or in my case as I spied on these times from across the years. For me they are in the past. Just before I was born. But Neave himself was asleep. I know because it was his dream state that I felt. He was seeing vivid images of Jews – the images that the Nazis adopted. Mostly he saw drawings – cartoons I think. Blond girls having sex with horned men with enormous noses, large wetted lips, eyes close together and greed-infested grins on their faces as they defiled the Aryan race.
>
> Neave was feeling sick. So was I the one who shared the dream – I would have liked to have comforted him then. Reassured him that he was not like those men. But even so many years later the dream had remained vivid for him. And now for me.
>
> Then suddenly his legs disappeared. Was he dreaming about falling over? Was he dizzy? Had the dream caused him physical pain?
>
> Then there was a deafening noise. Vibration. Smoke. Agony. Stillness. I couldn't understand – then I remembered. Later I read about it. He had died that way. Even in 1945 he sensed how he would die. I shudder even now.

The indictment party moved on. Each cell contained different nightmares for this group of visitors. The nightmares of the inhabitant of each and the nightmares they had inflicted on countless innocent women, children and men – and the unborn. Each one complicit in the mass exterminations but each one with different fears, different expectations as to how their personal stories would be received.

Erika remembered Albert Speer. He projected a repellent sophistication and emptiness. Speer didn't see it that way – clearly. He patronized the team delivering the indictments. He tried to smile. Show he was reasonable. Repentant. His tall, dark frame might have been attractive. His manner might have been engaging if you didn't know about the slaves he used up – worked them to death. Punished them inhumanely and replaced them with others imported from the decimated, and the most beleaguered countries of Europe.

Many of them naturally were Jews.

Neave didn't trust him.

'Speer is young – around my age, and intelligent. None of us expect that he will come through the trial with the worst punishment.'

And nor did he.

Before they all parted Neave took hold of Erika's arm.

'Thank you for sharing what you did. I believe I know something more. You're not to worry – the truth is that the dead woman was working for the "opposition".'

'What?'

'I'm afraid so. She was tasked with ensuring one of our prisoners was not to stand trial. She was to prevent that by any means. Now she can't. Justice shall be done.'

CHAPTER 39: THE AMERICAN PSYCHOLOGIST

All the indictments had been duly served shortly before Gustave Gilbert, the American psychologist, arrived at the Palace of Justice. The prisoners were all in solitary confinement by now while awaiting the trial itself. Erika had been in Andrus', now familiar, anteroom when Gilbert first entered carrying his own signed copies of the indictments with each defendants' opinions.

'I had no idea you were already here.' Gustave Gilbert had immediately sought out Erika for an informal briefing. They had been introduced long-distance by another American psychologist visiting the Tavistock Clinic – an increasingly famous institution with refugee first generation psychoanalysts on its staff. Even Rudolf Hess, Hitler's erstwhile deputy, was among its clinical subjects of investigation.

Erika as a native German speaker, medic and a trainee psychoanalyst, trained by Freud himself, complemented the perspectives held by Gilbert, a German speaker with a more traditional take on psychology. Both shared a curiosity about these evil men alongside the need to find justice.

Gilbert wasted no time after their brief introductions, in getting down to business.

'And you went with Andrus and Neave to deliver the indictments?'

'Yes, well most of them. Yes, I did'.

'Well what did you make of them so far? The prisoners?' Gustave Gilbert seemed excited but also, Erika sensed, put out perhaps that she might know more about what was going on than he did. She wasn't sure if he were slightly envious that she had got there first, but she wanted to put him at his ease. She had no need of enemies in her own team. There were enough of those in the cells. He was a young, like Neave, not much older than she was. He had a kind face with a wide, intelligent forehead. Brown eyes and hair. And very slightly overweight – as all Americans seem to be. It was a common feature. He was enthusiastic about his own ideas while Erika felt he was unsure of her role.

Perhaps he is a little anxious about who I really am?

'I'm hoping to work on translating and analyzing Hans Frank's diaries – the ones when he was a full-blown murderous Nazi and the newer ones - now he has found religion. But even he doesn't expect his conversion to save his body – just his soul.'

I could not bring myself to tell him who I really wanted to confront – Ernst Kaltenbrunner. He would not have understood.

She almost found herself smirking at this idea about Hans Frank's discovery of his human essence, before feeling the pain of the reality of Frank's work. Frank, Hitler's erstwhile lawyer, Governor-General of Poland, murderer of European Jews - transported, tortured and murdered under his command. It was strange, she thought, how she herself could live in the moment. See the prisoners here as men. Human.

Frank was a lawyer like my father. And so was Ernst Kaltenbrunner. Both were such cruel men. They turned on their own as well as those they declared to be their enemies.

And then she almost doubled up with the pain as she visualized the extent of each man's evil. Erika returned to earth.

These men were professionals – experts in their fields expected to work to a code of ethics. Arbiters of justice. But there was no justice during the Nazi years. There's no point in my saying yet again "how could this have happened?" "what kind of men could do what they did?" it remains pointless. I don't even think they themselves really knew what they had done – not really - not the crimes against humanity.

I would imagine that they were acting as if they had been playing what in the 21st Century might be a computer game – ordering death from a long distance. Not seeing it, feeling it or smelling it.

But no that could not have been how it was. They went to those camps. They heard the screams. They smelled the stench from the living and the dead. There is no excuse. Now or ever.

But I still can't grasp it. He, Hans Frank, couldn't see his prisoners as human. Or else how ….

'Ah. Erika. I have seen Hans Frank's comments on his diary. They're here'. Gilbert tapped the pile of documents he was holding which she considered a little patronizing.

'Perhaps we might meet with him later? Maybe then we might discuss some of his diary data?'

She looked up, smiled feeling pleased that he obviously had recognized her role – the legitimate part at least - and even trusted her. Gilbert then sat down, placing his paperwork on the ubiquitous table, trying to keep it separate from other files. It was strange that such an organized man like the colonel, whose shoes always shone, whose uniform was always so neatly pressed, with his well-disciplined military staff, would not have a more precise filing system.

'Here it is. Frank.' Gilbert handed the sheets of paper to Erika leaving her to ruminate while he watched her carefully. He shuffled some of the other files.

'Oh - so that's the way he's moving is it?' she tried to sound casual and stop herself from trembling as she attempted mentally and orally to make light of Frank's statement:

"I regard this trial as a God-willed world court, destined to examine and put an end the terrible suffering under Adolf Hitler".

She wondered how far Frank truly believed he could submit himself to justice from this particular Court.

Did he understand the extent of what he had done? Did any

of them? Were they trying to hide it from themselves? The fear of punishment must be immense.

Her stomach lurched. She tried to be self-possessed – she needed to look professional. Gilbert and the prison psychiatrist, Dr. Kelley, were to have their fingers on the pulses of evil. She had to be there too to share it with them. Without too much deliberation both Colonel Andrus and Dr. Kelley had already agreed she might assist in some of the other prisoner assessments. She was a psychiatrist and psychoanalyst in her own right. So why not? She needed Gilbert's support too. Gilbert's German revealed him not to be a native speaker. Erika was, which might turn out to be her trump card just in case he should decline her help with his work. But he wasn't going to do that.

'I do hope you are also happy for me to work with you and the psychiatrist?' *I have got to trust this man.* Erika could see he was a decent, competent person but also that his method of working veered towards the American take on psychology.

Measurement. Replication. Hypothesis testing. Despite this, he understood the European model which gave credit to the unconscious.

Well that was why I am here with him. But did he really understand psychoanalysis?

Erika sat holding Frank's papers looking into the distance and drumming on them with a pen. Gilbert sighed, and grabbing a chair lit a cigarette, and took hold of the already brimming ash tray currently weighing down the pile of papers. He looked around for a bin to empty the cigarette butts without success. He sighed again and drew the first flush of tobacco into his lungs.

Gilbert knew of Erika's reputation, connection to the Freud family and the clinic in London and was determined to find out more about Freud as a person.

But that would be later. He had to busy himself initially attaining the defendants' responses to their indictment. He still felt cautious about Erika's meeting with them before he had had the chance to do so himself.

She was rather pushy for a European woman.

Then he remembered she was a psychiatrist and knew about the murderous regime first-hand. He too was Jewish. He had resounding doubts about her being there even so.

She had not been particularly forthcoming about her initial impressions. Was she hiding something?

He could think of no reason for her to do so. At least not from him. Gilbert was aware that she would have little sympathy for the prisoners but there was a feeling he had about her.

Can I truly trust her?

He inhaled another breath of smoke.

'I've just been to visit Robert Ley' he told her. Erika raised her eyebrows and looked at him waiting for more.

'He's really not functioning well. Pacing his cell. Stammering. He even intimated that he was to be sacrificed, Christ-like, by those he calls 'victors'. He deeply resents being identified as a criminal. He told me he couldn't bring himself to even say the word.'

'Huh!' from Erika. 'What did he think he was doing over recent years? From my understanding he was a frequently drunken slave driver. He abused Russians in particular. And I know he embezzled funds meant to assist German workers. I'm not sure that Hitler particularly liked him either'.

'You're well informed'.

Erika was unsure whether Gilbert's remark had a deeper meaning, but she nodded in agreement.

'Yes. I have made sure of that. I had to', she recounted.

Gilbert continued to smoke, leafing through the piles of paper he had brought into the room with him. He paused and looked at her. 'Tell me' he said. 'What was it like working with Freud?'

That came out of the blue. But she rallied. She smiled. 'It was truly wonderful'. She paused looking into the distance. 'I don't say that about many things. Not now. Not after ...'. She gestured towards the paper on the table. 'You know ....'.

He nodded. 'But well, he was kind. But also made me work hard and had little patience if he thought I hadn't understood something. Or if I had let anything, any idea, pass by without examining it in full'.

She laughed slightly.

'But that was the point. The method. Everything. Every look, word or gesture. All data. You know?'

He nodded and grinned slightly in acknowledgement of her enthusiasm.

She is clearly lost in it. Entranced.

But he was impressed.

Erika laughed at herself and looked at him: 'you either love it or you hate it I guess. A very *Jewish* science so it is said. What about you Gustave? May I call you that?'

'Of course. And I don't know which view I take on Freud'.

'You know what happened in the end don't you? Anna his daughter was arrested by the Gestapo for a short time but long enough to cause panic. The family were constantly harassed by the Nazis and eventually Sigmund and some of his closest family moved to London. To Hampstead. Near where I eventually worked during the war and where I live now'.

Gustave Gilbert nodded. Erika remembered the incident well and how distressed Freud had become. He had wanted his old Vienna back.

'He died soon after. Before England entered the war against the Germans.'

'Yes. I know. Cancer of the face. From smoking cigars'.

He inhaled once more before rubbing the remainder of his cigarette against the over-filled ash tray. They both looked at it and laughed.

'The Freud family helped me to leave Vienna'. She looked down at her hands. For that she would be forever grateful to them.

'And after he died, it was through Anna's contacts that I gained a place to work and complete my training at the clinic'.

He nodded. They both sat in silence for a while.

'You know …' Erika wondered whether she should say more, then: 'several of my patients there, in London. They were like me.'

He looked at her quizzically.

'Jews from Europe. Vienna. Berlin. Salzburg. Even France. Refugees. Didn't see it as important before. It was simply what we were'.

He understood at last.

But Erika's patients were not really like her. She had lived in London throughout the worst of the hatred and murder of Jews. Her patients were survivors of devastating destruction of human life on a mass scale. Even after the liberation of the majority of the death camps in 1945 it was unclear exactly what had happened in those places.

Why had it happened? How had it happened?

Most people now knew that unspeakable crimes had been committed by Nazis, but the extent of their evil was beyond imagination. Erika knew. Her parents were lucky. Her family. Few survived. But even they had lost much of themselves in what they experienced and what they saw.

So had Max.

CHAPTER 40: ONE MORE DEATH, NUREMBERG, 1945

'Andrus has let them all know today,' Gilbert told her.

Erika nodded 'You mean about Ley?'

'Well they have been told he is dead. Not sure whether Andrus will be free with details. What do you think?'

Erika had heard that Robert Ley, the virulent anti-Semite and labour leader who was staunchly loyal to Hitler had more or less hanged or strangled himself with part of his towel and tied himself to the toilet pipe.

'I guess as he died slowly. It was strangulation' she said unnecessarily. Gilbert nodded confirmation even so.

Their conversation faded. It was difficult to decide on the overall impact of Ley's suicide on their work.

'Is it our failure Gustave?' Erika asked.

Gilbert raised his eyebrows and looked at her.

'Well in your case …'

'I know. You don't think I have any responsibility for these people. An ancillary. A parasite even?'

Gilbert flushed. 'I don't think that!' he almost barked at her. 'But it is not your job to look after them. You know that'.

She sat quietly thinking.

He really is thinking I might upstage him. We're both going to be writing our books! Is he worried that mine might be more appealing than his?

'OK. Yes. I know there is my specific project with Frank.

But both you and Dr. Kelley are up to your eyes. And besides – a woman gets different information'.

Gilbert looked at her.

Would she share that information I wonder?

They both decided unconsciously to let the matter drop. There was a pause. Gilbert and Erika were in the anteroom, normally overcrowded and smoke filled. Today it was quiet. The chance to work. But Ley's death had been a distraction for everyone. It was imperative to prevent further suicides. Andrus had quadrupled the guard. There was to be a 24-hour watch on each of them. But how would they prevent panic? Even the psychology experts were unclear.

'Do you know what Goering said?'

Erika looked expectantly. She knew Gilbert had been in his cell with him earlier.

'He told me it was a good thing!'

'About Ley? Really? Why?'

'Ley, according to him, was a drunk and would be a liability for them all during the trial'.

'They are still fighting a battle for power – over what? It hardly makes sense now does it.' Erika remained thoughtful.

'Well I suppose they might think that if they are top of the heap here, waiting to go on trial then something might rub off. Some positive image or feeling – odd though. They're not being tried for popularity in the prison are they?'

'Don't know – but I guess there is some logic in that.' He smiled and shook his head.

'Isn't it strange how easy it is to become part of this? This strange world. It's as if this were the real world. Like nothing exists outside. And nothing predated us being here. With them!'

Gilbert laughed in acknowledgement. 'It really does seem a total reality. I agree'.

'And anticipating the trial. I feel really nervous ..... and yet this trial should mean – what? I hope that - well – justice. You know? But even so I feel the tension as if it were me about to stand trial'.

Erika looked at her watch and started to stand up, smoothing down her skirt. She took a deep breath

'Now I have another appointment with Kaltenbrunner'.

Gilbert looked at her. She saw he was desperate to ask why, but she guessed he might still be slightly embarrassed by his earlier remarks about her responsibilities. He simply nodded.

'I'm not sure he is back in his cell yet. You do know he's had another stroke – a brain hemorrhage it appears, don't you?'

'No.' She was shocked.

He mustn't die. Not yet.

'I'll check with the guard. He should know. Tell me though – what is so important about him?'

Erika sighed. 'I have a patient in London. A man I knew vaguely from Austria. He has told me about Kaltenbrunner – he's ....'

She let her words fade and noticed that Gilbert was not going to let on to her whether or not he cared about her motive. Luckily Kaltenbrunner didn't appear to be of great interest to anyone other than her right now.

'See you later then. Good luck with that one.' And Gilbert's attention turned back to a file he was reading.

Erika moved quickly. She knew that the chief prison psychiatrist, Dr. Kelley, was with Rudolf Hess. There was still a question mark over Hess's sanity and consequently his ability to stand trial. Erika had only a vague interest in him – for now anyway. Her immediate focus was elsewhere.

She moved swiftly down the corridor, the military police guarding the cells acknowledging her as she went towards Kaltenbrunner's cell. She wondered what it would be like to see him again. When she was alone. To look into his eyes. The eyes of extreme evil. He was a psychopath as far as she could tell. He had also been ill once again – brain hemorrhage. They had brought him back from a brief stay in hospital in a wheelchair.

But he was not frail. He had condoned extremes of torture like some evil lord – dishing out commands against his enemies. He ordered the massacre of millions as it became clear that the Nazis were defeated. He had perceived no consequences for himself. He probably considered that he was a man who had fought to get to where he was – or at least to where he had been as a Nazi. That he was worthy of all rewards that might be offered. But he'd also shown himself to be a coward.

But it was the victims of his personal vengeance that she was interested in – those he had tortured after the attempt on Hitler's life. Colleagues of Gisevius and by association – colleagues of Max.

CHAPTER 41: THE LAWYER FROM LINZ

Erika showed her pass to the Military Police officer guarding Ernst Kaltenbrunner. Not something that anyone had thought important before Ley's suicide, but security was now more severe. Erika understood. Keeping to regulations was essential if unnecessary questions were to be avoided. The MP stood aside slightly, looked through the spy hole and banged on the door.

'I shall be here all the time. Thump on the door if you want me Miss. Er – Doctor, sorry. He is a very big man and violent – take care please.'

'He's probably harmless enough at the moment though.' She smiled kindly at the MP who had her interests at heart.

'He's still recovering from the stroke. But I won't forget you are there. Thank you.'

And with that the MP opened the cell door enough for her to pass through. They both peered in as Erika entered. She suddenly didn't feel quite as brave as she had done five seconds earlier. The prisoner was enormously tall – around seven feet it was said, but he managed to give the impression of being even taller. One or two of the guards claimed to be intimidated simply by his physical presence. His size was of minor importance to Erika though. Kaltenbrunner was unwell. He had headaches and blurry vision. This was a Godsend for her as it meant she could visit whenever she chose to discuss his health problems, and she was also able to recommend, and even administer, medication if she chose.

She had control.

She was conscious of the heavy door closing behind her followed by a snap of the lock. A musty smell hit her first – sweat disguised by cheap soap. She expected the inmate to stand and move towards her, but nothing happened. She recognized that she couldn't simply stand there gawping at this huge figure sitting upright on the bed, so she stepped slowly towards him. He continued to sit, lazily and heavily she thought, there on his bunk trying to look nonchalant. But his eyes gave him away. He was unwell and seriously weakened. Her sympathy didn't rise to the occasion though.

He may still be on drugs for the brain bleed. I think he might have an idea why I am here though.

He was about ten years her senior in age. Tall, heavy, lumbering.

Rather like an ox. An Austrian. Like Hitler. Like me.

He rose to his feet. She held her breath worried he might collapse. But she need not have worried. Kaltenbrunner was surprisingly agile for a man of his size, age despite his recent health problems. A giant with a scarred face and a receding hairline. Thin lips and a very slight sneer that remained a permanent part of any expression he made.

But there was something unexpected – tears. And he was shaking.

Is he crying?

She suddenly recalled something Neave had said after delivering the indictments.

'He had tears in his eyes. He was almost pleading'.

Erika had not been near enough at the time to see that, but she had intuited a degree of fear – but then most of them had been scared – terrified especially when they heard the charges against them.

A bunch of cowards. And here he is crying once again.

She continued to stare not knowing where to begin. She thought the cogs of his mind had brought him to the view that it was polite to stand and greet a guest even such an unwelcome one. To assume a sense of normality.

Just like Goering does, she recalled.

But without the charm. Without the bravado – the sense of entitlement. And yet this was the man who ordered and watched the torture of many. Cruel. Vicious.

He remained standing until she sat on his bunk despite the lack of invitation. She breathed deeply inhaling the tang of recent sweat from the stale air more deeply.

He is nervous. More than that – this ox – this ugly giant is a coward! Good. He should be terrified – he had made so many others cower in dread.

Kaltenbrunner lowered himself onto the bunk again, sitting uncomfortably as far away as possible from Erika. He stared. She wondered if he was beginning to relax because she was a woman. She had no need to remind herself how this man, a lawyer, a total coward, had assisted the Anschluss. *Handed over our country.* But that was hardly the full extent of his crimes.

'My name is Dr. Erika Adler. I am a psychiatrist ...' she chose to avoid mentioning the psychoanalysis and later wondered why '....and along with Drs. Gilbert and Kelley I am talking to you and the other prisoners.'

He nodded towards her. They had been in each other's close company before, when the indictments had been delivered. But she had taken a very back seat then and she hoped he had not registered her presence. She needed shock tactics. She needed to consolidate any available power. Now before the official proceedings took up everyone's time and thoughts.

'Why are you here?'

A good question!

'Because you might want to tell me things – about how you are feeling, about anything you might wish your lawyers or others in authority to know. We gave you information about lawyers I believe, didn't we?' She hesitated, watching him react.

Does he recall that I was here when the indictments were delivered?

'And because …. And because I want to know why you did some of the things you did.'

Erika took a deep breath as subtly as she could. She didn't wish for him to have a clue about how she was feeling. Being face-to-face with someone under these circumstances was unusual. Unnerving – not merely because of who they were but because it subtly shifted the power between them.

'But' she reminded herself 'these men are now prisoners and very likely to die soon. I still have influence.'

And, of course, there was Max. She had to know about Max. Besides she also needed to discover whether the information she had been provided on the night she had taken food to Helga had any real meaning.

What was the truth in all of this?

Ernst Kaltenbrunner had been a lawyer in Linz. But the dye had been cast some time before that. A Nazi through and through. He had been leader of the Austrian SS, the Schutzstaffel, guarding Nazi leaders. He had guarded Hitler.

Erika recalled how Max, *my Max,* had talked about him: 'Kaltenbrunner had been arrested and charged with conspiracy. He was even put in prison for a few months.'

And here he is again. I expect. Hope. For the last time.

Max had made it clear to her: 'After Anschluss Kaltenbrunner was promoted, became a member of the Reichstag and later, crucially, after Heydrich's assassination he was made Chief of the Security Police and the SD. Hitler loved him. He was my boss now at the Reich Main Security Office in Berlin – after Heydrich's death – you know?'

Erika had known. She also remembered that Max had told her that Kaltenbrunner was no better than the monster Heydrich. Kaltenbrunner had ordered the death of millions at Auschwitz.'

But did Max respect him? What was their relationship?

She needed to know. She wasn't sure why she had begun

to feel so uncertain about Max and this man. She desperately wanted to be sure. Clear. Convinced. As she ran those thoughts through her head, she realized she didn't know or trust Max as she needed to do.

'Herr Kaltenbrunner. Do you understand that it is important for you to talk to me?' She repeated.

Erika smiled. She tried to look gently at this brute of a man. He seemed calm. He looked curious. His mind was swimming. Many things were unclear to him. He needed to think but it was becoming harder.

What is she going to say? Her accent is Austrian. Do I know her?

His brain gradually formed a sense of what was happening. Pictures emerged in his mind.

> The memories and dreams of the people expunged by this man were present even as Erika sat there with him. I still have them, even now, long after his death. I know some of their dreams very well. Fear. Disbelief. Terror.
>
> I travelled along the Austrian length of the Danube from Vienna in the east towards Bavaria in Germany. We passed Linz sitting peacefully on the river. Was I the only one then to remember the lawyer? That man.
>
> The tour guide talked enthusiastically about the local architecture, the town's merit as a holiday destination and about its Museum of the Future. Nothing was said about its past. History. Hidden. Forgotten. Just as those who suffered and died in Mauthausen – not very far away – they remain hidden and now forgotten. At least by those wanting to enjoy the borderland.
>
> Was Hitler's defeat and suicide enough to whitewash the area? Did Kaltenbrunner's execution end Linz's reputation as a crucible of hatred magically collapse as time passed? Or did it have to wait for the capture and execution of another son of the Danube, Adolph Eichmann, before we could all point at the buildings and chat about the local cuisine with no thought for the evil past? Perhaps Hannah Arendt's dismissal of evil as banal did actually put an end to the belief that so many souls had putrefied into pure evil in that Austrian city?

'Herr Kaltenbrunner ...'

He looked at her, lethargically or perhaps slightly hazily. He was shaking.

'I want you to tell me about people who worked for you when you were head of the Security office.'

He continued to look at her. He didn't flinch and she couldn't decide whether or not he understood what she was asking him.

'I was only the head in title. I didn't know the people. But you will know that of course. I was merely an administrator.'

Erika sensed an obsequiousness.

That is not going to work!

Kaltenbrunner was a man who had remained in deep denial. He had, reportedly, tried to kill himself twice after he was captured, attempting to cut his own throat.

But that was cowardice, not guilt. No sign of repentance from him.

Almost everyone awaiting trial in Nuremberg had found the means to rationalize the reason for incarceration and potential guilt - blaming Hitler, loyalty to Germany or following orders. Kaltenbrunner had simply declared himself not guilty of any war crimes.

'I have only done my duty as an intelligence organ, and I refuse to serve as an Ersatz Himmler', is what he had, ostensibly, said to Gilbert in the aftermath of hearing his indictment. But Gilbert was not so focused on Kaltenbrunner. Erika was.

That is a bonus.

Gilbert had placed Kaltenbrunner second to bottom of the prisoners according to their IQ scores. Only Julius Streicher scored less. Kaltenbrunner's 113 was barely above normal.

Although of course you have to be fairly low level to be normal, Erika knew. The other Austrian lawyer, Hans Frank had reached 130.

Perhaps the more intelligent among them realize they needed a strategy beyond that of holding onto the lie. "I am innocent" will not work in this complicated forum.

There was nothing innocent about Kaltenbrunner, which was the reason Erika had to see him. He had signed the death warrants for so many. He had ordered countless others to be tortured before their murders. He had relished the torture of his enemies. Erika had little fear of this man despite his reputation and former role in the Nazi system. She had a covert power over him that she needed to call on before the trial began. She had planned to let him know that she had inside information about his culpability.

But now it seemed that her "informant" had been loyal to Kaltenbrunner, not her. Not to Gisevius. She needed to warn him, although from everything she understood Gisevius was home and dry – he had the very best allies and an impeccable reputation.

This man, this drunken, sniveling, murderous brute had been dreaming. Sometimes it made no sense that someone so brutal, so evil and without any moral sense could do something as ethereal, as human, as dream. But I could feel it. Hear it. It was about everything that he had jumbled up in his head. He was attempting to justify himself – to exonerate himself for himself. That's how it felt anyway.

But it is so hard to believe that this man had been in love. He dreamed constantly about this woman. But this woman had let him down. She had betrayed him. He would work himself up over this – his muscles would tighten and his jaw would hurt him as he clenched it in his sleep. What on earth had she done to make him so angry? This is not just a man in love missing the object of his affections is it?

Several nights later I was able to piece together the origins of his pain. Don't get me wrong. I'm delighted he is suffering but curiosity also needs assuaging. Like most Austrians he loved mountains. He could walk up hills, climb rock faces -to an extent – and he enjoyed bathing in some of the streams and lakes high up, away from unwanted eyes and bodies.

The weather was warm, the skies were clear blue. No clouds. No planes overhead. He had been married for ten years. He lacked interest in Frau Kaltenbrunner – Elisabeth. She had produced five children and each time she became fatter. Less attentive to him. But that wasn't true of every woman. Gisela had given him twins – the babies Ursula and Wolfgang. He wanted to see them. He couldn't see them up here in the mountains.

His breathing became more rapid. More laboured. He muttered. Deeply. Loudly. It was hard to bear for someone like me sharing the dream with him.

'Doctor. Doctor.' No. But that is the end of the dream. It was of course the end of his dream as the Americans brought him down from the mountain. And brought him here. Where Erika could meet him. Where he was soon removed to hospital. And after that, the gallows.

For Erika, Gustave Gilbert and the other psychologists and psychiatrists being in Nuremberg with these men – was about making sense of evil. And getting it held to account. In public. So that everyone could be a witness. Erika was already getting used to being next to evil. To staying with it. Holding it. Facing it. Responding to the sad, demanding, aggressive, depressed, anxious emotions that each prisoner flung at her and anyone else who took an interest in them.

'Can you tell me anything about Max Mayer? A policeman, Major Max Mayer - working at the Reich Main Security Office?'

Kaltenbrunner looked up suddenly. His expression was one of shock, changing rapidly to surprise. That made Erika think he might more slightly more alert than he would have others believe.

'You do know him. He sends regards to you.'

'Who are you?'

'I have told you – a psychiatrist. I'm here to see whether you are coping with imprisonment and are fit to stand trial. Also to answer questions.....'

'You are a liar. You are a Jew, aren't you?

The venom that accompanied that statement made her stomach clench. She could visualize for the first time what it must have been like to have been at the mercy of this man who had hitherto been a terrified, sick and self-absorbed prisoner. Now she found herself looking at a terrifying brute

– whose cruelty was his primary motivation.

'I am Jewish, yes. I am also an Austrian and I know what you yourself have done to my country.'

She immediately regretted saying that – she wanted him to trust her and now that may have been breached. But not quite.

His eyes lit up. The electricity that emerged from behind the earlier tears made her feel sick. For a few moments she forgot about Max, the reason she was with this man.

'Herr Major Max Mayer saved my life. He is loyal to the Thousand Year Reich. A man worthy of every honour.'

Erika almost fainted. It was not what she had expected to hear. Her hopes had just been smashed to pieces. She wanted to leave this place. Return to London. Try to feel better about herself and her judgement.

I almost thought I loved him. But he is a mortal enemy. What did he want from me?

She attempted to pull herself together and talk more to Kaltenbrunner. To extract more substance.

Has he made a mistake? Perhaps he is thinking of a different man – the name is common in German speaking lands.

She wondered then when Kaltenbrunner's life had been in danger other than from his illness. She considered the way that he had been discovered and arrested – a woman had, inadvertently given him away.

Maybe that had been deliberate. Was there a plot against him? He had tortured members of the Abwehr as well as his own men – Arthur Nebe for one. Head of the Kripo and Max's boss. Did Max betray Nebe?

Erika attempted to carry the interview further and to enable Kaltenbrunner to talk more about himself and what he did. She realized that, given his proclaimed innocence and claim to be a simple administrator, that he would be fabricating his evidence. But that would doubtless be of interest in itself.

These men – the prisoners - were all terrified in their

own manner and there was no reason to think this one would be exceptional. She recalled the tears and the shaking almost no time ago, but for Erika they belonged to another world. The world that existed before she knew Max's true story.

She thought the best way to manage her own emotions would be to see Kaltenbrunner as a patient. Nothing would have changed for him. He would still be living in fear.

Did they fear that they were going to experience something like they had given out when they were in power? Were they even able to comprehend a system that wasn't cruel, violent, vengeful? Is that why some might want to take justice into their own hands? Like Ley? And, of course like Kaltenbrunner – he had attempted to kill himself too. But before them – their bosses – Hitler, Goebbels, Himmler – all of them. Cowards. Is that why some tried to lie about their role in the plan or even their regrets? Self-flagellation. Separating themselves from their leaders.

Erika didn't want to spend a great deal of her time looking into the eyes of any of these men. That was not what she was used to professionally and personally she was unsure she could bear it. But she needed to do so.

Patient and analyst did not look at each other during the fifty minutes of treatment. The patient lying on the couch could see their hands, their body, especially the ceiling – but not the clinician behind them. Watching the patient. No eyes meeting. Out of each other's sight. As part of the patient's mind. Receiving projections, transferences.

The analyst wasn't supposed to be themselves, who they really were. They were to be whomsoever the patient felt them to be. The violent father. The loving uncle. The vicious teacher. The self-absorbed mother. The competitive sibling. The analysts absorbed and returned how they had experienced the unconscious desires and instincts to the patient as if they themselves were …. Well no-one. The product of the patients' mental mechanisms. The analyst was not expected to feel or even be in the room with the patient.

Although they were expected to be with the patient. Inch by inch. Emotion by emotion. The analyst was there to receive and return and eventually interpret.

'A woman. An English woman. She had been sent by my personal enemies. At the end. Enemies who claimed they held the interests of the Reich. She had been sent to kill me. They wanted to save Goering.'

Erika was amazed. She held her emotional position as an analyst with extreme difficulty but was pleased that she managed to do so.

'Herr Max Mayer – he made sure she was destroyed before she could commit that crime. A crime against me. A crime against the Reich.'

Max killed Mary Hart? But it was a woman who killed her.

Erika's mind flashed back to her meeting with Helga. The man who dropped the paper. And what had been written there – in German. Words badly formed but their meaning clear:

> Mary Hart worked for the Nazis. An English woman had made sure she did not achieve her mission.

Could Kaltenbrunner have been aware of his potential fate? If he had been killed before the trial, then he would have escaped justice. He also knew things that would have died with him.

'Please visit me again. I am not the man they say I am. I was simply an administrator following orders.'

Some years later – merely following orders – that's what they claimed. Kaltenbrunner's childhood friend. Captured in Latin America. Wearing dirty underwear – how he had fallen! Eichmann told the Jewish courtroom in 1961 – long ago now – "I was only following orders."

An American psychologist later demonstrated that it was indeed possible for people with no history of sociopathy, to act against an anonymous person. It seems that if an impressive white-coated experimenter told you to harm someone after giving even a half-hearted reason you were highly likely to do it. Does that let Eichmann off? Does it let Kaltenbrunner and the rest of them feel that none of what happened was their fault?

Another psychologist, Milgram's mentor Solomon Asch, had demonstrated a decade earlier that most of us, at least publicly, agree with the majority. That was the case even when we know the majority are wrong. Perhaps even when we know the majority are wicked and cruel. For a quiet life? Because we are all undeclared psychopaths? Because we are innately cruel? But as we shall come to understand not everyone who had done wrong to others will see it out to the bitter end. Many take the easier way out.

Erika stood up slowly and moved towards the cell door. She noticed that Kaltenbrunner stood for a while – a gesture of long-rehearsed politeness before sinking down onto his bed. She had a sense that time was winding back. He looked pathetic, still emitting a stale smell. Tearful and shaking with fear. For a short time he had provided a vision of power, evil and hate that the German people, the members of the Reich Main Security Office and even the intelligence services had to manage as they made sense of their lives. This knowledge pierced her being reminding her of the true nature of the occupants of the prison set beside the palace of Justice at Nuremberg.

CHAPTER 42: ANOTHER LUNCH WITH MARION, PRESENT DAY

Wilson's examined his work diary during breakfast. That was his normal routine although he knew today was another lunch with Marion. He tried to confine appointments and follow up work with the students and the patients he saw at the Tavistock to the day he worked there – he didn't wish for thoughts, plans and anxieties to spill over into his *own* time.

I wonder exactly what I mean by my own time?

He was enthusiastically engaged with the work at the clinic. He enjoyed the passing acquaintances with friendly colleagues such as James his office mate. He found the few patients he worked with to be interesting, and the students too. They were more exhausting than the patients in some ways. He wondered whether he ought to consider retirement. Although he rarely thought about his personal life, he did have friends beyond work. His remaining rugby crowd from his student days, many of whom like Wilson had gravitated to London. He still enjoyed the theatre and thanks to his current work and excellent pension, he was able to see a play wherever and whenever he chose. Perhaps his social focus needed to shift?

Then Marion – I like her. She's stimulating company. But I don't know what to make of her. I'm not comfortable around her – increasingly uncomfortable actually. The request to discover her true identity has not helped of course. Actually, I am worried about seeing her today – I can't fathom what it is she wants. I have no real idea what is disturbing me. But something almost tangible is getting me anxious. Making me not want to go into work. Wow! That is powerful. What the hell?

As he processed his thoughts, he had to acknowledge that she was casting a shadow over him. He was agitated merely thinking about her. Not in any pleasant way. He didn't count her as work-related and not in any sense a potential friend. It was hard to work out why. The encounter with Gabriel and Black-Beret hadn't been the cause – his awareness of his reticence predated them. He had only realized that later though. Several of his friends were women, so it wasn't that that had bothered him. His was well able to enjoy women's company without any sense of romantic or sexual interest. No-one could replace Hanna. Before knowing and loving her, he had had several girlfriends. So long ago. What was all this about? But for whatever reason he felt the way he did, Gabriel and Black-Beret had made him feel slightly more grounded. More like the person he had believed himself to be. He now had a mission, and he didn't expect them to stop him – maybe they would even help him discover everything he needed to know – about Marion and about her grandfather – if indeed he was – and the murder of this woman Mary. Also how these people were connected to the Nuremberg trial and even the Nazi regime. Discovering the truth was compelling.

I think someone, or some organization, wants me to do the digging for them. But what has alerted them to activities so long ago? We are still only looking at some dead people. Their time is long past surely? And they can do no more harm.

He moved his plate of cereal to the side and while still considering his diary he grabbed the few grapes he had prepared, enjoying the sweet liquid feel in his mouth as they burst. Something was bothering him still. Gradually he began to recall the dream he had woken from and realized it was a repeat. He moved towards the coffee maker, taking hold of the jug now filled with the fresh brew. He poured himself a cup.

What does this dream mean?

> Round and round he ran. Up the hill from Finchley Road to the clinic, up the stairs to his office. There he sifted through endless files that covered his desk. He then left the office, locked the door, jumped down the stairs three at a time, pushing his way through the students, patients and staff gathering in the vestibule. He could feel the cool breeze entering his lungs as he jogged through the car park, through Maresfield Gardens and back towards Finchley Road. His heart pounded but now his lungs struggled as he was desperate to reach to reach the end of that burst of exercise.
>
> It was not enjoyable. He was driven to this highly energized state by extreme levels of anxiety that he could not identify. There was no pleasure in the sense of strength and mobility that in real life he had not had for many years and would never have again. He was left feeling depressed and perplexed as he returned to the building.

I just can't work this one out. Obviously, it's about anxiety. No resolution to whatever is worrying me. But why am I worried? What has it got to do with the clinic? Is it merely about my disabilities? I don't think so. Not now after so long. And I am here, thinking about the appointments at the clinic and worrying about Marion.

He recalled that for many years he had woken from dreams where his injuries had gone. Dreams where he had been able to live and move freely without pain. The awful emptiness and depths of despair he experienced when he awoke to remember the painful reality were awful. Even the occasional dream produced a similar watered-down effect. But not this one. This was brutal and it was a pleasure to re-enter physical reality with the morning alarm.

He sighed. He was to have lunch with Marion again. He was not looking forward to it. This was the first seriously negative thought or feeling he had had since joining the team at the Tavi. The work was hard, but there was nothing that he hadn't wanted to do. Now there was. He knew she had been lying to him. Gabriel knew. Black-Beret knew. But they didn't yet know why.

And this has to be what my dream is about.

As he walked from Swiss Cottage underground station towards the clinic, he saw James heading in the same direction. He stopped where he was waiting for James to join him. Nothing different about James. I still like him. Good company. A little pretentious but that's James. Wilson smiled to himself. They entered their shared office and James volunteered Wilson to go to the general office to check whether either had any post.

'I'll do us each a coffee if you do!'

He happily agreed. He hated to admit it, but he always enjoyed James' coffee made from pods, to the canteen variety.

Wilson scrabbled through the pigeon-holes where staff mail was deposited three times a day. He didn't find any post for James, but a bulky padded envelope had arrived addressed to "Dr. Wilson Coffee, Psychological Investigator."

He assumed it was an essay or clinical notes left for him by a disdainful or immature student or colleague aware of his interest in political intrigue and making fun of his name. He didn't think for a moment that the sarcasm referred to his being a reluctant spy. He grabbed the envelope, feigning lack of interest and returned to his office.

Setting any thoughts about the package aside he caught up with James' news while they drank their coffees.

CHAPTER 43 : THE PACKAGE

James drained his second cup then looked at his watch.

'My lecture. I'm on in five!' He sprang from his chair, gathered his notes, memory stick, and marker pens for the whiteboard, looking back at his desk to check nothing remained. He waved cheerfully to Wilson almost skipping out of their office.

He loves his work – particularly the attention he gets! Wilson felt a wave affection towards his colleague. He sighed, stretched as he turned his consideration to the papers on his own desk. He looked at his watch. There were five minutes until he had to go to the seminar room at the end of the corridor to meet with the students writing the essay about social dreaming. He had long been interested in that subject gaining expertise alongside his enthusiasm so there was no need to gather papers or anything else. He knew his subject. The students were expected to do the work anyway.

'Sugar! I forgot the damn package'.

Wilson had spotted the bulky envelope that he had deposited on his desk. Chatting to James and the coffee had deflected his concentration. He hoped it wasn't anything important or that he needed to read before the seminar. But if it were an essay draft it was late and not his fault if he'd not had a chance to read it.

So he relaxed as he opened it. He had to push his fingers through a wad of bubble wrap to discover the contents and was beginning to think he was right, that it was some kind of joke. That he had been sent an empty parcel or the packaging equivalent of an apple-pie bed. But he was wrong. The bundle he eventually uncovered comprised a brown and white photograph of a woman and a bright pink memory stick. There was also four sheets of paper containing old fashioned typewriter script that were stapled together. It looked, through his long-sighted eyes, as if it had been set out officially – a title in capital letters, underlined. Then an introductory sentence or two followed by a subtitle and an indented list - from a) to h). In a red pen along the top of the first page THIS IS WHAT TRUE EVIL LOOKS LIKE was written.

Wilson put on his reading glasses.

Then he jerked into a minor panic: *The time! Tavistock rules – I can't bloody well be late.*

He saw that he had precisely one minute to reach his seminar group. Fortunately, he could make it in thirty seconds even without his walking cane. He had the presence of mind to put the envelope and its contents into his desk drawer as he moved away from his desk, locking the office behind him.

The seminar room door was open. Several students were there taking their seats, some turning to chat to others while two of the young women were setting out their notes for the discussion. He casually wondered why it was always the women who took their studies more seriously than the men. But then he thought again that that wasn't always the case.

Just a wee stereotype.

He was in the room completely on time. Only Wilson was aware of his near panic - that he had almost been late along with the vague frisson of anxiety about the contents of the parcel he had received.

And the way it was packaged and addressed. That is very disturbing. Is someone getting at me?

The seminar went predictably well, reassuring Wilson that his enthusiastic expertise on dream sharing was engaging the minds of his trainees. He had no papers to collect when the seminar ended, so nodding to the departing group, he left them to go their own way while he slowly and thoughtfully returned to his office.

There were many ideas floating, or flashing, through his mind, but he acknowledged that he had to be more systematic if he were to understand the information he had been sent. And indeed, what any of it had to do with him. Firstly, he looked again at the envelope he had received to see whether it had any postmark. He felt a little stupid not to have worked out earlier whether or not the package had been sent via the external mail. It didn't appear to have been franked in any way so either it had been hand delivered or was delivered internally. He called up the office manager to ask if anyone she hadn't recognized had handed in a package for him. She told him they hadn't, but she had to leave the office for a number of reasons during the course of any day. Wilson acknowledged to himself that he only came in once a week so the parcel could have arrived any time over the previous few days – or evenings. Was he any nearer to discovering its origins?

It doesn't necessarily mean it is an insider. Whoever put this together necessarily had to be a bit canny. But it could have arrived at any time.

The second question he faced was why was it addressed to him in that flippant, or was it threating manner? It suggested that someone had put the package directly into his post tray. If it had been left to the office staff to distribute, then they might have found the way he was addressed either amusing or disrespectful. They would probably have commented.

So why? What did they gain from the apparent "attack"?

Thirdly he wondered what the contents of the envelope pointed to – the photo and the memory stick were waiting for his examination.

Is this connected to Marion? Is it a dissatisfied, vengeful student?

Wilson was increasingly concerned about the order he had received from his erstwhile masters MI6. He was charged with finding out who Marion was working for. And indeed who she really was.

His musings were disturbed by a hearty knock at the office door, which opened almost immediately heralding Marion's arrival, clad in a jacket with her handbag over her shoulder. Wilson momentarily horrified looked at his watch.

'Hi Wilson, a little early, I'm sorry but ... well not that much.' She glanced at her wrist. 'We're due to take lunch in about three minutes. You hadn't forgotten?' She laughed.

'Of course not, Marion. How could I? I was thinking about an essay I have just read. Troubling and enticing in equal measure.' He grinned. 'Some of these guys are hugely talented – makes me feel a bit over the hill you know.'

Marion nodded and laughed. 'You? Never. But come on I'm hungry and I know you're going to have a few interesting things to tell me.'

Wilson stood and looked out of the window. Reassured by Freud's continuing, watchful, presence, he noted that he too ought to wear his coat. It was autumnal – gusts of wind whipping up clusters of leaves and a grey but unthreatening sky. Normal stuff. His body felt strangely heavy as he smiled at her and moved to get his coat from behind the door. He didn't want to go to lunch with this woman.

Is it because I want to spend more time on the package I received? Do I think she has something to do with it? Am I being silly? Or tired?

He sighed and it was clear that Marion had noticed. She peered at him, quizzically, but he had spotted an almost imperceptible sign that her first expression was anger. He reflected that she was behaving towards him as if he were under an obligation to her – she was his boss. That he had done something wrong or that he was a friend or lover letting her down. Something like that. Her expression did not represent reality as he perceived it – that they were friendly colleagues, and he was doing *her* a favour – even if it were an interesting one. That put him on high alert.

They went to the Turkish café they had visited before, but now his heart was heavy. His appetite had vanished. He felt strained and anxious and Marion seemed tense and on edge. Conversation did not come easily which made Wilson wonder why on earth they were there.

What does she really want from me?

He decided to take the initiative so they could move ahead, eat lunch and he could go home and work out the meaning of the missive he had received.

'So, Marion, I am only a little further on with our – he had decided to be friendly – "quest".'

'Oh?' she looked excited briefly.

'I know you could have read everything as well as I have ....'

'But I haven't had the time!'

And I have? Heavens above am I just being asked for a précis? I wonder how she treats her students.

'I think you must wonder why I've not read the papers in depth.'

She looked down. A sad expression passed across her face. She then turned from the table to order two more coffees. The waiter arrived, cleared the plates shortly to return with small steaming cups of espresso. Wilson watched her carefully. He decided that she was demonstrating a faux distress. To what end? He couldn't decide.

'I am very nervous about what you might discover about my grandparents – Max and Mary. Their lives are important to me. I want to make certain they were happy and survived all they had to go through. Do you get it? I am simply worried that you will discover they died in vain.'

Wilson looked at her. For a short moment he felt convinced by her emotion. But there was something awry. He understood that none of us wants to know about our close ancestors suffering. Perhaps more so we want to ensure that they are good, decent people. Not Nazis as might be the case here. He leaned back in the chair and scratched the back of his head, smiled and drank the remainder of his coffee.

'Okay. I need to do some more work of course and will let you know whatever comes from my searches. I understand from what you've said before that you want me to find out any additional information – that you want me to follow up what I can from beyond the dossier you have given me.'

'Please Wilson. I will be forever in your debt.'

'Come on then, back to work.' He looked at his watch. He was feeling more comfortable now. More in control but he guessed that Marion had not realized that.

She really does see me as an old guy. Weak. A bit of an idiot.

He wanted to think how he might unravel the truth about Marion herself and what it was that was so urgent that she needed to know about Mary Hart and Max Mayer. Judging by Erika Adler's account Mary had probably been a Nazi agent and Max worked, at least some of the time, for the Allies alongside Hans Gisevius.

So Max was most likely a good guy. And an English woman had dealt with Mary Hart.

They parted in the foyer.

'I need to nip into the library' Wilson turned to the left. He smiled at Marion as she headed for the stairs to the offices.

'I'll catch you next week then' she said.

Wilson entered the library on the ground floor, nodding to the librarian at the desk, then choosing a seat by the current periodical stand. Scanning them half-heartedly he waited long enough to have had a genuine pursuit before heading back to his office and the contents of the package.

Back at his desk he looked at the photograph. It was of a young woman. She had a fringe reaching half-way down her face. Although the photograph was faded, he guessed her hair had been quite dark.

Brown, rather than black, I think. Maybe that is the

photograph? A bit ordinary looking?

Her grey-looking skirt and jacket were unremarkable but in the fashion of the war years, he was certain about that. She wasn't wearing make-up as far as he could tell.

Unusual for a woman of her class – she has a dull appearance, but quite privileged, I think.

He stared at her for a little longer.

Actually, she looks nice. Possibly a bit of a blue stocking.

He turned the photograph over. In faded ink he could make out *Sylvia Ricks*. The name was familiar, but he couldn't imagine why.

'Ah – it's one of those English women in Nuremberg with Mary Hart – her father was a psychiatrist she said.'

His interest increased as he realized that the package was connected to the Hart murder. It occurred to him as he continued to look at the woman that Marion had had no connection with the package. Otherwise surely, she would have quizzed him?

If it was Marion who wanted me to have this, she would either have handed it to me or somehow pushed me to discover something about Sylvia Ricks. So where has this all come from?

He decided to leave the memory stick to last and placed the typed sheets on the desk. Cautiously he put the photo in his desk drawer in case anyone might enter the office and ask about it. A memory stick and a typed document were hardly worthy of a comment by any passer by.

The document, despite the recently added description in red ink, he recalled was titled formally as:

Operation E. K. head of RMSO.

That must be Kaltenbrunner. What has he got to do with the English women? I know about Max Mayer now – him and Kaltenbrunner but he had no connection to Mary Hart and presumably not to Sylvia Ricks!

He read on. It was a summary of Kaltenbrunner's interrogation by an American lawyer whilst in the prison at Nuremberg. Few stones were left unturned – the lawyer had done his research. Kaltenbrunner's contacts, personal history along with his roles and responsibilities in the Nazi regime were described. Most importantly the orders he signed were detailed and included persecution and murder of prisoners including Jewish concentration camp victims. He was also instrumental in ordering the execution of allied prisoners of war. Unsurprisingly Kaltenbrunner's denial of knowing anything about the outcome of the signed documents only served to emphasize his guilt.

He was a very stupid man. He even denied his contacts with Adolph Eichmann – we all know they were childhood friends and collaborated on Eichmann's murderous policies.

Wilson found this report fascinating. He was gripped as he read it. But then wondered yet again: *why have I been given this? Who would need me to read it?*

He guessed the answer might be on the memory stick that he chose to take home with him.

As he sipped his whisky standing inside his picture windows gazing at the Thames, he now understood how things had come together. From the memory stick an internal SIS memo confirmed that Mary Hart had indeed been a Nazi agent, tasked with carrying out the murder of Kaltenbrunner. Hart had been involved with *Werwolf*, Himmler's resistance group. Reading this, Wilson realized why he had been informed in this way and probably that Gabriel and Black-Beret had a role in letting him know. There was also a clear statement that Hart had no children.

Sylvia, the SIS agent had had orders to execute her to ensure that Kaltenbrunner stood trial, without suspicion falling on the British. She had been successful with some credit going to a small resistance group living in the district of the shared lodgings. The American investigation had concluded that German nationals had taken random revenge against a former enemy.

That left the problem with Marion.

That is what they want from me. I'm not sure I have the

stomach for this anymore.
    But then he remembered *Werwolf*. And Hanna.

CHAPTER 44: SHARING DREAMS OF SALVATION AND EXCLUSION, EARLY IN 1946

The run up to the trial itself proved to be a fertile ground for dreams. There was little alternative means of sharing anything. Prisoners were kept locked up and alone before the trial began and so conscious and unconscious sharing of ideas, antagonism and solidarity was accomplished in dreams. Dreams like those recorded by Charlotte Beradt – the woman – a Jewish woman - whose work had been acknowledged by Sigmund Freud and discussed many years later in Dr. Wilson Coffey's seminars. What she found throughout the reports of dreams she recorded during the early years of the Third Reich was evidence of a collective unconscious among those of us who shared experiences and a possible fate.

Individuals then didn't share dreams in conversations like some of us do now – but Beradt's study provided evidence of ties between waking reality and unconscious life found in the recall and recording of dreams. Dreams of those ordinary people – loyal German citizens. They always had been. But then they were scared of what they were hearing. They had inklings of what the everyday meanings might lead to. Dangers for them. Fears of mind-reading, control by the Devil, demonstrations, banners, posers and loud angry voices. Maybe there will be something here, among the prisoners, all of whom shared common values for at least the last 10 years, that could show us how evil too can be shared.

It wasn't difficult to disentangle some of their dreams. There were themes. One was about groups of men, women and children who were standing in line, holding hands. Stopping the dreamers from getting what they wanted – recognition, money, promotion – any types of success. Some dreamers saw men stealing blond, tall, athletic women from under their noses. Men with no entitlement – but men who prevailed. And won. The rage from these dreams precipitated headaches when the dreamers awoke. Sometimes these same dreamers awoke feeling triumphant. They had destroyed these enemies. The corruptors of their women. Their country. They looked around for others who shared their visions of an Aryan future and discovered they were not alone. But they also discovered that they had to watch their backs. Those who shared their vision would do anything to prevent their achievements – not quite like those strange alien groupings. This was more about who could be father's favourite. Albert? Martin? Hermann? Who was the best? Who could be the one to make sure father got his way. When father was their father *he could make everything better. At least at first. Towards the end the dreams and the dreamers turned away from each other. The dreamers felt the need to destroy. Quietly, secretly – not like the destruction of those in the early dreams. These dreams had to be secret. If they were not it was likely that few dreamers would awake.*

However hard Erika tried to convince herself that she was here in Nuremberg to ensure justice – fair justice – was carried out she could not feel anything beyond revulsion. Self-loathing was actually worse than her conscious, aware, sentient thoughts about these men. She talked mostly to Gustave Gilbert and when he was available, to Airey Neave as well. Each had different perspectives on the care of the prisoners and the forthcoming trial.

Gilbert, like her, was intrigued by the men's relationships to each other particularly the ways in which they disregarded and disparaged some, such as Julius Streicher and Rudolph Hess, while lauded others, particularly Goering. At least for a while.

'They are consumed with self-justification. And they want to exonerate themselves – either they "knew nothing" about the fate of the Jews and others, or they were "following orders". Most are in the first category' Gilbert thought at this stage of the trial that would be the easiest defence. Erika wondered, not by any means for the first time, whether these men were actually able to take in the extent of their crimes.

How could they live with themselves?

And she realized that Hitler, Goebbels, Himmler could not – but perhaps for different reasons. She also knew that Kaltenbrunner too had made more than one unsuccessful attempt to emulate them and although he himself had taken so many lives, he could not manage to end his own.

'Do you think it is a leader they're looking for – someone who will make it all alright for them. Like Goering perhaps?'

'They are demonstrating weakness. Cowardice. They don't know how to manage themselves here do they? You may be right Erika.'

'One thing I do know about Kaltenbrunner – he is not

the brightest of them, but he is one of the most vicious. He doesn't care who he kills, how cruelly he kills them if he believes them to be weak – or worthless and his definition of both is that they are not like him. He hates – not all of them do. He is prepared to watch former allies – maybe not friends – but people like Wilhelm Canaris for instance – he watched and exacerbated his torture. It was torture for the sake of it. Revenge for his part in the July plot. Revenge too because he had believed he might succeed Canaris as leader of the intelligence service, the Abwehr, but it was too late. Fate had spoken. Gratuitous hate was the answer.'

'I understand but I still want to know why – don't you?'

'Partly Gustave yes I do although I doubt we ever will. But I also want them to stand trial – I want the world to see and judge them.'

He nodded slowly.

Erika had become animated. 'Although you probably know Hess better than I do – I've hardly spoken to him so far – I am certain he doesn't hate like that – not like Frank, Kaltenbrunner or even Streicher. Thinking about it Streicher hates in a different way from those two. And vile as he is and despite taking an active part in ordering exterminations, I don't think Goering hates. But does that make him worse than those who hate?'

As I shared the fallout from the early morning deep sleep of Julius Streicher, former editor of the anti-Jewish journal – Der Stürmer - I found myself waking to a warm sense of self-righteousness. I doubted that was being shared with any others here in the prison next to the Palace of Justice.

This man felt vindicated and in our shared experience I experienced smiling guards and advocates.

'Please forgive my mistakes Mr. Streicher' was the common response every time his dreams led him through dark corridors past heavily locked doors. In the dreams, like Streicher, I could hear the sounds of crying, wailing and groaning from each cell as we glided through the maze of dark passageways into the light. A man, dark, powerful but generous to his friends sat at the end behind a large, polished oak desk.

'We know you are the expert on Jews and the Talmud' this man told us. 'You have told us the hidden meanings behind those Hebrew texts. You have helped us more than anyone – you have helped the German people to understand what has been happening in their midst. For years. You have been the one person to identify the problem. Only you have recognized how those people – the Jews – have pretended to share ideals with Christians. They were lying. You have told us how they have schemed to fool us. You have impressed me with the threat they pose to the Fatherland.'

We felt warm. Loved. Appreciated by those kind words as we awoke. But then the noises from the other cells. The banging from the guards brought our consciousness to the knowledge that the Leader who had treated us so warmly was no more. And we were here. And Streicher was alone. But he didn't seem to be afraid.

Erika attempted more than once to ask this man Streicher about his state of mind. The opening phase of the trial was well underway by now, although its activities and potential consequences were remote from prisoners and staff at this stage. It was essential that each prisoner was deemed fit for the trial and remained so for the protracted process that they would need to endure if justice were truly to be seen to be done.

'Erika – I have received the diagnosis from Dr. Goldensohn, and he thinks the same as Dr. Kelley – Streicher is not psychotic. Fit to stand trial so we keep him here and keep an eye on him.'

Erika smiled and nodded. 'I find him repulsive …'

'Well that's hardly surprising. What makes you say that about Streicher in particular?'

She screwed up her face and looked at Gilbert. He had returned to his somewhat guarded response to her.

He thinks that I have a different agenda – he's still suspicious about the psychoanalytic method.

'He sexualizes everything. You know that. You yourself told me how the young woman interpreting for the Russian doctors doing the physical examination felt sick as Streicher attempted to draw her attention to his body – his fat, disagreeable body. Those lewd comments.'

'Yes, I see what you mean. So you're saying that you don't want first refusal on working with him?'

Gilbert actually grinned. 'Well how about Rudolf Hess then? He was at your London clinic – the Tavistock for a while, wasn't he?'

'Dr. Rees – Jack – he worked with him until last year – in secret while Hess was in prison in Surrey. And others too I believe. How did you know about that?'

'Dr. Goldensohn and Dr. Kelley – they both told me.

THE BROKEN COUCH

Warned me I guess – their way of telling me that Hess may be practiced in getting out of things – knowing about psychoanalytic evidence.'

Erika made a mental note. Not only was she a lone woman among this company but she was apart from the other two psychiatrists – Kelley and Goldensohn in their distaste for Freud's ideas albeit distinct from Gustave Gilbert's perspectives too – as talented as he was, he was concerned with psychological measurement.

She thought she ought to see Hess. Although she had given Hess little thought she was aware of his dreams that had seeped into her unconscious mind a few nights earlier.

A dreamer, nearly as happy as Streicher, Hess dreamed of flying. Well no-one who knows what happened will be surprised by that, but dream interpreters over many years have made the point that it is common to have flying dreams. They don't necessarily bear any relationship to the act of flying an aeroplane. Most dreamers with that experience are connected by optimism. A sense of control and power over one's fate. Hess though ought to be unsure. Even before the trial there were many differing opinions among the clinical and army teams and among his peers – if indeed they are his peers – the other prisoners.

But as we both had dreamed his dreams I did not get a sense of control or optimism. I only felt his confusion – excitement, adrenaline rushes – but not fear or uncertainty. Possibly Hess was at least a little bit mad. Who can tell if he started his journey that way or took off because he was just reaching the extent of his sanity. Like Streicher though his mind brushed around figures of strength. Dark men. Powerful men. Memories of prison. And like Streicher he felt loved. Cared for. Attended to. But he was also suspicious of some of the other characters surrounding the dark man at the centre of the dream. His guard was up.

Erika was shaken back to the present and the work she needed to do with everyday behaviour and the conscious mind.

'Come with me and talk to them during the lunch hour. You've not done that much yet – not really met any of them properly. It will help you when you visit them in their cells. What I see when they are all together exemplifies a hierarchy – partly matched by IQ and partly by their former roles.'

'That would be helpful. I have been made slightly anxious being a woman among those people as the guards and Andrus in particularly constantly comment about that and ask what I am doing here. Implying that I ought to be at home doing housework and child-care no doubt. I don't think it has hit any of them yet that women had been active in war work.'

Erika wondered how far a collective experience of a central, powerful figure might occur across the group of prisoners. Certainly their behaviour in the cells and during meal-times were varied as with most human beings. A bit like a boys' boarding school. But these men were hardly typical. Or were they? While it was easy to see how Hess and Streicher were avoided by the majority, both she and Gilbert attempted to identify potential leaders among the prisoners and assess any impact they might have.

She shuddered as a fleeting thought wondered whether they were in fact ordinary. She knew something of Freud's ideas about the human need for a leader – a father figure. One who makes things alright. One who takes care that you are not hurt too badly. A father who can punish. The father who can let everyone down very badly. And in the end damages those who relied on him. The man you should not kill. But their choice of who to follow, and how to follow, was surely in the own hands? Every one of these men had made a bad choice at least once. A fatal choice and they had been let down. That man decided to escape – from them, from himself and from those who could judge.

I'm not sure why, when I am the centre of attention at a party – rather a celebration – and champagne is flowing freely, exactly why I feel so on edge. I am experiencing a heaviness. There is so much physical pressure on me that I can barely move. My worry though is that the people celebrating alongside me seem unable to help me along, or move me along, either.

Move me along? does that mean physically or does it mean that I am stuck in a set of ideas – an internal broken record? It could be because part of me wants to meet someone – someone I know who will recognize me for the important person I really am. But of course I was not important. I was merely an administrator in the main security office. We did nothing there that was wrong. Perhaps Himmler had done. Perhaps Heydrich had done – with him that might have been possible. But I took over the reigns – all I did was ensure that the wheels continued to turn. I keep informing everyone at this party that whoever they are looking to celebrate – it was not me!

But no-one will help. No-one will recognize me as a functionary. Nor will they see that I am a very important person in the chain of command. I fear I am destined to remain here – at this party – stuck forever.

I want to go home. I want to walk in the mountains and breathe the fresh air. But I'm told it cannot and will not happen. Celebrations continue and I am enjoying those parts of the dream. I'm at the forefront.

But this dream – it happens almost every night. But I never really enjoy the party. I never truly celebrate. There is something dark. Something bewildering that I can foresee. If I keep motionless here, taking part in this celebration, then I know I will never have to come face to face with it. With my accusers. With my murderers. With my trial.

Erika watched as the sentence was read out:
Death by Hanging.
The man with the scarred face simply repeated the word 'death'.

CHAPTER 45: ENDINGS

October 15th 1946 had now become October 16th, the morning that justice was effected in the gymnasium next to the Palace of Justice in Nuremberg. Three black-painted scaffolds were visible as the men accompanied by military police officers, were led towards them. Two gallows for consecutive hangings and the third was there to provide extra capacity to speed the process. Erika was there in the gymnasium alongside several colleagues and international journalists. She felt very little. She was also unsure whether this death was punishment enough.

How could it be?

Could fair retribution really be achieved for those millions of innocent people murdered by these men? Jews mostly – but not only them. Gypsies, Slavs, Communists, the mentally disabled, gay people. Ordinary, nondescript Germans who spoke out against the regime.

Everything was surprisingly fast that night. The prisoners were taken from their cells one by one. News of Goering's death had reached them. Reactions varied as did their final journeys. Bravery, defiance, fear and prayer. Most had last words.

Ribbentrop's body was removed from the gallows. His head still covered by the black hood. The military police attendants carried his remains to the far end of the gym behind a black curtain out of the sight of those who were to follow.

Then, two army doctors appeared – an American and a Russian. Bearing stethoscopes, they pushed their way behind the black curtain to pronounce death, cut the rope and remove hoods. The dead were all to be displayed with the noose still around their necks to demonstrate their final frailty as evidence to the world.

It was 1.36 a.m. A tall, ox of a man was led in. He was **wearing a sweater beneath his blue double-breasted coat**. Thinning hair brushed back, displaying his scars grimacing, menacingly, to those who saw him. Despite the hushed atmosphere of the execution chamber, a journalist whispered to Erika that Ernst Kaltenbrunner looked as if he had been dribbling – his lips were wet. All she noticed though was that he walked steadily towards the gallows having answered his name in a calm, characteristic voice. He sounded as if he might choose to talk to her about himself once again, later on in the day. That was not going to happen. She didn't know whether she was relieved or disappointed. Numbness filled her soul once more. He offered his last words:

'I have loved my German people and my fatherland with a warm heart. I have done my duty by the laws of my people and I am sorry my people were led this time by men who were not soldiers and that crimes were committed of which I had no knowledge. And finally, as his head was covered by the black hood:

'Germany, good luck.'

That was the last time she was to hear his voice.

EPILOGUE

Wilson watched the docudrama on the Nuremberg trial for the third time. There was so much there to think about – the Nazi regime, the Holocaust, the evil among the leaders most of whom turned out to be cowards. *Perhaps that was no surprise.*

Most turned on each other. Some claimed loyalty to Hitler with a hint that they were under his thrall and consequently only liable for a small share of blame for the devastation of Europe.

What was the rationale for the trial itself? Had Nuremberg enabled the world to understand? Had that understanding prevented a repeat of the hatred, murder and evil? Could what had happened ever be communicated in mere words? He was still not certain about any of that but believed that the trial at least gave the world pause to consider what we humans at our worst were capable of doing to others. It also provided an impetus for psychologists and others to examine human hatred and violence in depth.

Even now there are those who dismiss the validity and generalizability of experiments on obedience, bystander apathy and all forms of social control and influence. Without such everyday evidence though should we write off the Nazi regime as banal?

He knew he wasn't going to get to the bottom of such conundrums – no-one else had managed it so far. He poured himself a whisky and reflected upon his bit-part in a parallel drama. The drama orchestrated by Dr. Marion Morgan – his former colleague. Mary Hart, whom Marion had claimed as her grandmother, and who was *not* the partner of Max Mayer, had been a Nazi agent. She had been tasked with the killing of Kaltenbrunner. That had been intended to take place before the trial. The reason? That Kaltenbrunner had failed to kill Goering as he had been instructed to do before their arrests. The remaining elements of the Nazi command had feared Goering's potential for blabbing and giving away secrets about their escape routes – to Latin America, but also to parts of Germany where Nazi loyalists lurked. The reincarnation of the Thousand Year Reich was still a living dream.

The efforts of MI6 - Black-Beret and Gabriel in particular had confirmed that Marion Morgan was in fact a right-wing activist with links to a group operational in both Germany and London. When he found out Wilson was surprised that someone like that would be involved with the Tavi.

She was a trained and accredited psychoanalyst for Heaven's sake!

He remembered his final lunch with Marion. He had felt uneasy. But he had needed to discover the meaning of the contents of that package left for him at the Tavi and pressed her on the reasons for her requests to him to discover her grand-parents legacies, although now of course he was well aware that they were not related to her in any way. Wilson had attempted to confront Marion about Mary Hart – suggesting that maybe she had been misled? Maybe her own mother had misunderstood the familial relationship? Wilson was shocked by Marion's sudden change of mood. She raged at him. Called him a silly old fool. A has-been. A disgrace for someone who had married a German.

Wilson recalled how he had begun their relationship, which he always preferred to consider a connection, by pursuing the mission of examining the life or rather the death of Mary Hart. The story turned out in reality to be of Max Mayer and Erika Adler not the story Marion had commissioned. Max and Erika had married a few years after the war following which their lives had melted into peaceful anonymity.

ACKNOWLEDGEMENTS

It was Gustave Gilbert's Nuremberg Diary and Airey Neve's personal account of his work with the Nazi war criminals that inspired me to think what it must have been like at the prison and Palace of Justice before, during and after the first Nuremberg trial. I have drawn upon their thoughts and experiences and I trust ensured that their legacies are acknowledged.

I am also pleased to have been a student at the Tavistock Clinic for three years after taking early retirement from my post at Royal Holloway, University of London where I learnt so much about psychoanalysis.

ABOUT THE AUTHOR

Paula Nicolson

Paula Nicolson is Emeritus Professor of Health and Social Psychology at Royal Holloway, University of London. Her academic career spanned 40 years at the universities of East London, Sheffield and latterly Royal Holloway.

She trained in the psychoanalysis of organizations at the Tavistock Clinic in North London, acting as a consultant to several universities after that, as well as leading a research project on leadership in the British National Health Service.

Her numerous academic articles and books are about the psychology of development, motherhood, domestic abuse, the unconscious mind and social influence. Her most recent book published by Taylor and Francis (2022) links genealogical research to the transmission of trauma across generations.

Her novels, 'Containment' featuring Dr. Coffey Wilson the reluctant spy and 'Believe Me', and 'Bystander' featuring Dr. Nancy Strong the psychological profiler are all available in eBooks and paperback.

Paula, married to Derry Nicolson is mother to Kate and grandmother to Malachi and Azriel.

Printed in Great Britain
by Amazon